The Founders' Plot

by
Frank M. Victoria

Copyright © 2011, Frank M. Victoria
ISBN: 978-0-9846559-0-8

Library of Congress Control Number: 20011916011

All Rights Reserved. No part of this book may be reproduced or transmitted in any form or by any means, electronic or mechanical, including photocopying, recording, or by any information storage and retrieval system without written permission from the author, except for the inclusion of brief quotations in a review. Printed in the United States of America.

This novel is dedicated to my wife, Gloria, and my entire family—living and deceased—and to my friends, who are, to me, like family.

To Sarah,

Hope you enjoy
Read it in good health.

Frank

Acknowledgments

It took four years to write this novel—and I'd probably still be writing it if not for my editors. First, there was Ann Colette of the Helen Rees Literary Agency. She, however, stopped working with me because of a previous commitment to write a book of her own with another author.

But then I stumbled onto the gold standard in book doctors, Susan Mary Malone, of Malone Editorial Services. Virtually every page of my manuscript was marked with advice and corrections. And that came with a twenty-page evaluation clearly pointing out the strong and weak points of my work. Moreover, her follow-up assistance was spectacular. Via e-mail or phone, she advised me on my rewrites over and over again. Susan has written five of her own books and edited several best sellers.

In the middle of all this, I met Sara Wolski, a literary agent who founded her own firm, Calliope Content. Sara looked over my work-in-progress and was a great spirit-lifter when I had doubts about my writing. I'm grateful, also, to Valerie Brooks, of TheWriteEdit.com, who did a remarkable final proofreading of my novel.

And thanks to all the instructors at the many writers conferences I attended—in particular, Mary Buckham and her *Break Into Fiction* workshops, who stepped in to help me at a critical time. Also, to Donald Maass of the Maass Literary Agency, whose writing conferences were indispensible in improving the writing and content of this novel.

Finally, I have to mention that in addition to drawing on my knowledge as a teacher of American history and government, I also spent numerous hours researching the subject matter of this novel. In that process, I found *Men in Black*, by Mark Levin, a recognized constitutional scholar and radio talk show host. It provided a detailed account of the development of the U.S. Constitution, insightful information on the Founding Fathers, and a penetrating look at the history of the U.S. Supreme Court, its justices, and their opinions.

Chapter One

Mike's mouth was parched. If he could spit, it'd come out something like cotton. His gaze fixed on the colonel's collar, the silver eagles flickering in the harsh light of the bulbs strung along the top of the green canvas tent. He stood at ease, legs spread, and hands clasped loosely behind his back. But he was far from at ease.

"I can't accept it, sir," he said.

The colonel frowned. "Why not?"

"I had a serious lapse of judgment and I was responsible for—"

"I thought that was it," the colonel said. "Lieutenant DiGrasso, the investigation was thorough, and it cleared you of any wrong doing. I understand your reluctance to take the medal. You lost a lot of marines."

An image of his men under fire flashed through Mike's mind. His jaw tightened. "Five dead, nine wounded."

"I know. But you couldn't have foreseen what happened. And your behavior under fire warrants the Silver Star. Why don't you give this more thought, and we'll talk about it again?"

"I've given it a lot of thought already, sir. I think about it all the time. And I can't in all good conscience take that medal. That mistake cost—"

"Mistake? *You* think it was a mistake. No one else does. The way you reacted in that fire fight was exemplary. Take the medal for that, and put the rest out of your mind."

"That's true. I reacted well. But that was *after* I misjudged. If I'd sized up that terrain properly—"

"*If*," the colonel said. "*If* you had a crystal ball. *If* pigs had wings they could fly. *If* my aunt had balls, she'd be my uncle." He leaned forward and put his hands on the desk. "You're doing yourself a disservice, Mike. Losing men in combat is tough. I know. I've gone through it. But you've got to get past this. You're an outstanding officer. Don't do this to yourself."

Mike almost succumbed. It would be so simple. Just take the medal and forget about the whole thing. But he couldn't. He looked away. "I can't, sir. I just can't."

The colonel sat back. "You know, Mike, you've got a strong sense of duty and fair play, and you're adamant about what's right and wrong. I've seen it in the way you handle your men and the way you work with other officers. In this case, though, it's hurting you, and you might want to ease off. This isn't a black-and-white circumstance. Be a little compromising with yourself."

"Sometimes you can't compromise, sir. Sometimes there *is* just right and wrong, or, as you said, black and white. I don't have a right to that medal."

The colonel sighed and shook his head. "Okay. That's it then. I think you're wrong. But I admire your integrity. And I can't very well *order* you to take the medal. What about the Purple Heart? I assume you'll at least accept that. How's the arm and leg?"

"They're fine, sir. Thanks for asking. And, yes. I think I've got that coming."

Mike reflected on that conversation now and then. Not very often, though. Even now, almost forty years later, the memory of that fire fight haunted him.

The medal itself was meaningless. Five months later, he accepted a Silver Star and another Purple Heart. Those he'd earned, having been hit by shrapnel while carrying wounded to a Medevac helicopter under heavy fire and refusing to board until his men were safe.

Looking back on it now, Mike still believed he'd made the right decision by refusing the first medal. He really didn't deserve it. He'd gotten those men killed.

He eased back into the sofa and sipped his wine, feeling puzzled. Why on earth was he was thinking about this on the night before his inauguration as governor of California? A wry smile crossed his lips. Maybe he didn't think he deserved to be governor either.

Ah! A little too much vino. He spent fifteen minutes going over his inauguration speech and went to bed. As quietly as he could, he slipped under the sheets. But Josephine was a light sleeper.

"Goodnight, *Governor*," she said, putting her arm around him.

Mike grinned. "I think you sleep with one eye open."

"Yeah. Well, look who I'm married to."

Chapter Two

The sky shone clear blue and cloudless as Mike took the oath of office with Josephine and his three daughters standing by his side. The solemn words were humbling, making him almost feel smaller than his six-foot-two-inch frame.

His brief inauguration speech emphasized the bedrock issue of his campaign—solving the illegal immigration problem. "The people who elected me are not against immigrants," he said. "They simply want them to enter legally."

He waited for the applause to fade. "And they want them to assimilate into American culture as others have. They see nothing anti-immigrant about their dislike of having to 'press one for English, *y dos por espanol*,' or neighborhoods where storefront signs and billboards are in a foreign language."

More applause. Then, "Soon, we will have the serious immigration law I promised during my campaign. It will prevent illegals from entering our state, find those who are here, and return them to their countries of origin. It will make this state an uncomfortable place in which to reside for those here illegally."

After the swearing in, Mike spent the afternoon with congressional leaders before being driven to the inaugural ball, where hundreds of dignitaries were among the thousands of guests. The most prestigious of them, however, was President of the United States, Martin W. Ballard, a friend of Mike's since they attended Yale Law School together almost thirty-four years earlier.

Mike noticed that even after six years in office the president retained much of his youthful appearance, despite his graying hair and the deepened crowsfeet lines creasing the sides of his blue eyes.

He greeted Ballard and the First Lady and led them to his family from Chicago and then to the head table where Josephine waited. She extended her hand to the president and when he took it, bent forward and kissed him on the cheek.

"What a pleasure to have you here," she said and did the same with the First Lady.

Ballard stood back to look at Josephine. "You never change. You're always beautiful."

Mike knew he meant it. There was little gray in Josephine's long black hair. Her large brown eyes sparkled, her lips were a constant invitation, and her figure wasn't much different from when he married her.

Following dinner, the president leaned toward Mike and whispered, "Let's step outside for a little fresh air."

They walked to a courtyard patio, previously cleared by the Secret Service and state police. Mike had a waiter bring two snifters of cognac, and two cigars.

"Ready to go?" Ballard asked softly.

Mike nodded.

"Okay," Ballard said, "you've got the ball. Make sure it's tough. Otherwise, we'll have to start all over on something else."

"I'll get things moving right away."

"Are you sure they'll cooperate?"

"As sure as I can be. The election sent a message."

The president exhaled deeply. "This is it, Mike."

"I know," Mike said, his emotions mixed—excited, but a little nervous. "Let's hope nothing goes wrong."

They talked for another fifteen minutes, then returned to the ball and took their wives to mix with guests. Mike acted as if he were enjoying himself, but his mind was on the conversation with Ballard.

The presidential couple left at eleven o'clock. Mike and Josephine departed an hour later. Settling into the back seat of the governor's limousine, Josephine said, "What a great night. It was wonderful having Marty here. But the best part was having all the girls together with us. That doesn't happen much anymore."

"What?" Mike replied. "Oh, the girls. No. It doesn't. But to be honest, I kind of like being an empty nester."

"Want me all to yourself, eh?"

"You bet."

"Well," she said, "do you feel like the governor of California yet?"

"It's sinking in."

"Nervous?"

"Not really. But sometimes I feel like the dog that caught the fire truck. Now that I've got it, what do I do with it?"

"You? Put in a bigger engine and paint it a different color."

Chapter Three

DiGrasso's election was an ominous portent for illegals in the state. They too knew his reputation, first as an effective deputy district attorney, then for making good on promises as a state senator. There was no reason to think he wouldn't get an immigration law that could end their days in America.

The night of the gubernatorial election, Carlos Costellano sat with his wife Marisol on the gray cloth sofa in the living room of their Los Angeles apartment, their three children tucked in bed. Julio and Carmella Perez, friends who lived in the second-floor apartment of the two-story building, were with them watching news coverage of election results.

They'd finished dinner hours earlier, but the aroma of freshly baked homemade tortillas and the smoky, sweet-sour scent of carne asada still permeated the apartment. The redolence would normally impart in Carlos a placid contentment. But not now, not with the future in such doubt.

"This is bad," Carlos said when DiGrasso was declared the new governor. *"Muy mal."* He stretched his thick arms above his bulky physique, then clicked off the TV.

"Don't worry too much," Julio said. Carlos glanced at his friend, a little shorter than he, about five-foot-eight, with a slighter build.

A deep scar on his upper lip suggested a cleft palate as a baby. But Carols knew it was, in fact, a lasting reminder of a fight in which he was hit in the mouth with a beer bottle.

"They have promised tough immigration laws before," Julio went on, "and nothing's changed."

"Maybe," Carlos said. "I hope you're right. *Cervesa?*"

Julio nodded. "Yeah, a cold beer sounds good." Carmella shook her head. Carlos looked to Marisol. "Anything?"

"No. Nothing thanks," Marisol said, with a smile revealing gleaming white teeth that blended perfectly with her classic Castilian features—light complexion, shoulder-length raven-black hair and wide brown eyes.

"This is different," Carlos heard Marisol say as he walked down the narrow hallway to the kitchen. "This man means business. I cannot say how I know, but I can tell. He'll get his law, and he'll enforce it."

As he grabbed two cans of beer from the refrigerator, Carlos tried to tell himself that their concerns were exaggerated, but his gnawing stomach told him Marisol was right.

He returned and handed Julio the beer, then snapped open his can and sat back next to his wife on the sofa. He took a swig and put his feet on the coffee table.

"I don't know what to think," Carmella said, her blue eyes darkened by worry. She shifted her short, somewhat stocky frame in the chair. "I hope to God Marisol is wrong. But this DiGrasso. *Un toro.* Maybe we should think about moving. But where?"

"Another state, maybe," Julio answered. "Our relatives in Texas are doing well. There's plenty of work, and the pay is good."

"No, we can't leave," Marisol said. "You and Carmella might. Your children are grown and out of the house. And how can I pick up and move while I'm like this?" she said, spreading her hands across her well-rounded stomach.

Carlos grinned. "And only four months pregnant. Such a fast-growing belly must mean triplets."

She gave him a playful elbow to his ribs. "I'm serious. It would be very hard to make that kind of move with me like this. But the worst part is that we have roots here. We've made so many friends. We'd have to sell the building. Giving all that up would be horrible."

"Especially the building," Julio said. "We put almost everything we had into it."

Carlos winced at the thought, remembering how ten years earlier, Julio got him a job with his construction crew and taught him to install drywall and plaster, which paid much more than his previous job at a meatpacking plant. Both families scrimped and saved, then pooled their resources to buy the building together. He recalled him and Julio spending months refurbishing the "handyman special," making it a domicile better than anything they could have had in their home country.

His gaze went to the room's left wall, covered with photographs of their families in Mexico. He shivered as he looked at the narrow, littered streets and ramshackle buildings of his hometown, which he left at seventeen to find work in Mexico City, where he met Marisol.

"None of us want to think about this," Carlos said. "But we have to deal with it. You heard what the governor said during his whole campaign. If he gets a law that works, other states will do the same thing. That's a long way off, if it ever happens. But if it does, we might have to return to Mexico."

"Not me," Julio said. "My family depends on me to send them money."

"We all face that, my friend. I'm just saying that if things turn out the way the new governor wants, we need to consider Mexico, even if it's temporary. We have to save enough money so that if we *are* forced to move we'll live a decent life."

Julio sighed. "That's true. We can't deny it. We've got to face reality. What we must do is build a . . . *como se dice* . . . *ahorros mas grande*."

"A bigger nest egg," Marisol said in accent-less English. Carlos beamed with admiration for her, knowing she'd started studying English in grammar school, where it was taught from first grade, and later honed her skills well enough to work as a host in a Mexico City hotel filled with Americans.

He remembered Marisol insisting they speak English at home. But Carlos objected to his children losing their native tongue, so they compromised. One week they spoke English and one Spanish. This week was English. His use of the language improved greatly under her tutelage, but Julio and Carmella still had notable accents and sometimes reverted to Spanish to make a point.

Julio nodded. "Yes, that's what I meant. A bigger nest egg."

"I'll look for more work," Carlos said. "We'll cut spending and save more."

Marisol raised her eyebrows. "That will be difficult. There'll be medical expenses, even though Dr. Menendez charges us very little because I work at his office. And what else can you do? You already work ten or twelve hours a day."

"I can work weekends," he said, then held up his heavily calloused palms. "But let's not get ahead of ourselves. We have time. This isn't going to happen overnight."

"Carlos is right," Julio said. "It'll be months before a new law is passed, if it's passed at all. And it will take months, maybe years, until it's in place. We shouldn't panic, just be prepared, have a plan."

Voices came from the street. Carlos stood and stepped to the window. He lightly pushed aside the earth-tone serape acting as a curtain. Five boys huddled on the sidewalk to the left of his building wearing oversized sweatshirts with the hoods pulled over their heads. *Gangeros*. Gangbangers. During the day, the neighborhood was reasonably safe. But at night, the vampires came out.

He glanced down the block. Parked cars lined both curbs, and small widely-spaced streetlights cast circles of light on the black asphalt, spotlights on a dark stage. The bleak scene reflected his feelings.

Carlos turned and rubbed his face, feeling the creases in his dark skin, which reflected the many hours he'd spent working under a blazing sun. "Well," he said, "I'm ready for bed. The early morning comes quickly."

"Me too," Julio replied.

Carlos walked them to the back door in the kitchen that opened to a porch where stairs led to the second-floor apartment.

When they entered their apartment, Carmella sat at the kitchen table, her head lowered. Julio sat next to her and put his hand on hers. "Try not to think about it."

"You're toying with me. Holding things back."

"No. No, Carmella. Believe me, things will work out. We don't yet even know if the governor will get his law passed."

"I suppose. Did you mean it, that we'll be able to sell the building and move?"

"Of course I did. And it made sense, no?"

"I guess so," she said, and stood. "I'm going to take a sleeping pill and go to bed."

The pill put Carmella out quickly, but Julio lay in bed remembering that his wife hadn't always been so prone to distress. But five years ago, she had a minor stroke, plaque cutting off blood to a spot in her right eye, leaving it partly blind.

That was the start. She worried incessantly that she'd have another, and slipped into deep depression. Despite seeing a psychologist regularly for more than a year and taking antidepressants, she couldn't shake her morose attitude. It seemed her entire psychology had been re-wired, and she fretted constantly.

Nothing he said or did helped, making him feel inadequate and helpless. He remembered when just a hug and kiss dispelled her concerns. Not any more. Now, only their twenty-three-year-old son, Roberto, and twenty-two-year-old daughter, Erika, afforded her any joy, as if she'd invested all her emotions in them. She was filled with pride when they graduated high school, found good jobs, and went out on their own.

If the governor got what he wanted, Julio didn't know how she'd deal with it.

Chapter Four

Mike was edgy about the upcoming meeting. It was only a week since his inauguration, and the opposition party, which had just lost both the House and Senate for the first time in twelve years, might not be in a cooperative mood. He'd considered first working with them on another, less controversial matter. But no. That wouldn't work. Illegal immigration was the key, and it had to be up front right away. This was his first test—and he couldn't afford to fail.

Mike was among the governors and state lawmakers swept into office as voters, frustrated by federal inaction, turned to local and state politicians to tackle illegal immigration. But he knew there was more to his election. He was highly regarded for his competence, hard work, and honesty. People knew where he stood and knew he'd stand by it. And he also knew that his imposing appearance—athletic build, full head of black hair, rugged but handsome face, marred only by a two-inch scar his on his left cheek—gave him a powerful presence.

At 9:15, Senate Majority Leader, John Stone, arrived, and Mike's secretary showed him in.

"Good to see you, John," Mike said and held out his hand, once again noticing how much younger Stone looked than his actual sixty-four years. Mike attributed that mainly to his tall, slender frame, bright green eyes, and clearly defined features.

"Likewise," Stone replied as he shook Mike's hand.

Mike motioned to the brown leather sofa running along the right wall. "Have a seat. The others should be here soon."

Stone eased into the sofa. Mike sat in a chair at the end of a marble-topped coffee table in front of it, recollecting how Stone helped him when he first entered the Senate, and they gradually became close friends.

Stone stroked his pencil-thin mustache. "You think Stern and Griswold will go along?"

Mike shrugged. "We'll find out. But I don't see how they can fight us. It's too big an issue."

"If there's a way, Stern will find it. The election made her senate *minority* leader instead of *majority* leader. And that sticks in her throat. She could try to obstruct whatever you want just to make you look bad."

"I know. I'm going to have to be careful."

"You know how she'll come at you, don't you? Immigration is mainly a federal matter. If we pass a tough law, it could be challenged in court and might be ruled unconstitutional."

"Yeah," Mike said. "And if she fights us, she'll argue that we're wasting time creating a law that'll just be struck down. And the damn Supreme Court would probably hear the case, too. Stern would love that."

"Sure would. She likes activist federal courts and wants the Constitution interpreted liberally as,"—he twitched his fingers to signal quotation marks—"'a living, breathing document.'"

"And I think she's dead wrong. That's not what the Founders wanted."

Mike's secretary buzzed his intercom. "The minority leaders are here," she said.

Mike stood and looked at Stone. "Well, this is where the rubber meets the road."

He welcomed Senate Minority Leader, Elizabeth Stern, and House Minority Leader, Tom Griswold. Stone stood and they all shook hands.

It was always hard for Mike to imagine Griswold, just five-foot-seven inches and on the hefty side, leading an infantry company in the first Gulf War. But he had, and a serious hip wound left him with a permanent limp. Mike worked with Griswold on several pieces of legislation and considered him generally cooperative and trustworthy.

Stern was another matter. He knew she was fiercely partisan, shrewd, and an expert at legislative maneuvers. Looking at her as they shook hands, he reminded himself that her appearance—youthful, shoulder-length blonde hair, vivid hazel eyes, and bright smile—belied her ferocious political nature. Mike once said she had Angelina Jolie's smile and Jack the Ripper's eyes.

Stern and Griswold sat in chairs across the coffee table from Stone. They chatted until House Speaker, Manuel Mendoza, arrived ten minutes later and they greeted him. Mike liked and respected the burly House Speaker, who'd spent twelve years in the Los Angeles Police Department before entering politics. Mike considered him level-headed, and his face rarely reflected his feelings, although Mike noticed that his right eye sometimes twitched when he was nervous or upset.

Mendoza sat on the sofa. "Sorry I'm late. I miss anything?"

"Just some small talk," Mike said.

As Mike took his seat, he couldn't help but notice the unintended symbolism of their positioning—Stone and Mendoza on one side, Stern and Griswold on the other, and he in the middle, on the sidelines.

He leaned forward. "I called you here because I'd like you to make an immigration bill your first order of business. I'm hoping we can get bipartisan support on this."

Stern glanced upward. "What a surprise. That's all we heard about in your campaign."

"You weren't listening," Mike replied. "There were plenty of issues. But, yeah, I pounded on immigration, and apparently the people liked what I had to say."

"Gloating isn't very becoming, governor," she said.

"That wasn't gloating, just a simple statement of fact. Now, can we get down to business? I think we agree this issue needs to be addressed quickly. It affects both sides of the aisle. We've all got a horse in this race."

Stern tilted her head away from Mike. "We'll do what we can. As you said, we're all under the gun on immigration."

Mike studied her. That didn't sound too sincere. Was she already hedging?

Although they eventually agreed to work together, Stern had concerns—exactly what Stone predicted. "Hate to be the skunk at the garden party," she said, "but immigration is generally a federal issue and if the law is challenged—"

"Let's not even think about that right now if you don't mind, Liz," Mike said. He didn't want to get bogged down on this issue right now. He'd handle it after the bill was written. "We'll grapple with its constitutionality if and when it goes to court."

She rested her hands on the chair's arms, tapping her right index finger four times, then did the same with her left. Mike had seen her do similar things. She applied moisturizer on her hands frequently, probably because she washed her hands unusually often. He'd been in her office several times and everything on her desk was always in the same place. Three small metal-framed photos stood on one side of her desk and three on the other, each roughly the same distance from the edge and facing at about the same angle.

"All right," she said. "Just making a point."

She sounded calm, but Mike saw her face turn a light shade of red and knew she was angry about being cut off and her comment being taken lightly. "I appreciate it," he said. "But I'm sure you folks can come up with legislation that'll make it past judicial review."

They spent an hour discussing possible provisions of the legislation, not without some disagreement, and everyone but Stone left.

"What do you think?" Stone asked.

Mike took off his suit coat, threw it on the chair, and put his hands in his pockets. "Stern's going to be a problem."

Stone fingered his mustache. "Well, she's a scrapper and if she's not on your side, she's trouble personified."

Mike nodded. "It's a good thing we've got the majority."

"Not much of one. Two in the Senate, six in the House. We have to be sure we get every one of them. Stern knows how to play the game.

She's been around for a long time. She could sabotage the bill just to discredit you and our whole party."

"I know," Mike said. "I wouldn't trust her with a pair of sharp scissors. We need to keep a very tight rein on this. We've got to get a good immigration bill passed, or we'll look like fools."

Chapter Five

"He's overreaching," Stern told Griswold after they left the governor's office.

Griswold nodded. "I think you're right. Especially about the courts. If we write the bill as tough as he wants, somebody's going to challenge it."

"No doubt about it, and that's why I'm inclined to go along with him," Stern replied, smiling. She'd love to see the governor's law struck down by the courts, love to see him stew about that. Stern wasn't a big DiGrasso fan. When he won the election, she sat in the recliner in her study sipping vodka martinis and planning how to deal with the new political landscape.

She considered him competent and honest but despised his politics—small government, free market, anti-affirmative action, anti-abortion. Stern didn't see the government as an enemy the way the governor and his ilk did. If you left it to people like him, blacks would still be using separate bathrooms, and women would be getting back-alley abortions.

"But we've got to at least be seen as playing his game," Griswold said, limping along. "There's a lot of discontent out there, especially with violence from Mexican border towns spilling over into the States. It's getting pretty nasty down there."

"Well, let's give him what he wants and let him live with the consequences." She almost said, "Give him the rope to hang himself," but thought it better to keep her bitter aspirations to herself.

Stern stepped into her spacious office and sat at the maplewood desk in the center of the room. Instead of the governor's plans, she focused on the charity function she was holding tomorrow for the American Cancer Society. Her mother and grandmother died of cancer, and she'd sponsored many benefits for the organization as well as for other charitable groups. Her legislative record also spoke to her compassionate instincts, having helped write California's Medi-Cal program, which provided healthcare to the poor, and consistently fought to increase its funding.

Aside from her only child, a daughter, politics was the center of her universe.

And when she plied her trade, every detail had to be perfect, probably a symptom of her obsessive-compulsive disorder, for which she took medications. She was devastated by her party's loss in the last election. But it was only round one with the new governor. And a lot could happen in four years.

Chapter Six

Four months elapsed before the immigration bill passed. It hadn't been easy. The opposition, and some of his own party members, balked at key stipulations. But Mike conceded nothing. He knew the wind was at his back, and he and Stone and Mendoza were engaged at every step of the process. In the end, the bill included everything Mike wanted.

He'd signed it into law two days later, in front of a pool of reporters with House and Senate heavyweights looking on. Now, before his 11:00 a.m. news conference announcing the bill's passage, Mike went through its main provisions one more time.

Declaring English the state's official language had been an absolute must, as was having citizens show valid identification before voting. Equally important was mandating that realtors and landlords make certain that buyers and renters were American citizens or had legal status in the United States. The same requirement held for employers, who were also obligated to use the federal government's E-Verify system, which matches social security numbers with names. And it called for extending and strengthening the fence along the California-Mexico border and having it meticulously patrolled.

His intercom buzzed. "They're ready in the press room, governor," his secretary said. He'd lost track of the time. Putting on his suit coat, he walked through his large outer office and headed for the press room.

When he entered, flood lights switched on, hand-held cameras clicked, and flashes popped. Television cameras began whirring. He stepped up to the podium with the Seal of California embossed on the front. More than forty reporters sat in neatly arranged chairs.

Copies of the legislation were given to the press that morning, but he quickly summarized its major provisions and opened the forum for questions, calling on a young woman representing *ABC News*.

"Governor, people are already saying this legislation is too harsh and too far-reaching and that it may affect your standing in the Mexican community. What's your reaction?"

"I frankly don't see anything harsh about this law. Its intent is to prevent illegal immigrants from entering this state and to identify those who are here, then work with the federal government to deport them and penalize those who house or employ them. And I doubt that I'll lose support in the Mexican community. Remember, there are many Mexican-Americans who spent years following the process of getting here legally, and they resent their former countrymen bypassing the system."

He pointed to the reporter from the *Sacramento Gazette* sitting at the far right of the first row, a comely blond with a traffic-stopper figure.

"We're already hearing comments that this law is anti-immigrant and racist," she said.

"Is that a surprise to you? Because it isn't to me," Mike said, pointing to himself. "Some people can find a racial motivation behind almost everything. It's the first thing they fall back on when they have no real argument."

Such comments had earned Mike his reputation for speaking out on issues that most politicians would shrewdly sidestep. He, too, could be subtle, but he generally preferred a straightforward approach.

"The race card is an emotional response, not a logical one, and I'd like any of those critics to specifically pick out any provisions of this law that are racist. What illegals are doing is unlawful, and we will enforce the law regardless of race or nationality."

Mike grinned. "As far as being anti-immigrant, suffice it to say that my parents were immigrants. And it's a good thing they came here, too, because if they hadn't I'd be trying to grow tomatoes someplace in Sicily."

A ripple of laughter went through the reporters before Mike went on. "I welcome immigrants, legal immigrants. And I believe most Americans do, too. They are immigrants themselves or descended from immigrants. They look at them the way I do—people who are part of the fiber of the United States, people who built, and are still building, this country by doing dirty, backbreaking work to give their families a shot at the American dream."

He motioned to the reporter from the *Sacramento News and Review,* a grizzled veteran who looked the part with a slightly disheveled suit and a tie that wasn't pulled tightly into his collar. "Do you really think you can round up and deport all the illegals?"

"We really don't have to. The purpose of the law is not only to deport illegals, but also to create an atmosphere that causes them to stay out of our state or move somewhere else. As other states see our law working, they'll be encouraged to pass similar legislation."

Mike looked to the rear of the room and called on a tall, lanky reporter from NBC. "You're asking for trouble by outlawing sanctuary cities in this law. Can you legally do that? Aren't there home rule provisions?"

Mike expected that one. He'd insisted on the sanctuary ban, and he wasn't about to back off. "Naturally, we looked into that, and the conclusion was that in this case state law supersedes home rule. We'll negotiate with city officials. The state has some leverage because we provide monetary assistance to the cities."

"Follow up, governor?" the reporter said.

Mike nodded. "Shoot."

"You'd take away state funds from those cities?" the reporter asked.

"It's one consideration. Keep in mind that sanctuary cities not only take some bite from our immigration law, but those cities are violating U.S. law, which requires local governments to cooperate with ICE—that is, Immigration and Customs Enforcement—to report illegals. But sanctuaries don't. In fact, they don't even report illegals who commit crimes. That gives these criminals a free ride. And I want that to stop."

Reporters scribbled notes, and some held out small tape recorders. Others paged through their copies of the legislation, underlining passages and making notes in the margins. It reminded Mike of a college lecture hall.

The questions gradually shifted to other issues—mainly education reform, the state budget, crime, and expanding and improving the state's highways and bridges. Mike smoothly answered them in detail, then ended the conference.

Chapter Seven

"It's already happening," John Stone said.

Mike pressed the phone to his ear. He'd just walked into his office the day after the press conference. "What's that, John?"

"There's a lot of pissed off people out there, especially the sanctuary city mayors. Mayor Dawkins is holding a news conference in L.A. today, and he's hinted he'll tell you what to do with your sanctuary ban. I wouldn't be surprised if others did, too."

"Let them blow off steam," Mike grumbled, remembering that he'd thought of contacting the sanctuary city mayors prior to pushing though the bill, but decided against it because he thought they'd fight the legislation. "It's all show."

"I think you're right. It's political theater. If they don't speak out against it, they lose votes. Farmers will raise a stink. And businessmen will lean on the mayors and city councils because they like the cheap labor, too."

Mike's face flushed, and his grip on the phone tightened. "Yeah, well, there are ways to deal with them. I'll have health and safety inspectors up their asses every day."

"Be careful, Mike. Get a hold on your temper. Don't do anything rash. If something like that gets out, you'll catch heavy flack. It'd be red meat for the media."

"All right, John. I'll call some mayors from the smaller cities. A few of them owe me favors. If I can turn a few, others may fall in line. But, John, if they don't buckle, I'm ready for the fight! I'm not going to let them undermine this law. I'll pull state funding! I'll have the sons-a-bitches arrested! I'll file suit to make them obey that law."

"I know. I know. But wait a day or so before you call them. Let the dust settle a bit, and give yourself time to cool off."

Mike exhaled deeply. "Okay. I will, John. I will."

Later, Mike watched Los Angeles Mayor David Dawkins's press conference. Dawkins didn't pull his punches, daring the governor to enforce the sanctuary ban. Mike had an amiable relationship with Dawkins, but he knew Dawkins was as quick as he to lose his temper. The situation was going to heat up fast. That was fine by him. Bring it on. But he wondered how stiff resistance from mayors like Dawkins would impact enforcement of the law.

Nonetheless, three days later, Mike announced that unless the sanctuary mayors complied with the law within a week, he'd yank state funding and take legal action to have them conform with the ban. When the week passed and the mayors still refused, he ordered state funds cut and instructed his attorney general to begin litigation to require compliance.

The sanctuary mayors fired back the following day, holding a joint press conference, with Dawkins as spokesman. The war of words continued for nearly a week.

Then, the president called.

"Didn't you anticipate a problem with the sanctuary ban?" Ballard asked.

"Not this bad. I figured the mayors would scream, but I thought threatening to withdraw state funding would bring them in line."

Ballard was quiet for a few seconds, and Mike could picture him rubbing his chin as he considered what to say.

"You know, Mike, this is drawing a lot more attention than it should. Maybe you should think about amending the law and cutting the sanctuary ban. Or, maybe let it be known that you won't enforce it."

That was a shocker. He hadn't expected Ballard to say that, and he felt a twinge of anger. "What? I can't do that. The ban is important. Without it, the law loses some of its teeth."

"Maybe. But it would still serve its purpose. Give it some thought."

Mike sighed. "All right. But I don't like backing off. It's a bad loss of face."

"There are worse things than a loss of face. Think about the big picture. And see if you can come up with a compromise you can all live with."

Mike hesitated. "Okay, but I'd like to play this out a little before I'm forced to cave."

"Fine. Stay in touch."

With that conversation in mind, Mike spent the next day calling sanctuary city mayors, hoping to defuse the situation enough to at least keep the issue out of the news. The mayors, however, were adamant. They'd fight the ban.

When another week passed with the mayors refusing to budge, Mike thought about what Ballard said. Was his ego more important than everything else? Ballard was right. Maybe it was time to bite the bullet and order some humble pie. Then, he remembered something else the president told him. What was it? Find a compromise?

Mike wasn't used to compromising. He usually just got his way or got knocked on his ass, which had happened more than once in his career. "If you can find a piece of my butt without scar tissue," he'd say, "you're welcome to it."

He pinched the bridge of his nose. What kind of compromise? How would he find a middle ground? Then, he tensed and sat erect, eyes wide. He smiled and hit his forehead with the heel of his hand. "Dammit! I could have had a V-8," he said out loud and laughed. Why hadn't he thought of that before? It was so simple, and it just might work.

He snatched the phone and called a sanctuary mayor, whom he'd helped on a regulatory issue not long ago. "Let me ask you something," Mike said. "Would you be willing to eliminate your sanctuary policy for illegals who commit crimes if I accepted you not turning in the illegals who aren't criminals?"

A long silence. "You know, Mike, I think that's doable. Let me give it a little more thought. But I think you're on to something. I think I'd go for it."

"Great. Do me a favor, will you? If you think this will work, quietly call a few other mayors and bounce it off of them. Tell them to keep it mum. If I can secretly get a dozen or so, the other mayors might look like uncompromising punks for not going along."

"I'll do that," the mayor said. "I'll get on it right away."

"Thanks. I'll get back to you in a few days."

But sanctuary cities went on the back burner a few months later when Mike learned that the immigration bill would be challenged in court by the American Civil Liberties Union and the National Center for Immigration Justice.

Mike kept the lawsuit pretty much out of his mind for the next few months, but occasionally monitored the litigation as it wove its way through the legal system and eventually went to the California Supreme Court. However, that court refused to hear the case, saying it was a political matter better handled by legislators. But Mike knew this wouldn't stop here. It was too hot an issue.

Next stop, United States Supreme Court.

Chapter Eight

It all came to a head two weeks after the new year. Lunching in his office with Stone, Mike's secretary buzzed. "Jason Glenn is calling from Washington." Mike clenched his teeth. Glenn was chief legal counsel, representing California at the Supreme Court on the immigration bill. Mike grabbed the phone and heard what he'd expected.

"The court ruled against us," Glenn said. "Sorry, Governor. We did everything we could."

"I know you did. But you were fighting an uphill battle. We'll talk when you get back," he said and hung up.

This was it. The final stage.

And he felt the tension building.

He looked at Stone, who said, "Sounded like bad news."

"Yep," Mike answered, reaching for the TV remote.

"They ruled against the law?"

"Yes, they did. But no big surprise, huh?" Mike flicked on the wide-screen TV on the left wall. Coverage of the decision had just begun, starting with a reporter standing on the oval plaza in front of the Supreme Court building, a dignified structure of classical Greco-Roman architecture with a Vermont marble exterior.

"Less than a half hour ago, the Supreme Court struck down, by a lopsided vote of six to three, the controversial California immigration law. The court ruled that although some provisions of the law passed muster, others created a new immigration regulatory regime independent of the federal system. The decision said the law, and I quote, 'violates the supremacy clause of the Constitution by attempting to regulate immigration, which is a federal matter.'"

The show switched to a panel of political and legal commentators, but Mike turned off the television. "I don't really care what they have to say, do you?"

Stone shook his head.

"Well, I've got to do some thinking about this, John. And I know you've got plenty going on in the Senate. I'll set a meeting for tomorrow," he said as he guided Stone to the door. "You and Manny, Stern and Griswold."

"There's going to be some I told you so's coming from Stern," Stone said. "She'll revel in this."

Mike smiled. "I don't know about you, but I didn't need Lizzy foreseeing the future on this one."

Chapter Nine

Mike glanced at his watch. They'd be here in fifteen minutes and then it would hit the fan. Mike didn't need their approval, and there was no way they could stop him. So, he thought, let the games begin.

His intercom sounded. "Everyone's here for the meeting, Governor," his secretary said. "All walked in at once."

He greeted them and motioned to the sofa and chairs. As in their last meeting, Stone and Mendoza eased into the sofa, and Stern and Griswold sat in the chairs. Mike stepped in front of his desk.

A few minutes of chitchat, then Stern asked, "Okay, Governor, why did you want us here?"

"It's the court ruling," Mike replied. "I've been thinking about this for quite a while. I suppose we all expected this might happen and, to be honest, I decided a long time ago what I'd do if it worked out this way. You all know how I feel about the court meddling in areas where it has no authority. They've done it too many times."

Stone sat forward, squinting as if peeking into Mike's thoughts. "You're going to ignore the ruling, aren't you?"

Mike spread his arms. "I don't see what else I can do and maintain any semblance of integrity."

Stern looked as if she'd been jolted by a cattle prod, snapping erect, eyes wide, mouth agape. "Are you *serious*? You're going to defy the Supreme Court?"

Mike nodded. "Yes, I am. As I see it, I have no other choice."

"There's plenty you can do without taking it that far," Stern said, staring hard into Mike's eyes. "Remember, I warned you the court might step in. I said immigration was a federal concern."

Mike suppressed a smile as he thought, I told you so.

Stern shifted her chair toward Mike. "I think we should draw up another bill that won't get struck down."

"That wouldn't work," Mike responded. "You'd have to cut the guts out of the law, omit vital provisions. It'd be another watered down non-solution."

"I think Liz is right," Griswold said. "There's no point in taking this to the edge. I'm sure we can come up with something that's workable and avoids a confrontation."

Mike shrugged. "I can't tell you what to do. That's not within my powers. If you want to put another bill together, I can't stop you. But I'd prefer, and greatly appreciate it, if you don't. I'd like to see this through."

"I can't say I'll go along with that," Stern said, crossing her legs and folding her arms across them. "I think this is absolutely unnecessary and wrong-headed. And where do you get off cutting funds to the sanctuary cities and filing suit against them to comply with the law when you refuse to obey the Supreme Court of the United States? That's just plain hypocritical!"

Mike held back his anger at being called a hypocrite. "Those are two different issues. And you know it."

"I don't see it that way. You can't just defy a Supreme Court ruling."

Mike had prepared for this for so long that he was almost completely at ease with this otherwise tense atmosphere. "Yes, I can, and I will. The court should never have ruled on that case. It shouldn't have even agreed to hear it."

"Why not?"

"Because this is a state legislative issue and the court has no authority to get involved."

"Oh. I should have known. Same old bugaboo."

"Yes, you should have. I'm not going to debate judicial philosophy with you right now. It's a waste of time. The fact remains that I will not abide by the court's decision."

"I don't condone this at all," she said, her hair falling to the right side of her face as she shook her head. She brushed it back, then did the same on the other side, even though there was no need to. "I think we should come up with a new bill, and I'm going to get that moving tomorrow. You have the majority in both Houses but I think enough of your own people will jump ship on this and it can be passed."

Mike walked behind his desk and sat. "You may be right, Liz. But I'll veto it, and I very much doubt you'll get the votes to override."

The others were temporarily only spectators. Mendoza sat forward, elbows on his knees. Stone got up and stepped to one of the bookcases stretching along the wall, leaned against it and put his hands in his pockets. Griswold looked at the floor as if not wanting to see a train wreck.

"Pardon me, Governor," she said, spitting out the words, "but now you're just being obstinate. To satisfy your personal pet peeve, you're going to disgrace this government. This is a terrible precedent you'll be setting. Ignoring a court order is going to create chaos, shift the balance of power in the three branches."

"That's the point, Liz," Stone said. "The balance has already shifted, and the judiciary is exerting too much influence. I think Mike is right. This had to happen sooner or later." He looked at Mike. "I'm with you on this."

"Thank you, John," Mike said and looked at Mendoza. "How about you, Manny?"

Mendoza was silent, staring straight ahead. Then, he turned to Mike. "You could end up in jail, you know."

"I accept that," Mike said flatly.

Mendoza looked down, and his jaw muscles flexed. "I don't know, Mike. This is a pretty drastic move." He turned his head away. No one spoke. Mike saw his right eye twitch, signaling his consternation. Mendoza pinched the bridge of his nose, then looked back at Mike. "I don't have the legal background that you and John do. I'm just not sure that this is the right thing. I'd like to go along with you, but I've got to tell you that this is a real quandary for me. I need to think it out."

"That's all right, Manny," Mike said. "It's a tough call. Go ahead, think it over. And take your time."

Stern glared at Mike with what he read as a satisfied grin. "You'll be seeing a lot of that, Governor. I hope you're ready for it." She turned to Mendoza. "You're instincts are right, Manny. This is a dangerously insane move. The repercussions will be incredible. And," she said, her gaze darting back to Mike, "there'll be plenty of your people who feel the same.

"Don't overdo it, Liz," Mike said, his eyes meeting hers.

"I'm not overdoing *anything*," she said, her voice sounding as if she were holding back an angry shout. "Sure, some people think the court overreaches occasionally. But sometimes it's necessary. Sometimes we, the lawmakers, don't get the job done and the court has to step in."

"Liz, you know that's not the way this government is supposed to operate," Mike replied.

She got up and approached Mike. "You've got to obey the law, Governor," she said, shoving a finger at him, "just like everybody else."

"That's what this is all about, Liz," Mike responded as he leaned back in his chair. "It's not the law. It's government by judicial edict." He moved his eyes to both Stern and Griswold. "Look, I called you all here as a courtesy. I didn't have to. This was my decision. I could have just announced it at the press conference I arranged for tomorrow. But I didn't think that was right. I thought all of you needed to know what I was going to do and not get blindsided."

He stood. "Listen. I'm the one who's going to take the arrows," he said, pointing his thumbs to his chest. "This doesn't directly affect the legislature."

Stern was breathing heavily. Everything he said obviously made her angrier and more stubborn. "I still say you're going far further than you have to."

Mike spread open his hands. "My requests are simple. Don't pass a new immigration law, and don't pile on when they start trying to take me down. I'm not asking anyone to defend me. Just be noncommittal."

Griswold turned to Stern. "I doubt there's anything we can say that'll change his mind, Liz. Maybe we can go along with this. He's right. This really doesn't affect the legislature, and we certainly know how to be noncommittal. Mike's been straight with us in the past, and he was good enough to give us this heads up."

Stern whirled around, bonfires flaring in her fierce hazel eyes. "I don't like this, Tom! Not at all!" Now, she *was* beginning to shout. "I don't like establishing a precedent that allows the executive branch to snub its nose at the Supreme Court. Where does this take us? I won't be a party to it." She grabbed her briefcase. "I'm going to leave now, if that's all right with the rest of you."

They agreed and were silent for a few moments when she left. "Put on your helmets," Griswold finally said. "She's just declared war and I'm not . . . I can't, stand against her. It's a matter of party unity."

Mike sympathized with Griswold. He wasn't a weakling, but this was a critically serious issue. If he split with Stern and his party on something this important, it could be a political time bomb for him.

"I'll talk to her," Griswold said, "but I doubt she'll budge. I've seen her like this before. When she gets that way, she's tenacious as a crab. I really wish you'd reconsider."

"Can't do it, Tom," Mike said. He walked to Griswold and clasped his shoulder. "And I understand your situation. Do what you have to."

"Mike laid it out for her pretty well," Stone said, still leaning on the bookcases. "There's really no downside for the legislature."

"This is a mess," Griswold said. "Especially coming just a few days after the corruption investigation in Congress started. It doesn't make this government look good."

Mendoza's eye twitched. "How's that going?"

"The investigation?" Griswold said. "I don't know. Might be nothing. Might be serious. It's a wait-and-see game." He shrugged. "I'm going to leave, too. I have to mull this over." He got up, shook hands all around, limped to the door and left.

"He's not going to get anywhere with Stern, if he even tries," Stone said. "He's right. She feels like a cornered rat, and she's going to fight."

"What can she do?" Mendoza asked. "If she gets a new immigration bill, Mike vetoes it and that's the end."

"Don't be so sure," Mike said. "She was right about defections, Manny. Look how this affected you."

"I'm sorry, Mike, but—"

Mike raised his hand. "No need to be sorry. I started this and I don't want to jeopardize anyone else. You let everyone know that. Refusing to adhere to a Supreme Court ruling is radioactive and I can't blame anyone who doesn't want to be contaminated."

Stone stepped to the sofa and sat. "Mike's right, Manny. Just the same, this is the right thing to do, no doubt about it. The courts have gotten way out of hand."

Crossing his legs, Stone leaned back into the couch. Mike smiled. Stone was about to give a lecture, and Mike loved when he did that. Stone held a doctorate in early American history and a J.D., the equivalent of a doctorate, in law. A Rhodes scholar, he often lectured at law schools.

Stone stroked his mustache. "The Founders were afraid of this. They'd be stunned to see the power the courts have assumed. James Madison, the Father of the Constitution, said that allowing the courts to judge constitutionality generally was wrong and that they should be limited to cases of a judiciary nature. In fact, most of the Founders agreed with constitutional opponents on that point. Do you know who Robert Yates was?"

Mendoza shook his head, and Stone went on. "He was a delegate at the Constitutional Convention, where the Constitution was crafted, and an ardent opponent of it. Yates feared that errors made by federal courts couldn't be corrected, and they would have unprecedented power because they'd be independent of both the people and their legislators. He said they might overwhelm state governments by extending the federal government's power. And, of course, he was right."

"So," Mendoza said, "the Founders were concerned about this way back then."

Stone nodded. "That's right."

"More food for thought," Mendoza said and stood. "I'll get back to you on this, Mike."

When Mendoza left, Stone said, "This is a problem. Without Manny in the House twisting arms, we could be in trouble."

"Yeah." Mike sighed. "It's a predicament all right. Look, John, if you want to back off too, I won't—"

"Not a chance," Stone said. "This needs to be done. And I've got to give you credit, Mike. This is a gutsy move, and it's not going to be easy."

Chapter Ten

Stern slammed her briefcase on her desk, sending papers flying. She washed her hands and applied moisturizer, pacing like a caged mountain lion. Finally, she sat and made calls to set a meeting with party leaders as she reached around picking up the papers and setting them on the proper stacks.

That finished, she called her legal counsel. "I just met with the governor, and guess what he intends to do about the Supreme Court ruling?"

"I don't think I'm going to like this," the counsel said. "What's his plan?"

"He's going to ignore the ruling," she said, and just speaking the words sent another tremor of anger through her. "He's going to ignore the Supreme Court."

Silence for a moment. "Did I hear you right? Did you say he's going to ignore the ruling?"

"That's exactly what I said."

"Wow. That's incredible. I would never have expected that."

"Neither did I. Who would have? The question is, what can we do about it?"

"I'm not sure. But you've got to give him credit for having a pair."

"Yeah. And I'm going to cut them off. How about a court injunction, a restraining order that prevents him from enforcing the law?"

"We could try that. And we'd probably get one."

"That's what I wanted to hear. Get working on that right away, would you?"

"Sure. But there's a problem."

"What's that?"

"What good would it do? This guy's going to ignore a Supreme Court decision. What makes you think he'd abide by a local court ruling? He'll just ignore that, too. He's the state's chief executive. Is he going to order someone to arrest him?"

"Yeah. That's true. But get things moving on it anyway."

"I'll do that first thing tomorrow."

She ran her fingers across her forehead, then called the House Minority Whip, Thad McMasters. She related the governor's plans and told him to discretely ask around to see if there might be any support for beginning impeachment hearings.

"That's a pretty drastic step, Liz."

"No. *He's* the one taking the drastic step. *He's* the one defying a court order."

"What would we charge him on?"

Stern rubbed the back of her neck. "We'll have to research that. There's got to be something."

"I'll look into it."

"Please do. Maybe we need to put the cart before the horse on this one. Let's first see if there's a chance we can get impeachment hearings, and then we'll find the reasons for it later."

She felt better now that she was taking action, even if her plan at this point was basically throwing a lot of manure at the wall to see what stuck. But the key was pushing through a new immigration bill that would pass judicial review, leaving the governor in the unenviable position of enforcing a law ruled unconstitutional or a new one that *would* be constitutional.

She considered her next moves as light from the setting sun flowed in from two large windows behind her, illuminating the room in an almost eerie golden glow, ordinarily a relaxing ambience. But today it didn't come close to assuaging her anger.

It wasn't just a personal dislike of DiGrasso or even his intent to ignore the court that grated her so much. He was a manifestation of the reactionaries, the purists, who clung to the outdated notion that the Constitution should be interpreted strictly. How could you strictly adhere to a document written more than 220 years ago? But the governor was a clever bastard, a real snake charmer. He'd no doubt convince a good many people he was right.

Standing, she smoothed her skirt—three times with her right hand, then three times with her left—and sat on the corduroy sofa against the right wall. She kicked off her shoes and put her feet on the coffee table thinking of how strongly her youth had molded her.

Her parents divorced when she was ten and when her mother died two years later, she lived with her grandparents. Although financially comfortable, they would have been sorely pressed to make ends meet if not for Social Security.

She took a large government loan to attend Pepperdine University Law School and graduated with honors, then worked for a Fresno law firm. Her grandfather died a year earlier, and she wanted to be near her grandmother, who was battling cancer. It wasn't long before the frail old woman was put into hospice and died four days later. Stern often pondered what kind of care her grandmother would have received without Medicare.

During her grandmother's hospitalization, she began dating a young doctor. They were married a year later, and Stern shortly had a baby girl. But the marriage soured, and they divorced after five years.

Stern got the house in the divorce and worked from there to be with her four-year-old daughter. Those were lean years, and as she recalled them, she had a surge of pride that it hadn't prevented her from continuing to do considerable pro bono work. And it was the people in the communities where she worked who convinced her to enter politics, then helped get her elected.

For more than twenty years, Stern had tussled in an environment of backroom legislative machinations. She'd made her share of deals, given her share of favors, made and forced concessions. She held markers on legislators in both parties, and she was ready to call them in.

Chapter Eleven

Mike and Stone talked for half an hour after Mendoza left, trying to anticipate Stern's next move. Later, Mike lay on the couch to relax before he went home. How events evolved now could destroy him, and others. But he knew that going in.

He remembered the phone call from his brother Anthony in Chicago twenty years ago. "They're going to evict Mom," his brother told him.

"What!" Mike said. "Who is? Why?"

"The city. Eminent domain. They're going to build a Chicago campus for a downstate university."

Three years earlier, Mike and his brother had bought their mother a home close to the neighborhood where she'd raised them, and she loved it because she was near family and long-time friends.

As a young deputy district attorney, Mike had plenty of work on his hands. But he postponed some cases and temporarily handed off some to others. Two days later, he flew into Chicago and he and Anthony were with their mother having coffee and nibbling on biscotti and sliced fresh fruit at her kitchen table. Sunlight filled the room, reflecting off the stove and refrigerator and the vinyl red-and-white checkered table cloth. She appeared nonchalant.

Then, Mike asked, "How you holding up, Mom?"

She raised her eyebrows. "What do you mean? I'm fine. I already told you."

"C'mon, Mom," Anthony said. "We can help."

Her dark brown eyes darted to him. "What help? What are you talking about?"

"The eviction," Mike answered.

She dunked a biscotti into her cream-lightened coffee. "Oh, that. Times change. You adapt."

"You're not worried?"

She turned away, the sun highlighting the silver in her short black hair, and nibbled her lower lip momentarily. Then, she looked back at him. "Listen, I lived through the Great Depression and I'm supposed to be worried by this? I was pregnant when your father went to war. Now, *that* worried me. This is nothing."

"Your friends say you're depressed," Anthony said.

Her face went red. "What? What the hell did they say? You tell them they better goddamn well stay out of it. This is a family matter. It's none of their fuckin' business!"

Marie DiGrasso had a wide beaming smile and a normally genteel, well-mannered demeanor. But when she got angry, she'd swear like a truck driver. People who didn't know her well were stunned when this pleasant, elderly lady unloaded. It was like watching Mother Teresa become possessed by the devil.

"Take it easy, Mom," Mike said. "They just care about you."

"Ah." She huffed. *"Que sera, sera.* What will be will be."

But now she was beyond pretense. Her lips quivered. Then, tears formed.

She stood, shifting her face away. "I've got to use the bathroom."

Mike put his arm around her. "No, you don't, Ma. You're trying to make a getaway. Don't want to show your feelings. You can't do that."

"It'll help if you let loose," Anthony said. "You're not a burden."

"Yes, I *am!*" she said and pushed away from Mike. Then, her voice trembled and a solitary tear from each eye rolled down her cheeks. "I am a burden! And I don't like it."

"It's going to be all right, Mom."

Her facial muscles tightened as she struggled to fight off more tears.

No good.

She put her face in her hands and sobbed. Then, she slammed her palms on the table. "Those sons-a-bitches! How can they do this? *Scarafaggi,* cockroaches! Why this neighborhood? Why not somewhere else?"

But as quickly as she'd lost her temper, she lowered her head and cried again.

Mike took her hands. "It's going to work out. You've got to believe that."

"I want to. But I can't see any good ahead. Sure, we can get another house. But where? My friends and family, they'll be scattered." She hesitated. "I— I just don't want to be alone. That's all. I don't want to be by myself. *Sono spaventato.* It scares me."

Mike wiped away her tears. "You won't be, Ma. I promise."

She lowered her eyes. "I haven't been this sad since . . . since Mariano was killed over there—and then I still had your father to share the grief. It's been so long, but I still think about him. I can see him in that starched uniform with the sharp creases in his trousers. The paratrooper emblem on his shirt. Those spit-shined boots. Like mirrors. You could see your face in them."

Mike swallowed hard, picturing his older brother. The torment, the agony, the emptiness they'd suffered back then were as alive now as when it happened. Mariano. Even now, it seemed impossible he was dead.

A macabre slideshow flashed through Mike's mind. Mariano with his friends on the corner, playing ball in the park, swimming at the beach, waving as he left for his second tour in Vietnam. And then the wind ruffling the flag on his coffin, the chilly, overcast day, taps sounding, the airborne trooper on one knee presenting the folded American flag to his parents.

"I know, Mom," Mike said. "Me, too. I still think about him. But that's behind us. Mariano wouldn't want us grieving like this."

Marie nodded. "I know. You're right. He wouldn't." She forced a smile, but melancholy filled her eyes. "I guess I'm not as strong as I used to be. Yeah, there was the Depression and the war and all that. But I was young then. It's different now."

"Mom," Anthony said, "you're sixty-eight. That's not exactly ancient anymore."

"Sure," she replied, "but it feels old at times like this."

"You'll get past it," Mike said, smiling. "You're a tough old broad."

She punched him playfully on the arm. "Tough old broad? Don't talk to your mother like that."

Mike laughed. "We'll get you another house. And you can still stay in touch with everyone. There's this new invention. The telephone."

At last, Marie laughed. "Now you're a comedian, huh?"

"When I have to be. You're able to drive, so you can go see your friends and relatives, and they'll visit you. You can still have those weekly pinochle games."

She nodded and breathed deeply. "Okay. Enough. No more crying. You two do what you have to, and I'll get hold of myself. Anthony, you were right. I had to get it out of me. Don't worry. I'll be fine now."

Neighborhood residents pooled resources and filed suit. Knowing Chicago, Mike figured the fix was in and they'd lose. He was right. But when the case went to the U.S. Supreme Court, Mike was hopeful. It was far removed from local politics. But the court also ruled for the city. Mike was furious.

He and his brother moved their mother to a new home, but for years she wasn't herself, her usual cheerfulness and optimism gone. She eventually adjusted, but Mike never forgot the effect all that had on his mother.

He'd never denied that the city had the right to apply eminent domain, but didn't believe it was justified or necessary. There were other parts of the city where the university could have built a campus without displacing thousands of people. And for the Supreme Court to condone the dislocation of so many families was beyond wrong. It was heartless and unconscionable.

But his mother's eviction in itself wasn't what incensed Mike now. That was only a small part of a far more significant problem, just the head of an inflamed, festering boil. It was the trigger that began his scrutiny of federal court decisions. And he didn't like what he saw.

The courts were ruling on issues where they had no jurisdiction. That's what infuriated him. They were exercising powers far beyond those granted them by the Constitution, and that was the core of Mike's angst.

The Founding Fathers never intended courts to have such power. And they were correct. The court had been wrong in the past and would be again. The Dred Scott decision popped into his mind as a prime example of the court's misjudgment, because it not only endorsed slavery but also had far-reaching consequences.

Scott was a slave whose master, an army surgeon, had taken him to posts in free states. When the master died, Scott sued for his freedom, arguing that his prolonged residence in free states made him a free man. However, Chief Justice Roger Taney wrote that because Scott was a slave he was not a citizen, so he couldn't bring suit.

The worst part, Mike recalled, was that Taney also wrote that since slaves were property, the congressional ban on slavery in territories of the Louisiana Purchase was unconstitutional, because it denied people of their right to property. What Taney essentially did was erase the Missouri Compromise, one cause of the Civil War.

For decades, Mike had scrutinized the unwarranted rulings of federal courts. Now, he was in the crosshairs of the ultimate federal court.

So be it. This had to be done. Off and running.

Chapter Twelve

Mike was ill at ease when he got home that night. The day after the court decision, Josephine asked him what he was going to do and he told her he wasn't sure. He walked out to the deck where Josephine was reading.

"Home on time," she said. "I could get used to that."

Mike sat on the lounge chair next to her and kissed her on her cheek. "Thought I'd give myself a break."

"Good idea."

"I get those now and then. What's for dinner?"

"Pot roast is in the oven."

"Sounds good."

He started to speak, then hesitated.

"Something wrong?" Josephine asked. "Is this about work?"

"Kind of," Mike said and looked away.

She put the book on the patio table. "Okay. Let's have it."

"It's about the Supreme Court ruling."

"What about it? You're off the hook. You did what you said you would. But the court struck down the law. It's not your fault. The people can't blame you."

"I'm going to hold a press conference tomorrow. I'll announce that I'm going to ignore the ruling."

Josephine's jaw dropped. "You're going to *what*?"

"I'm not going to obey the court. I'm going to keep enforcing the law."

"What! Are you kidding me?"

"No. I'm dead serious."

"Can you do that?"

"Yes, I can, and I'm determined to do it."

She stood and stepped away, her back to him. "That's crazy, Mike. That's insane. You can't just defy a court order, especially a Supreme Court order. Why on earth would you do that? Haven't you got enough on your plate?"

"It needs to be done. You know how I feel about federal courts being out of line."

"But why you?"

"Someone has to, Babe. It's got to be done, and I'm going to do it."

Mike got up and walked to her. He clasped her shoulders. "Try to understand, Jo."

"I'm trying. I'm trying. Believe me. But this is quite a bomb you dropped." She shook her head. "I think this is folly. I'm sorry, but I do."

"Don't worry about it."

She spun around to face him. *"Don't worry? Don't worry?* How can I not worry?" She threw her hands in the air. "My husband is going to defy the Supreme Law of the land, and I shouldn't worry?"

"The Constitution is the Supreme Law of the land," Mike corrected. "The court just interprets it."

"Oh, don't be so fuckin' technical. You know what I meant."

Mike smiled. "I just love it when you talk dirty."

She pushed him away. "Jokes. Now you've got to make jokes."

"I wasn't joking."

"Oh, stop it," she said and sat back down. "I don't get this. And I don't like it." She paused. "Are you still thinking about your mother's eviction? Mike, that was a long time ago. And it all worked out well. Why can't you just let it go?"

Mike shook his head. "It's not that simple, Jo. You've heard John and me talk about this. It's got to stop."

Josephine looked down. "Mike, I wish I could say I'm behind you on this. But I can't. I just can't. This concerns me big time. Can't you just amend the law or get a new one that won't get struck down?"

"No. That won't fly. That's what Stern wants. And I'm not going to do it." Mike sat next to her. "You've got to trust me on this, Babe."

"Sure. But I know what this is going to do to you. You're burning yourself out as it is, and now you take this on. It makes no sense. You're already in a pressure cooker, and now you're going to turn up the heat. How am I supposed to feel about that?"

Anger flashed through him. She'd been harping for months about working himself too hard, and he was tired of it. "Oh, stop with the pressure cooker shit! I've heard enough of that."

Josephine's shoulders slumped, and she lowered her eyes. "See what I mean, Mike? See what you just said and how you said it? That's not you, Mike. That's the job grinding you down, making you tense. And I don't like it."

She stood and walked to the back door. Mike walked after her. "Okay, I'm sorry. I shouldn't have snapped at you like that. But there are things happening. Very important things—"

"More important than our marriage? Mike, I feel like I'm a sideshow in your life."

"That's not true, and you know it."

"Why don't you pour yourself a drink and relax. The pot roast is almost ready. Help yourself. I'm not very hungry," she said and walked inside.

Mike sat back in the lounge chair and rubbed his temples. This was what he'd feared, what he'd wanted to avoid. He exhaled deeply, wishing he knew where all this was going, wondering how badly it would endanger his marriage.

Chapter Thirteen

The following day, Mike held a press conference on his decision. He kept it short and took no questions, telling reporters he'd have plenty to say in the weeks ahead.

"Very briefly," he said, "I will not obey the Supreme Court ruling regarding this state's immigration law, because it has no right to adjudicate on legislative matters. The court's decision is yet another example of the judiciary overreaching the mandate given to it in the Constitution. At this point, I won't waste time detailing my reasons or the legitimacy of my actions. All I'll say for now is that there is precedent for what I'm doing."

He paused for a moment. "I'll just add that for the court to strike down our law when it has already proven highly successful is regrettable considering the gravity of the illegal immigration problem. Illegals are an enormous drain on this state. And for the Supreme Court to prevent us from eliminating this burden is dead wrong, and I will not allow it to happen."

The words were barely out of his mouth when the critics unloaded on him. He was breaking the law, undermining the judicial system, throwing the country into turmoil, igniting a clash among federal, state, and judicial power that threatened to jar the country's political and justice systems.

He braced for a long, brutal battle.

Mike's defiance of the Supreme Court was instant national news. Media outlets across the country contacted him, including invitations to appear on weekday morning television news shows as well as Sunday morning appearances on NBC and *Fox News*. He accepted them all, and the next day technicians were in his office hooking up equipment for the telecasts.

That night Stone had dinner with Mike in his office to prep him for the interviews. "I don't think I have to tell you this, Mike, but answering questions isn't the only objective. I know you'll handle that well. But try to steer the conversation to the issues you want to stress."

"That's my plan."

"Be sure you get into *Marbury versus Madison*," Stone continued, referring to the 1803 case pitting then Secretary of State, James Madison, against William Marbury, who'd been appointed by President John Adams to justice of the peace in Washington, D.C. But that was just before Adams left office, and the commission papers hadn't been delivered to Marbury when Thomas Jefferson became president. Jefferson told Madison to hold Marbury's commission papers. Marbury sued, and the court ruled in his favor.

"Absolutely. There are probably people who don't understand the impact that had," Mike said, meaning the Marbury case ushered in the practice of judicial review, which gave federal courts the power to decide the constitutionality of legislation.

They worked for almost two hours, then Stone asked, "Nervous?"

Mike smiled. "A little. But not much. In fact, I'm kind of energized by it."

"I figured you'd be."

"What bothers me sometimes, John, is that I wonder if Stern's right—that this whole thing is aimed at satisfying my own pet peeve about the courts."

"That's not likely, Mike. It's not like you. And this is a lot bigger than a pet peeve. This is a serious constitutional issue that you're taking on. Are you having second thoughts?"

"Not really. But there are times when I ask myself, who I am to take this on? And who knows how this will all shake out? What effect it will have. Am I the wisest of the wise?"

"Maybe not. But you're defending the work of some very wise men—the Founding Founders of this country."

"Yeah. That's really what this is all about."

"I know you're prepared to take this on. And I'll be here for you no matter what."

"Thanks, John. I know you will. But Josephine is dead set against it. She's worried about the stress. It's straining my marriage."

"That's too bad. I'm sorry to hear it. How bad is it?"

"I don't know for sure. Sometimes Jo is hard to read."

Chapter Fourteen

When the makeup artist finished with Mike, a technician placed a tiny radio receiver into his ear, then explained the procedure they'd follow going on the air. Three cameras were pointed at him from different angles, and a TV monitor was a few feet from his desk. Behind the cameras, floodlights were attached high on tall silver poles. Cables and wires snaked through the equipment, and two large boom microphones loomed above, huge serpents hovering over prey.

"One minute, Governor," a cameraman said.

Mike straightened his tie and folded his hands on the desk. At the entrance to his office, Stone gave him a thumbs up.

The floodlights flashed on, and the cameraman pointed to Mike. The TV in front of him lit up, showing the program's regular host, a smartly dressed, attractive blonde woman sitting on a high-backed leather stool. After welcoming Mike, she asked, "Why are you doing this, Governor?"

"The immigration law that the court struck down was passed because the people in my state, and throughout the country, are tired of the difficulties created by so many illegal aliens. Schools are overcrowded because of the heavy influx of immigrant children. Crime has increased, much of it attributed to gangs recruiting illegals. Hospital emergency rooms are packed beyond capacity, because illegals are using them for non-emergency care, as if they were doctors' offices. In Southern California, some hospitals closed, because it was financially impossible to operate under those conditions. What does that mean for the people in those communities? It's wrong and it's unacceptable."

"But you're breaking the law, Governor," the host said. "And as the state's chief executive, you're the top law enforcement officer. Doesn't that strike you as ironic?"

"Not really. Because I don't believe I'm breaking the law." He leaned back slightly and rested his hands on the chair's arms. "Please remember that judicial review is not specifically noted in the Constitution. In fact, there's very little in the Constitution about the Supreme Court, only that it should be established. It doesn't say how many justices there should be or even the qualifications they should have. The president and the Senate could make a one-eyed twelve-year-old a justice if they wanted. That's obviously hyperbole and would never happen. But it's a fact."

"Just the same, judicial review was established in *Marbury versus Madison*."

She'd done her homework. That was okay with Mike as long as her comments led him to where he wanted to go. And this was a chance to dismiss the notion that the Constitution gave the Supreme Court the right of judicial review.

"That's not necessarily correct," he said. "That case set a precedent and became a tradition, perhaps even doctrine, but it's certainly not an enumerated power given by the Constitution. It's based on the willingness of the people, their legislators, and chief executives to accept it." He shrugged. "And I just don't accept it. The United States Supreme Court should not have involved itself in my state's legislative business. The California Supreme Court correctly declined to rule on the issue and it all should have ended there."

The host frowned. "Hold on a second, Governor. Federal court rulings have generally been accepted since the beginning of our republic, and lawmakers have routinely abided by those rulings. Most of our legal opinions are based on decisions of past court cases. I'd say you should be concerned by the precedents you're threatening. After all, even Thomas Jefferson went along with the Marbury decision."

Mike grinned. "Well, just goes to show you even Jefferson could be wrong once in a while. Remember, he didn't want to make the Louisiana Purchase, which doubled the size of the country and opened the way west. He had to be persuaded to do it."

Whoa, he thought. Don't get too cocky. This interview is going well. Don't come off as arrogant. Just stay on message.

"Now, regarding your point about precedents, I'm sure you know that this isn't the first time the court has been defied. In 1832, the court ruled against the state of Georgia moving Indian tribes to government reservations in the West. Andrew Jackson refused to enforce the court order. He said, 'John Marshall'—the Chief Justice—'has made his decision, now let him enforce it.' And Abe Lincoln ignored a federal district court that said he couldn't suspend *habeas corpus*."

"You're reaching way back there, Governor," the host said. "A lot has happened since then."

"Sure, but the fact remains that what I'm doing is not unprecedented. And I can give you other examples that aren't exactly ancient history. Back in the '50s, I think it was '57, the governor of Arkansas, Orval Faubus, defied a unanimous Supreme Court decision saying segregated schools were unconstitutional."

"Yeah, I read something about that. They stopped some black kids from going into an all-white high school."

"That's right. After the court order, segregationists stood in front of the school to block the black kids from entering Central High School in Little Rock. Faubus activated the state National Guard to support the protesters. President Eisenhower nationalized the guard troops and ordered them to return to their armories. Then, he sent in a contingent from the 101st Airborne to escort the kids into the school."

"Even so, this is a hornet's nest you're stirring up, Governor. You still think it's worth it?"

Mike jumped on that. Here was an opportunity to expound on the core motive for defying the court. "You bet it is. I represent the people. I was *not* appointed. And one of the chief reasons I was elected was to do something about illegal immigration. This is what the majority of our citizens wanted, and we gave it to them. And I don't believe the Supreme Court was justified in striking it down."

Before he was asked another question, Mike quickly said, "Let me get to the crux of the issue. Judges are legislating from the bench, and that's not how this republic is supposed to operate. Legislators are elected representatives of the people. If they don't meet expectations, the people can vote them out of office.

"Federal judges are *appointed for life*, which is one reason why the Founders limited their power. They don't normally have to worry about getting kicked out of their jobs, so they're not usually susceptible to public pressure."

"That's a pretty good overview," the host said. "But how about specifics?"

"All right. Look at it this way. If a majority people favor abortion, they can work through their representatives to make it legal. Or, vice versa. Now, contrast that to *Stern versus Carhar*, where the court ruled against a federal statute outlawing partial-birth abortions. How you feel about that issue is moot. The point is that millions of people who oppose that procedure can do little or nothing to stop it."

Without skipping a beat, Mike continued. "Here's another one. Some years ago, the people of California voted by a sizeable majority for a proposition against legalizing gay marriage. But the California state court struck down the proposition.

"You see, there's always the chance judges will override the will of the people. That's why everything we know about the Founders makes it clear they were skeptical of federal judges exercising power beyond those specifically given in the Constitution."

The host began to say something, but Mike held up his hand. "Just a few more seconds." Mike wasn't pedantic, but he knew many Americans didn't fully understand how their government is structured and operates or why the Framers created it that way.

"The men who designed this government intentionally separated its powers into three branches," he explained, holding up three fingers. "Legislative, executive, and judicial, each having specific authority. And they put into place checks and balances, so one branch could not become more powerful than another. The president, for example, has a check over Congress because he can veto legislation. And Congress has a check on the president, because it can override that veto with a two-thirds majority vote. For decades now, the judicial branch has gradually steamrolled that carefully thought-out arrangement."

"Thank you for explaining that, Governor," the host said. "It's good background for our viewers. Even so, wouldn't it be easier to just scrap the law or amend it or get a new one?"

"Sure, it would be easier. But it wouldn't be right. It wouldn't solve the immigration mess and, most of all, it wouldn't be standing up to the excesses of federal courts. This needs to be done."

"Okay, but are you sure this is the time or that this is the issue? And why you?"

"I don't want to sound flip but look at it this way—if not now, when? If not me, then who?"

Mike held his palm to his chest. "I don't claim to be the ultimate patriot, but I love this country dearly. My father fought for it, my brother died for it, and I got shot up a bit for it. I'd do it again if I had to."

"That's very commendable," the host said. "I applaud your service. But what does that have to do with fighting the court?" Mike sensed sarcasm in her tone, but he let it go. "Very simple. I cling tightly to the fundamental concepts this country's based on, what makes it worth loving and risking your life for. And because I love and respect the men who created this government."

He pointed to the camera. "You know, if there is a God, he has definitely blessed America, starting with the Founding Fathers. Think about it. All those brilliant, educated, courageous men in exactly the right place at exactly the right time. It wouldn't be too far of a leap to call that a miracle of sorts, would it?"

The host smiled. "Not quite walking on water. But maybe a miracle nonetheless."

"And," Mike continued, "I'm convinced that if the Founders are looking down on us, they're fuming at how the federal courts have twisted and circumvented the intent of the Constitution. The judiciary has not only assumed powers they weren't granted, but has expanded the scope and power of the federal government. I wonder what kind of plan—or even plot—they'd have hatched to set things straight."

"Interesting thought. But it would be dangerous."

"Ah. That wouldn't have stopped them. They put their lives on the line when they signed the Declaration of Independence and fought the war against England. And it's not like they had nothing to lose. Most of them were well off and well educated—lawyers, wealthy merchants, large plantation owners. They knew the risks and did it anyway. Why? I know this quote by heart. It's the last line in the Declaration of Independence: 'For the support of this declaration, with a strong reliance on the protection of divine providence, we mutually pledge to each other our lives, our fortunes, and our sacred honor.'"

Mike squinted. "Did you hear that? *Our sacred honor.* When was the last time you heard a politician say something like that? These were great men. They've been my heroes since grade school."

"All well and good, Governor. But what does that have to do with what you're doing?"

"Because the Constitution they wrote is a magnificent document that's been a model for fledgling democracies across the world. And I just can't allow it to be defiled and adulterated any longer. It's got to end."

"I have to admit," she said "that was nicely put, Governor."

"Thank you."

"Okay, you get the last word. Sum it up."

"I think we should just take stock of what the judiciary has done in the last forty years or so and ask ourselves if we think most Americans agree with it. Activist judges have exerted influence over school systems, prisons, hiring and firing practices in business, farm quotas, and quite a bit more. They've banned pretty much any religious activity or symbols in public.

"At the same time, they've protected virtual child pornography, flag burning, the seizure of private property, and partial-birth abortion. That's a pretty abysmal record, and we have to prevent it from continuing."

When the interview ended, Stone walked to shake Mike's hand. "You were great. I couldn't have done better myself."

"I don't know about that. But thanks. That's high praise coming from you. I thought it went pretty well, but I wasn't sure," Mike said. "I'm already thinking of other things I should've said."

"I know. There was a time limit. But I wish you'd gotten in more about the church and state thing. Brought up Jefferson and the Danbury Baptists."

"Who?" Mike asked.

"Tell you what, your next interview isn't for another hour. Let's have some coffee and a bite in my office and go over a few things."

Mike nodded. "I'll meet you in ten minutes."

Stone washed down a mouthful of a bran muffin with a sip of coffee. "You know, Mike, it's a pity that you have to go through this at all. The court was wrong. And you did a terrific job proving that this morning. Made your points clearly and crisply. And I loved that little history lesson you gave about the Founders."

Mike tipped his head, and Stone went on. "I was thinking you should bring up some court decisions that backfired in retrospect."

"Yeah. I was thinking *Dred Scott,* for one."

"That's a good one. And *Plessy versus Ferguson,*" Stone said. "That's where the Supreme Court, back in 1896, I think, ruled that Louisiana could require railroads to carry black and white passengers in separate but equal coaches."

"Absolutely. And *Brown versus the Board of Ed.* It reversed *Plessy.*"

"Right. Those are important."

"Anything else?"

"Oh, yes. There are other cases where the court has ignored or upended previous rulings. One that would be especially important these days is how we're now giving people who aren't citizens the same privileges as those who are. Goes back to 1915, *Heim versus McCall.*"

"I've heard of it, but don't know the details."

Stone filled him in.

"That's an awful lot to get into a five-minute interview."

"Well, not just in the one. But you've got upcoming radio show and newspaper interviews. And, of course, the big appearances on Sunday morning. Oh, and don't forget the church and state business.

It's really symbolic of perverting and expanding the aim of the Constitution. Which brings me to the Danbury Baptists . . ."

An hour later, Mike had his second satellite interview, which was remarkably similar to the earlier one. Afterwards, Mike lay on the office sofa reviewing his performance as TV crews dismantled and removed their equipment. He'd reiterated some of the points in his first interview, but also brought in material that he hadn't in the earlier one when the interviewer asked about political corruption.

"We've certainly had our share of corrupt and inept lawmakers," Mike said. "But that holds for Supreme Court justices as well. Some people seem to think the justices are virtually infallible, men of unquestioned wisdom and virtue. And that's just outright wrong. Did you know Justice Hugo Black was a member of the Ku Klux Klan? That in 1969 he had a stroke that resulted in a partial loss of memory, but stayed on the bench?"

Mike then noted that Justice Thurgood Marshall in his later years on the court became indifferent to his duties and often had his clerks write his opinions. He spent hours in his chambers watching soap operas. Even though his eyesight and hearing were failing and he was clearly unable to meet his obligations, he told his clerks that if he died they should "prop me up and keep on voting."

Mike pressed on, pointing out that Justice William O. Douglas was alleged to have sexually assaulted a stewardess he invited to his office. "But that wasn't the worst of it. His divorces from younger women left him financially unstable and he needed to supplement his income. It was reported that he got more than $100,000 from the foundation of Albert Parvin, a former co-owner of the Flamingo Hotel in Las Vegas, as well as an associate of mobster Meyer Lansky and 'Ice Pick Willie' Alderman.

"I'll let your imagination decide how he got that nickname," Mike said. "So, the idea that Supreme Court justices have the wisdom of Solomon and the character of Mother Teresa is mythology."

Chapter Fifteen

The Friday before Mike's Sunday morning talk show interviews in New York, the governor's jet took off at 8:00 a.m. But it wasn't headed for the Big Apple. It landed early that evening in a secured area of Reagan National Airport in Washington, D.C.

Awaiting was a black limousine with blue-tinted windows. Four men in business suits stood at each corner of the vehicle scanning the surroundings. As Mike approached, one of them opened the back seat door. Mike said thanks and climbed in. A sedan pulled in front of the limo and another behind. The four men surrounding the limo got into another car, and the small motorcade proceeded.

It swerved onto a blockaded road closed to the public and then into a well lit tunnel. Minutes later Mike was in the Oval Office of the White House where President Ballard waited with Karl Rostoff, his chief of staff.

Ballard grinned and held out his hand. "How are you, Mike?"

Mike shook it. "Pretty good, all things considered," he said and turned to shake Rostoff's hand. "Good to see you."

"Same here," Rostoff said. He was squat, somewhat unkempt and bald except for a band of graying brown hair ringing the sides of his head. His pudgy face overwhelmed his thin nose, and his eyes seemed in a constant squint. He didn't look it, but Mike knew Rostoff was a political genius.

"Want some dinner?" Ballard asked Mike. "We can meet in the dining room, or I can have something brought here."

"No, thanks. I ate on the plane."

As they sat, Mike eyed the office. He'd been there before, but was still awestruck and inspired by its ambience. He could almost feel the presence and power of its greatest occupants.

Pictures of Ballard with world leaders and celebrities were on the walls and his desk, but the office also displayed Ballard's modest personal taste, decorated mainly with oil paintings and sketches of California's picturesque coast and mountains. The mostly leather and dark wood furniture also reflected the president's down-to-earth persona, as did the bronze Remington cowboy busts.

"Justice Reynolds coming?" Mike asked.

Ballard shook his head. "No need. He's done his part. He's out of it now. The touchiest part was getting him involved. He could have blown the whole thing if he'd objected and disclosed our plans."

"Yeah, that was chancy," Mike said. "But we had to be sure the court would rule against my immigration law and he could have been the swing vote."

"Yes," Ballard said, "but I've known him for years and he was as disgusted as we were about federal courts overstepping their bounds and muzzling in on legislative turf. He was the one who concluded that someone had to refuse to obey a court decision—preferably a Supreme Court decision."

"Still trust him?" Mike asked.

"Oh, sure. He's solid. Very principled. He'll stay mum. He's convinced this is the right thing to do and knows we'd both be impeached if this got out."

"I think you're right," Mike said, then pointed his thumb at Rostoff. "And if I know this guy, he'll take it with him to his grave."

Ballard nodded. "I'd trust him with my life."

"Thanks, boss," Rostoff said.

Mike shook his head. "But you know, Marty, I still can't believe we've gone this far without a hitch. I mean, there were just the four of us, but that's a lot of people to keep a secret like this."

"I know what you mean. Ever since we all agreed on doing this, I've been waiting for a headline that said something like, 'President, Governor, Plot to Thwart Judicial Power.'"

"I think we were all edgy about that," Rostoff said, then looked at Mike. "You did really well on the TV interviews the other day."

"I concur," Ballard said. "I was especially pleased at how you laid out the legal and historical groundwork for your position. That was vital. People had to know you weren't some irrational gadfly."

Mike tipped his head. "Hope I do as well on Sunday."

"I'm sure you will," Ballard said. "We're close to the end, Mike, and I know you won't freeze. No doubt in my mind."

"No, I won't. But I'll tell you, Marty, I want this over with. I want it finished."

Ballard leaned forward. "So do I, Mike. Believe me, as much as you. But we knew this had to be done. Sooner or later, someone had to set a modern precedent for defying the court. And I knew that if anyone had the balls and brains to pull it off, it was you."

"Thanks."

Rostoff tapped Mike's arm. "We're planning to have you up to Camp David soon. We'll invite your two state senators. It's all show, so put on your best act. It's just a finishing touch, a few witnesses to the president and me trying to convince you to abide by the court decision."

"Sounds good. Your idea?"

"No. Actually, the president's. Sometimes he comes up with a good one without me."

Ballard chuckled, then pursed his lips and looked down at his desk for a few moments. "Well, now we go into the last act, Mike. Your part is pretty much over on Sunday. Probably a few more interviews here and there, but that should be it for you. You're in a good position at this point. Just keep enforcing that law. But this could be the riskiest part for me. I'll be in the midst of a furious uproar. The media are going to go nuts. And the opposition . . . well, they'll have their carving knives out. Hell, they might try to impeach me. Dereliction of duty. Failure to defend the Constitution. Who knows what they'll come up with? I'm not altogether sure how the guys on my side will react."

"Maybe," Mike said. "But I doubt it. You're still a pretty popular president."

"Right," Rostoff said. "And the ruckus is going to come from one side of the political spectrum. Have you seen some of the conservative blogs and commentaries? There are plenty of people who support Mike. Early polling shows the same thing. And as we keep making our case, more people will side with us."

"Perhaps," Mike said. "But you know what side the mainstream media will be on."

"Sure," Rostoff said. "But they don't have the influence they used to. Look at their ratings. They're biased, and it's become so blatant that most people see through it and resent it. That's why their audience has shrunk so badly. Aside from that, how's the sanctuary business going?"

"I may have defused it," Mike said and explained the compromise.

"Great," Ballard replied. "That should work."

Rostoff nodded. "I agree. It's a good plan, and if the sanctuary mayors don't agree, they'll look like a bunch of spoiled brats." He looked at his watch and stood. "Well, I've got to run. We're having guests for dinner, and if I'm late my wife will have my head." He shook Mike's hand. "Just stopped by to say hello. Great seeing you again."

"Likewise."

When Rostoff left, Mike said, "Good man."

"Yes, he is. Brilliant guy. Been with me a long time and never let me down."

Ballard leaned forward and looked directly into Mike's eyes. "So, what's going on, Mike?"

"What do you mean?"

"Something's wrong. I can see it."

"Didn't know I was that transparent."

"Not to most people. But this is Marty. We go way back."

Mike glanced down. "It's Jo."

Ballard jerked erect. "What about her?"

Mike sighed. "We're having some problems."

"That doesn't seem possible. What kind of problems?"

Mike told him.

"Wow! That's a stunner. You two are a paradigm of the perfect marriage."

"I'll tell you, Marty, that argument with Jo just about did it for me. I was almost ready to back out of this, maybe just obey the court decision and go back to a normal life without the problems between Jo and me."

"That's understandable. Something like this can strain a marriage, even one as good as yours."

"Oh, it wasn't just that particular argument. It's the cumulative effect of everything that's going on. The spat was just what could have been the final straw on the camel's back, that's all." He paused. "I wish I could tell her what's really happening and why. Maybe if she knew, she'd side with me, and that would make the whole thing a lot easier."

"I know what you mean, Mike. Keeping this from my wife has bugged me to no end. It's almost like I'm being unfaithful to her."

"Yeah."

"But you said it yourself. Just the four of us keeping this secret was hard enough. Letting anyone else in on it would increase the chances of being found out. Besides, what if you told Jo and it made her even more dead set against it?"

"Didn't consider that. I guess I'm just thinking out loud. Or, just needed to get it off my chest with someone I trust."

Ballard stood, walked to Mike, and his placed hand on his friend's shoulder. "You'll work it out. You'll find a way. I'm sure of it."

"I hope so, Marty."

Chapter Sixteen

Mike was put up in the Lincoln bedroom, and as he prepared for bed, he remembered how easily Ballard had picked up on the stress he felt because of the friction with Josephine. It didn't surprise him. Ballard had always been perceptive. Moreover, he and the president had often confided in each other. They were close, although Mike always marveled at that. He thought they were an unlikely pair, a case of opposites attracting. Although they agreed on almost everything politically, their lives could not have been more different.

Ballard's father, a successful real estate developer, made millions and invested wisely. He retired at age fifty with an enormous estate and resided in a huge San Diego oceanside mansion. Ballard, an only child, lived a life of privilege. He excelled in school and was offered scholarships to several elite universities, but refused them. His family could easily afford the expense, he told Mike, "so why take it from someone who really needed it?"

Besides, he said he preferred the Air Force Academy. After graduating as an officer, he was trained as an F-4 Phantom pilot. Shortly after earning his wings, he volunteered for Vietnam, but wasn't sent. Mike suspected that Ballard's father surreptitiously pulled strings that ensured his son would never get there.

By contrast, Mike came from a low-income neighborhood on Chicago's south side with strict immigrant parents who worshipped their adopted country. Joseph and Marie DiGrasso were hardened by the Great Depression, then joined the ranks of the "Greatest Generation" to win World War II. Joe was wounded twice fighting in the Pacific.

Unskilled and barely educated, Joe worked long hours unloading trucks and boxcars. At sixty-four years old, he did the work of a young man—and died of a heart attack a year before he planned to retire.

His sons emulated his traditional values and absorbed his patriotism. Not only was Mike's older brother killed in Vietnam, his younger brother served as a Navy corpsman. Mike chose the marines, enlisting immediately after graduating from the University of Illinois. After Officer Candidate School, he volunteered for Vietnam, where he served two tours, then went to Yale Law School on the GI Bill. Having fallen in love with San Diego while stationed at Camp Pendleton, he moved there after getting his law degree and became a deputy district attorney.

When he met Ballard at Yale, they didn't immediately take to each other. But they had some classes and study groups together, and as they got to know each other, a friendship emerged, and Ballard explained his original stand-offishness.

"Well, first of all, you were a marine. And, secondly, you were a marine."

Mike laughed. "But that's over, right?"

"Absolutely."

Their friendship was cemented after Ballard asked Mike to join his fraternity. Mike declined, saying he didn't think he'd fit. When Ballard mentioned this to a fraternity brother, the response turned him red.

"He's right," the other guy said, "he probably wouldn't fit. He's a street kid."

"What's that supposed to mean!" Ballard snarled. "He's not as good as us?"

Stunned, the other man backed away a step. "I didn't mean anything by it. He said he wouldn't fit. I just agree."

Ballard stepped toward him, almost nose-to-nose. "Listen, that guy is a decorated combat veteran. He was wounded. He got through college on a scholarship. How dumb does that make him? Believe me, his blood is as blue as yours. Say something like that again and you'll regret it! Fraternity brother or not."

Mike heard about the incident and met Ballard for a beer. "You didn't have to do that, Marty."

"But I did. And I'm glad I did. It just came out of me. The arrogance of the son-of-a-bitch. I can't stand that kind of attitude."

"I've noticed that. And I've always admired it, especially coming from someone with your background. It's hard to find humility at that level of society."

Mike didn't talk about his past very often, but Ballard was fascinated that Mike had come so far from such a humble background. So, at Ballard's prodding, Mike occasionally told him about his youth in "the old neighborhood."

Red-brick tenement-like buildings separated by narrow gangways lined the streets. Most were three- or four-story structures with a "garden apartment" below street level.

"Today, people might call it a slum," Mike told Ballard one night as they strolled along the path of a park near Ballard's fraternity house. They'd just spent hours in a study group cramming for midterms and wanted to take in some cool night air. "But it wasn't. The people wouldn't let it be. The buildings were old but clean and well-maintained, and people kept property litter-free. Crime was almost nonexistent because neighbors were friends who trusted and looked out for one another."

His family lived in a second-floor flat where Mike shared a bedroom with his brothers. "We were poor," Mike said, "but food was always on the table, and we had clean clothes to wear. Gifts were there at Christmas, and my brothers and I shared a bicycle. The school playground was right across the street, and a city park was two blocks away. What more could I want?"

He told Ballard about the hot days when someone opened a fire hydrant, then wedged a board underneath the nozzle to create a high arching spray so children in swim trunks could play beneath the shower of cold water. At night, people gathered on the front steps of the buildings as he and other kids played in the street.

"I remember the laughter and voices and the sound of the baseball game on the radio. There was the clean, fresh aroma of Lake Michigan when the wind came in from the east and the putrid odor of the stockyards when it blew in from the north."

Ballard's eyes teared when Mike told him how his mother would kiss a piece of bread too stale even for making bread crumbs, then make the sign of the cross and say, "God, forgive me," before wetting it and throwing it out to the birds.

"Is that why you always take a doggy bag from a restaurant, even though there's almost nothing left of your meal?" Ballard asked.

"Yep. It goes home to the refrigerator for another day. Waste not, want not. The Depression made its mark on my parents and, because of them, on me."

They sat on a bench, and Ballard leaned back with a wistful expression. "You know, Mike, I envy you that experience. You must be far more appreciative of what you've accomplished than anything I could feel."

That remark touched Mike, and forged his friendship with Ballard into kinship.

Chapter Seventeen

Over breakfast the next morning, Mike and Ballard chatted about what they'd discuss at the Camp David meeting. Then, Mike was driven to the airport and flew to New York.

The TV stations put him up in an expensive midtown Manhattan hotel. He spent the afternoon going over notes for the interviews and after dinner went for a walk, bundled in a white turtleneck sweater and suede leather jacket. Walking to Park Avenue, he followed it north to Central Park South.

At 6:30 p.m., the streets were active with people returning from shopping or going out for the night. Mike liked New York, thought it was made for strolling and sightseeing, even in winter. A light, fluffy snow covered the sidewalks. Cabs sped past, splashing through slush on the street, and occasionally a horse-drawn carriage carrying warmly clothed people clopped by. Street vendors were on almost every corner, and the aroma of the sauerkraut-topped hot dogs hung in the air. Years ago, he and Josephine visited New York, the first time for both of them. They sampled those dogs, and now his mouth watered remembering the salty-sour taste. If he wasn't so full from dinner, he'd have had one.

He crossed the street to Central Park, remembering him and Josephine spending almost a full day on a tour of the park, finishing with an outdoor concert at the ornate Naumberg Bandshell. He shoved his angst into a remote recess of his mind and reminisced.

What different times back then, he thought. Sure, his job was demanding because he put his heart and soul into every prosecution. But they were young and, even after their first child, almost carefree, filled with optimism and the exuberance of juvenescence. The blissful memories and the picturesque surroundings eased his tension.

Just over the snow-dusted trees on Vista Rock, he could see the gray rock structure of Belvedere Castle, its bell tower peeking out, and he faintly heard the sounds of the calliope at the huge carousel inside the park. Despite the cold, people walked and jogged on the park paths, their breaths forming vapors in the chilly air. He sat on a bench for twenty minutes soaking up the serene atmosphere, then returned to his hotel.

At NBC the following morning, the show's moderator, and one of the station's legal advisors greeted him as he entered the studio. "Welcome, Governor," the moderator said, holding out his hand. He was a stately man with thick, graying brown hair. The legal advisor, tall and stocky, shook Mike's hand, but said nothing. Mike thought that odd, actually kind of rude, but ignored it.

The moderator motioned to a chair at the end of an oblong dark wood table. "Take a seat, please," he said as he and the advisor sat to Mike's left. The wall behind the table displayed the station's logo, and about twenty feet to Mike's right camera and sound crews, wearing ear phones, inspected and tested equipment.

As Mike expected, the first five minutes of the interview were a rehash of the previous ones. But he eventually segued to the issue of religion and government. "Federal judges have done the same thing by misinterpreting what we call the Establishment Clause in the First Amendment. All it says is that 'Congress shall make no law respecting the establishment of religion, or prohibiting the free exercise thereof.'"

"That's it! The Founders wanted to be sure the government couldn't create a state religion. But the courts have molded that clause to the point where a nativity scene or other religious symbols can't be displayed on government property."

"Some people are offended by religious icons on public property," the moderator said.

"The Constitution doesn't give anyone the right *not* to be offended. Any more than it gives you the right to be heard because you have freedom of speech."

"What's wrong with a wall between church and state?" the moderator asked. "Thomas Jefferson believed in it. He coined the phrase."

"There's no such wording in the Constitution. Jefferson used it in a letter to a Baptist community in Danbury, Connecticut, which had written to congratulate him on becoming president. He wrote to thank them and noted that he wouldn't create national holidays of fasting and thanksgiving. In closing, he quoted the Establishment Clause and finished with the phrase, 'thus building a wall of separation between church and state.' That was the extent of it."

"Okay," the host said. "But why is this so bothersome for you?"

"Lots of reasons, but mainly because it's an example of how federal courts extend the intent of the Establishment Clause—and other constitutional provisions—in a way that can produce all kinds of ridiculous possibilities. Here's a hypothetical. Suppose a priest is saying mass and has a heart attack. Are you telling me that a fire department ambulance can't get him to a hospital?"

"Oh, come on, Governor," the advisor huffed. "That's a *reductio ad absurdum*. You can carry almost anything far enough out to where it makes no sense."

"That's what I'm saying. Read too much into the Constitution and you find yourself in very confusing and silly situations. This is why the Founders limited the judiciary's powers."

"Frankly," the analyst said, "this is all immaterial. You're diverting us from the base issue. The matter at hand is judicial review and you ignoring the court ruling."

"It's hardly immaterial," Mike responded, now understanding why the advisor said nothing when he shook hands—the guy didn't much like what Mike was doing. And probably didn't much like Mike either. "I'm pointing out how the courts misinterpret the Constitution. That's what this is all about. It's the basis for my actions. But, okay, let's take it where you want to go—judicial review.

"Consider this: James Madison took copious notes during the Constitutional Convention, and those notes show that judicial review was considered by the delegates and they rejected it. The *Federalist Papers* also give solid evidence of this."

The moderator cut in to remind viewers that the *Federalist Papers* were the eighty-five essays written by James Madison, Alexander Hamilton, and John Jay, who later became the first chief justice of the Supreme Court. He noted that the essays were intended to counter arguments of the anti-federalists, politicians who opposed the new Constitution.

Mike continued, noting that many of the Founders agreed with anti-federalists who feared the courts would shape our government into any form they wanted. "And, of course, they were right. That's why I'm here. And I'd bet that if the Founders were alive today, they'd stand with me."

The advisor chuckled. "Alexander Hamilton wouldn't. He was more concerned about the other branches overwhelming the judiciary."

Mike almost smiled. Stone had coached him well and he was ready. "That's a common misconception, because one of his essays in the *Federalist Papers* emphasized the need for the judiciary to be independent—free from the influence of Congress, the president, and the political winds of the time." Mike raised his finger. "However, even in that essay, Hamilton said he didn't believe the judiciary was a threat '*so long as it remained truly distinct from the other branches.*' Hamilton said there could be no liberty if the judiciary involved itself in legislative or executive issues."

"Doesn't matter," the advisor said. "You seem to be living in the past. There are many scholars who say the Constitution needs to be liberally interpreted so it can be adapted to contemporary circumstances."

The advisor's attitude was beginning to piss Mike off, but he held his temper. "That approach has produced judges who interpret the Constitution in ways that impose their personal ideas on society. Justice Thurgood Marshall revealed this attitude beautifully when he was asked about his judicial philosophy. He said, 'You do what you think is right, and let the law catch up.'

"That kind of arrogance has led activist judges to distort the intent of the Founders. A good example is their flagrant misuse of the 'necessary and proper clause' of the Constitution, the so-called 'elastic clause.' They've stretched it so far that the whole judiciary ought to be doing Spandex commercials."

The moderator laughed and turned to the advisor. "Maybe you should explain what the governor is referring to."

"He's talking about Article One, Section Eight of the Constitution, which gives Congress power to make all laws *necessary and proper* for carrying out its responsibilities. Some people think the court has used that clause too liberally and grossly extended the powers of the courts and the federal government."

"And I'm one of them," Mike said. "That same section gives Congress the power to regulate trade, and the courts have also applied *it* in ways that have done the same thing."

The advisor raised his eyebrows. "There's nothing in the Constitution about regulating airlines because the Founders couldn't envision such a thing. So are you saying the commerce clause was wrongly used when Congress made rules for operating airlines?"

"No, I'm not. But that was a legitimate use of the commerce clause because it *gave* reasonable power to the legislature."

The advisor snickered. "That's a distinction without a difference."

Mike momentarily envisioned his fist crashing into the advisor's mouth. "You're wrong. In that instance, the court didn't legislate. It allowed elected lawmakers to legislate. That's a far cry from . . . let's say, judges telling airlines how to spend their money or how to set their fares. I'm simply saying that rulings that are tantamount to legislation are inappropriate."

The advisor gave a condescending sigh. "Give an example of what you're talking about—if you can."

Mike glared at him. "Okay, let's take some hot-button issues. You know as well as I that there is nothing in the Constitution that guarantees a right to privacy. But the court managed to find that so-called right in the Fourth and Fourteenth Amendments—where that word never appears. And then they applied that fictitious right in a way that allows abortion."

"You want *Roe versus Wade* overturned?" the advisor shot back.

Mike waved his hand. "I'm not going to waste time arguing abortion. That's not the point. I'm saying abortion is not the concern of the Supreme Court, and it should never have ruled on that case in the first place. It doesn't belong in the judicial arena."

"Why not?"

"Because it's a public policy decision that should be made by elected representatives. What's happening is that interest groups who can't get the support of citizens and their lawmakers are sidestepping the legislative process and having the judiciary do their work for them."

"All right, Governor," the moderator said. "I don't think I agree with that, but I'll give you the benefit of the doubt."

But the advisor said, "I don't think we should. What the governor seems to want is an impotent judiciary that concerns itself strictly with legal and criminal matters. That's a step backward. It's reactionary, and I, for one, disagree with it."

Mike tensed. "I want to confine the court to the issues that the Founders wanted it confined to. Limiting the court in this way doesn't make it impotent. It just keeps it in the role the Founders intended."

The advisor was about to say something, but Mike didn't give him a chance. "In recent decades, the courts have gone so far as to tell state and local governments how to spend their tax money. For example, the requirement to admit children of illegals into our schools and allow them welfare wasn't made by lawmakers. It was made by judges. That costs taxpayers money, and it is not up to people in black robes to decide how we spend tax dollars. That's up to legislators accountable to their constituents."

"Yes, but that—" the advisor started to say.

Mike ignored him. "And there's more to consider. What ever happened to states' rights?" He pointed at the advisor. "You know the Tenth Amendment says the federal government has only the power specifically given it by the Constitution. All other powers go to the states and the people. What's developed, intentionally or not, is an alliance among judges, special interest groups, and politicians that swells federal power."

The advisor sneered. "You'd dare mention states' rights. You know how that was used in the South before Civil Rights laws were passed."

"Now you're making my point. That's the way it's supposed to work. Congress passed legislation to prevent what was going on from continuing. All the court did was give that legislation its seal of approval."

"That's all the time we have," the moderator said. "Thank you for being here."

The moderator at *Fox News* was relatively young but good at his job. Nonetheless, the interview began with questions Mike was tired of hearing and his pat responses made him feel as if he were giving a campaign stump speech that's repeated over and over. But he eventually steered the conversation to where he wanted to go.

"I don't understand the unquestioning faith people have in the Supreme Court, considering some of the decisions it's made. Look at the Dred Scott ruling," he said and summarized the Scott decision. "Do you think that was a wise ruling?"

The moderator shook his head. "No, I don't."

Mike listed the court decisions he and Stone had discussed, those which had been overturned by later court rulings and said, "In short, the Supreme Court has made some bad calls—meaning that just because the court rules on an issue doesn't mean its decision is right."

The moderator shifted in his chair. "These are landmark cases you're citing, Governor. But they're decades old and have been reversed."

"Yes, they were reversed. That's the point. The decisions seemed reasonable when they were made but didn't stand the test of time. And, unfortunately, sometimes logical, sensible decisions are made and overridden by later rulings. Here's one that I know sticks in the throats of a lot of taxpayers. The case was *Heim versus McCall*. The court said states that don't provide illegal non-citizens with public benefits *do not* violate the equal protection clause of the Fourteenth Amendment. Now, that makes sense, doesn't it? Why should non-citizens get the same benefits as taxpaying citizens? But later court rulings have upended that, and today illegals get public educations, food assistance, Supplemental Security Income and a lot more. And it's all paid for by American taxpayers."

The interview continued for ten minutes more with Mike giving short, comprehensive answers, and as he left the studio, he was satisfied with his performance. That reassured him. These appearances, more than most of the others, would be the ones where his comments would be widely aired on the news. He relaxed a bit. Ballard was right. His part was nearly finished, aside from a few more radio and newspaper interviews. Now, it was up to the president to bring everything to a successful conclusion.

Chapter Eighteen

Mike got home Sunday night. Josephine was watching television in the family room.

"Hi, Mike," she called out. "How are you?"

He walked to her and gave her a kiss on the cheek. "I'm okay. Just a bit tired."

"Sleep at all on the flight?"

"Tried to, but kept thinking about what else I should have squeezed into those interviews."

"I thought you did really well."

"Thanks. That's good to hear."

"That legal advisor on NBC really had it in for you."

"Was it that obvious?"

Josephine nodded. "Yes. But you came out way ahead of him."

Mike considered just saying thanks and dropping the matter, but he sensed a chance to change her mind. "I appreciate that. Did I convince you?"

She shook her head. "No, Mike. I'm afraid you didn't."

"Come on, Jo. Give it a little more thought, will you. I mean—"

She shut the TV. "No, Mike. I have thought about it. Quite a bit. I'm sorry, but I still think this is a mistake. I know it bugs you when I say it, but I'm going to tell you anyway. Your job is tough enough as it is, and this war with the Supreme Court is making it worse. Look at you. You're not just tired. You're exhausted. And that worries me."

"Just some jet lag."

"It's more than that, and you know it."

"Wow. This is a hell of a welcome home."

"I'm sorry. I really am. But you brought it up. I'm concerned, and you don't seem to care."

"That's not true. You know that's not true."

She stood and held up her palms. "Okay. This was a bad time to talk about it. Let's just drop it."

"All right."

"Good. You want something to eat? I can put something together for you real quick, and there are leftovers."

He shook his head. "No. I'm not hungry. I'm going to clean up and relax a bit."

As tired as he was, it took a while for Mike to fall asleep that night. Perhaps it was the nagging anxiety from what he was doing. Or, maybe the friction between him and Josephine. And when he finally did doze off, it was a short and far from peaceful slumber.

His eyes snapped open and darted around the dark bedroom. He blinked several times, then sat up and ran his fingers through his hair, which was soaked with perspiration.

He lay quietly for a few minutes, then got up and put on his robe and slippers.

Josephine rolled over. "Where you going?"

"Downstairs for a while. I woke up and can't get back to sleep."

"Heat some milk. That usually helps."

"Yeah, I'll do that."

He went to the kitchen, and in the moonlight from the windows heated some milk, poured it into a cup and sat motionless at the table. Almost two years since the last one, two years since the last nightmare, and he'd hoped he was past them. But the Vietnam images still simmered in the deep crevices of his mind, swirling and bubbling like white hot magma under the surface of a volcano. And tonight something forced a narrow crack in the cast-iron psychological lid he'd welded over his memories and they spilled out like molten-hot lava over the lip of the volcano.

Mike usually avoided relating specifics of his Vietnam combat experience, glossing over it, often humorously. He was vague about it even with Josephine. The details he told only to his father.

But years later he told Ballard. He wasn't sure why. He and Ballard had become close. But Mike had other friends and never mentioned his wartime experiences to them. Still, Ballard was different. He was a damned good sounding board with a very sympathetic ear. Mike actually felt better unloading his feelings on him. It was almost like going to confession.

Ballard didn't question him much about Vietnam. Mike assumed his friend sensed his reticence to discuss it. One night, however, an incident led Ballard to inquire. After working on legal briefs at Ballard's fraternity house, they went to the recreation room to relax and watch television. Someone flicked on a documentary about Vietnam, which included the My Lai Massacre. Mike was immediately uncomfortable. He looked away from the TV from time to time, pursing his lips tightly, struggling to shut out his thoughts. Halfway into the documentary, he said he was tired and got up to leave. Ballard suggested they go out for a beer and a burger.

They went to a nearby pub and after ordering, chatted and sipped from their frosted beer mugs as they waited for the burgers. Finally, Ballard asked Mike about his reaction to the documentary.

"Watching things like that irritate me," Mike said. "The way they portray the troops is distorted. You'd think all of them were on dope, demented, or sadists. It's just not true."

"Vietnam would have been a totally different experience for me," Ballard said, "being a pilot instead of a ground-pounder. How was it for you?"

"Tedium is a good word for it. You know the old adage, 'five days of boredom and thirty minutes of terror.' Most of the time you're training, keeping your post clean and prepared, staying alert and trying to keep cool. The weather was miserable. Hot, humid, rainy. Then, one day you're on patrol or your base gets hit and you're under fire and . . ." His voice trailed off.

Mike figured Ballard recognized his reluctance to go further, but couldn't contain his curiosity.

The burgers came, both very rare.

"So, what kind of action did you see?" Ballard asked as they both squeezed on mustard and added some salt.

"Some," Mike replied and took a bite of his burger, hoping Ballard would take the hint.

He didn't.

"What was it like, Mike? How'd you deal with it?"

"Most of it's training," Mike said, putting a few french fries into his mouth. "You just sort of react without thinking. You develop a mindset, convince yourself that you have two choices: You can chicken out or you can do your job regardless of the consequences. Then you just hope you do the latter."

Ballard bit into his burger, some of its juice dripping onto his chin. He wiped it with his napkin and took a gulp of beer. "Tell me, Mike, why haven't you ever mentioned the Silver Star and Purple Heart?"

Mike's head whipped toward Ballard. "How'd you know about that?" he snapped. He noticed Ballard's stunned expression and forced himself to calm down. "Sorry. Didn't mean to bark at you like that, Marty. It's just that I've never told anyone but family."

"Word gets around. I heard someone in admissions found out while verifying your military records."

"I think I'd like to visit admissions. Those are private records."

Mike took another bite of his hamburger. Ballard was quiet for a few moments and Mike could tell his friend was trying to stop the questioning—but couldn't.

"So," Ballard finally said, "are you going to tell me about the medals? I'd like to know, Mike. I really would."

Mike leaned his forearms on the bar and looked at Ballard. He really didn't want to go into it. But he and Ballard were tight. All right, Mike thought, but just part of the story. Just part of it.

"Okay. But you've got to remember that it all happens so fast, even though it seems like slow motion while it's going on. It's like you're not really there, like you're watching yourself from above or in a dream. You just react, do what you have to."

Then, he briefly related how he was hit by shrapnel as he carried the wounded to the Medevac.

"But you've got two Purple Hearts," Ballard said. "And there are rumors that you turned down another Silver Star."

Mike's head dropped. "How did that get started?"

Ballard shrugged. "I don't know. Is it true?"

"This is a tough one, Marty. It's hard to talk about."

"You've gone this far."

Mike exhaled heavily. "All right. But keep this to yourself. Don't feed the rumor mill."

Ballard nodded.

Mike pushed away his burger. He looked around the bar as if checking that no one was within earshot, then stared straight ahead.

"My platoon was moving into a village about twenty miles north of Da Nang. As we came down the dirt road through the jungle, the trees thinned out and gradually became a clearing with ankle-high grass that ran for five klicks or so before becoming foothills of the mountains behind them.

"The village was less than a football field away. The ground sloped upward, forming sort of a knoll," he said, raising his hand diagonally upward. "A dry river bed ran along the top of it. There was a ridge on our left, about eight feet high and maybe a hundred or so yards long, and covered with tall grass and boulders. On the right the jungle seemed to go on endlessly."

Mike ran his tongue across his lips. "I scanned the area with binoculars, then sent out two point men to reconnoiter. When they were almost at the village, I sent out two fire teams, four men each. As they neared the village, they dropped to the ground and formed a defensive perimeter, and I went out with a second set of two fire teams.

"We were about twenty yards out when they hit us," Mike said, and his Adam's apple jumped as he swallowed hard. "We weren't expecting it. The village was cleared only two days earlier. We were just supposed to set up a fire base and send out patrols. The rest of the company would reinforce in a few days.

"But the Viet Cong had set up an L-shaped ambush. They were ahead of us in the riverbed in front of the village and on the ridge to our left. There was a withering fire—machine guns, small arms, mortars. My point men went down immediately and one of the guys with me in the second set of fire teams was hit."

Mike told Ballard that the VC had chosen their ground well. The only cover was back in the trees, and it seemed they were a thousand yards away. Mike ordered one fire team to grab the wounded man and get back to the trees while he and the others laid down covering fire. When the first team was under cover, he and the others ran for the trees.

One of them was hit, and Mike and another marine grabbed him under his armpits and carried him to the trees, with bullets whining past, smacking into tree bark, pinging off the rocks and snapping through leaves.

Mike shook his head and smiled. "Funny what comes to mind when you think back on things like this. I can't get rid of the image of hundreds of those tree leaves raining down on us.

"Anyway, it's a miracle no one else was hit. The trees and boulders and a small dry gulch to our left rear provided pretty good cover. But the VC were raking our position. Three more of my guys were hit and taken to the gulch, where a corpsman had set up an aid station. What worried me most were my point men and the first two fire teams were pinned down and I knew some of them were hit, maybe killed."

He explained to Ballard that he was afraid to call in artillery because the VC were too close to his men near the village, and he didn't want friendly fire casualties. He radioed for a Medevac helicopter and air support, and Cobra gunships, but they wouldn't get there for fifteen or twenty minutes.

"That was way too long," he said, glancing at Ballard. "We were taking a lot of casualties, and that was going to get worse if I didn't do something fast."

Ballard leaned to Mike. "What was going through your head right then? I mean, under heavy fire, seeing those men go down, no help available."

"Believe it or not, I don't remember. If I was thinking at all, it was unconsciously." He stopped and looked at Ballard as if he were about to reveal a secret. "This is when it happens, Marty, where training and simple reaction take over. Some part of your brain switches off, and some kind of primal instinct takes its place."

Mike told Ballard he took two fire teams to the left, leaving his top sergeant in charge of the other men. He had to get to the right flank of the VC on the ridge and lay down enfilade fire on their position. If they could knock the VC off the ridge, they could move ahead to flank the ones in the riverbed in front of the village.

Mike led his men through the trees to the VC's right flank, just behind the tree line. But in front of them was about thirty yards of open ground with only some boulders and swatches of high grass for cover. And the flank was anchored by a heavy machine gun.

He had to take out the machine gun in front of him and rake the VC line from its flank—immediately. Keeping four men at the tree line for covering fire, he led the other four in a run toward the machine gun. Halfway to the edge of the ridge, they were spotted. The VC machine gunner swung his weapon around and opened fire. Two of the men with him were hit immediately. Mike grabbed one and dragged him behind a boulder into a small swatch of grass as bullets buzzed through the air and kicked up small explosions in the ground around him.

He pulled the pin on a grenade and tossed it. When it went off, he ran out for the other wounded marine. The men manning the machine gun had disappeared, but two more quickly replaced them and more VC joined them, although two were hit by the covering fire of the marines at the tree line behind him. He and the other marine pulled their wounded comrade behind the boulder.

The unwounded marine with him lay prone on the ground just in front of him returning fire. Then, the back of his skull exploded, and blood and bone fragments splattered Mike. Blinking a few times, Mike lobbed another grenade and after the explosion leaped up and ran through the smoke toward the enemy position, his trigger finger almost a blur as he rapidly squeezed of rounds from his M-16—but the rifle jammed.

Continuing forward, he grabbed his .45-caliber sidearm and fired. Then, the sharp, powerful impact in his right thigh and his leg giving way. He resumed firing as he got up and moved forward, dragging his right leg behind him. He signaled the four marines behind him and they advanced, firing as they moved ahead.

Mike ejected the empty magazine from his side arm and shoved in another. He trudged ahead, operating on pure adrenalin, and emptied the side arm's magazine. He rammed in another, his last, and hobbled forward, firing the .45.

At the top of the ridge, eight VC lay dead or wounded, but in front of him, others were moving toward him to retake their flank. Grabbing one of the VC Kalashnikovs, he emptied it into the wounded VC.

From the corner of his eye, Mike saw Ballard wince. "I couldn't fire on the VC coming at me and watch the wounded. One of them could have reached a weapon and greased me. It's one of those instantaneous decisions," he said, snapping his fingers. "No. Make that instantaneous reactions that happen in situations like that."

Mike went on, telling Ballard how he knelt down to take pressure off his wounded leg and make himself a smaller target. The marines from the rear took positions next to him. Mike reached for the enemy machine gun but was hit again, this time in his left forearm. It flew back, and Mike fell to his side, grimacing in pain for a moment before pushing himself back to his knees, his left arm hanging at his side. He pulled back the bolt on the machine gun and opened fire. A grenade exploded in front of him. A piece of shrapnel sliced his left cheek.

"That's when I got this," he told Ballard, pointing to the two-inch scar on his face.

The marines had good enfilade fire on the VC, Mike said, giving them the advantage, even though they were outnumbered. He recalled the pungent smell of cordite, bullets whizzing past, orange tracer rounds lacing the air. Finally, the VC pulled back.

As they disappeared, Mike heard the thwacking sound of Cobras and he lay down on his back. One marine tore open Mike's right pant leg and cleaned the wound as best as he could, then applied the dressing from his first-aid packet, all the while screaming for a corpsman. A second marine worked on Mike's arm as the other two went back to tend to the wounded man in the grass behind them.

Mike heard rockets exploding as the Cobras fired on the fleeing VC. Two other marines and a corpsman came to the ridge and carried him and the other wounded down to the now silent clearing, where two Medevac choppers had just landed.

"I blacked out when they put me into the chopper," Mike continued. "The next thing I knew, I was in a hospital tent with my leg bandaged and a cast on my arm."

Mike shrugged. "That's it. I saw other action, but nothing as bad as that. It put me in the hospital for a while, and I needed a cane for almost a month. The bullet that hit my forearm broke the bone, and I had to wear a cast for five weeks . . . in that miserable humidity and heat. Sometimes, I think that was the worst part. Itched like a son-of-a-bitch. When they took that cast off and cleaned my arm, it was like having an orgasm. It acts up now and then if there's cold or rain coming. Best weather forecaster in the country."

Ballard smiled and started to say something, then stopped. Mike waited and Ballard finally asked, "How many men did you lose?"

Mike looked down. "Five dead, nine wounded," he said, his voice choking. "They investigated and concluded that I hadn't done anything wrong. But I didn't agree with that then and I still don't. That's why I wouldn't take the Silver Star."

"What! Reacting the way you did under those conditions? Sounds like you did everything right to me."

"Oh, yeah. After I'd already fucked up. As far as I'm concerned, I got those guys killed."

Ballard cocked his head. "I don't follow."

"I should have seen it coming, Marty. I should have made sure that fuckin' ridge on our left was clear before I sent out the fire teams. There would have been a fire fight anyway, but if we'd discovered them on the ridge, I wouldn't have had all those men out in the open, wouldn't have taken all those casualties.

"I wrote to the families personally. Thought it might help them, help me, be some kind of catharsis. It wasn't. I can still remember their names and faces. Sometimes I feel like I died with them, like I left a piece of me back there and after all these years I'm just beginning to get it back."

"Good Lord, Mike. That's twenty-twenty hindsight."

Mike shook his head. "No, Marty, I'm afraid it's not. I should have sized up that terrain and recognized right away that it was perfect for an ambush like that."

"You can't carry that guilt around you for the rest of your life."

"Oh, it's not always with me. But sometimes something will bring it back to mind. It's just something I have to live with it."

Ballard put his hand on Mike's shoulder. They sat there silently for a while, then left—but only after Mike got a doggy bag for his uneaten burger.

Chapter Nineteen

Carlos Castellano was preoccupied as he and Julio drove to work, and Julio picked up on it. "You worried about something?" he asked.

Carlos ran his fingers against his lips. "This thing with the phony documents. I'm more nervous about selling them now than when I first started. I feel like I'm living on borrowed time. Two of the other guys were picked up yesterday. Maybe I've just been lucky all these months."

"Perhaps you should stop doing it."

"I don't know, Julio. I'm making a lot of money, and we'll need it badly if we have to go back to Mexico. Besides, I don't know if I can get out of it so easy."

Carlos started selling counterfeit documents to illegals five months earlier. It wasn't something he'd gone looking for. Just cause and effect, serendipitous.

There'd been bad blood between him and one of the other construction workers for years, ever since Carlos began working with Julio. Fortunately, they often worked at different job sites so the friction between them never sparked a serious physical altercation.

Juan Cortez was a smug bully prone to biting sarcasm and occasional outright insults. Julio had warned Carlos about him and said not to be provoked. "Juan is here legally. You're not. You're the one in danger of being deported."

Juan didn't bother all the workers. A jackal seeking the weakest prey, he directed his abuse at those who feared him. So, when Carlos ignored his degrading remarks or tried to make a joke of them, Juan misread it as cowardice and became increasingly obnoxious.

Carlos knew that a confrontation was inevitable. And it came shortly before Marisol would have their fourth child. Carlos was overjoyed. But another mouth to feed perplexed him, making him more susceptible to his emotions. The workmen at the construction site were breaking for the day, leaving the thirty half-built skeletal houses of the new subdivision south of L.A. Rain fell most of the day and the dirt on the job site was mud.

The sky was still overcast, and mist hung in the air. Carlos threw a light waterproof windbreaker over his flannel shirt which, like his blue jeans and boots, was splattered with plaster and white dust from the drywall. As he stepped out of the house where he and Julio had been working, Juan approached.

"I hear your wife is due pretty soon," he said.

"That's right," Carlos responded and began walking toward his pickup truck parked at the edge of the job site.

"Congratulations," Juan said.

Carlos turned, his head cocked to one side, confused by Juan's unusual friendly behavior. "Thank you," he said.

Then, Juan said loud enough for others to hear, "I'm surprised you can make babies. Didn't think you had the equipment. Are you sure it's yours?"

Carlos stared Juan directly in the eyes, unblinking, teeth clenched, muscles tense. His face flushed, then went white, as blood funneled from his head to the muscles and organs used to fight or flee. But Carlos wasn't readying himself to flee. Julio saw it and jumped in front of him.

"Don't," he said, putting his hands on Carlos's chest. "Don't do it, my friend. Let it go. It's just words."

Carlos looked past Julio at Juan and started to say something, then turned to walk away, rankled by some of the men laughing at him.

Juan sidestepped Julio, grabbed Carlos's arm and spun him around. "Don't turn your back on me, asshole! I'm tired of that!" he shouted, then shoved Carlos.

Until now, it had only been insults. Juan had never touched him, never pushed him. Julio tried to get between them again.

Too late.

Carlos uncoiled a solid right square on Juan's chin, buckling the bully's knees and knocking him back a few feet. Julio again stood between the two men, but Carlos pushed him away. "I've had enough of this," he growled, his chest heaving.

Juan was two inches taller than Carlos and weighed perhaps thirty pounds more, not much of it fat. But Carlos grew up fighting in the streets and alleys of his poverty-stricken home town and he'd many times used his fists in the rough and tumble oil fields of Faja de Ore, on the Central Coast of the Gulf of Mexico, just before coming to America. He was agile, quick, and strong as a bull.

Juan regained his balance. As the other workers formed a circle around the two men, Juan charged, trying to tackle Carlos. But Carlos quickly shot his spread legs behind him, not allowing Juan to pull his knees inward as he pushed forward to bring Carlos down. Carlos doubled his fists and pounded them into the back of Juan's head, knocking him to his knees. Then, he stepped back, hoping this was over.

But Juan got to his feet and stepped forward. He shot two left jabs at Carlos and followed with a hard right cross. Carlos ducked. Then, with his entire body and all the strength in his right arm, drove his elbow deep into Juan's rib cage. Juan grunted and doubled over. Carlos swiveled right, pushed down hard on the back of Juan's head and brought his knee up hard into his opponent's face. Then, he yanked Juan's head up by the hair and drove a crashing right into his mouth. Again, Juan's legs buckled. This time he flopped into the mud, semiconscious, blood flowing from his lips.

Someone grabbed Carlos around his neck from behind. Another man came at him from his right. Julio tried to pull the man off Carlos's back, but two men wrestled him to the ground and held him.

Carlos reached over his right shoulder and grabbed the arm of the man behind him just above the elbow. He swiveled left, simultaneously pulling his assailant's arm and bending forward, dropping his right knee almost to the ground. The man flew over Carlos's shoulder and landed hard on his back, spraying mud in all directions. Carlos dropped a knee on the man's stomach. His opponent grimaced and huffed out a huge breath. Carlos threw a roundhouse right to the man's jaw, pounding him unconscious.

Carlos hadn't forgotten the man to his right. He stood and turned to face him.

Not quickly enough.

As Carlos raised his fists, the man caught him with a solid right hook. Carlos's head flung right. He momentarily lost his balance, but didn't fall. A left hook landed on his chin, then a right to his jaw. Carlos fell, but deftly rolled away from the other man, at the same time pushing himself to his feet, dazed, but in control.

The man stepped toward him and threw another punch. Carlos ducked it and drove a powerful right into his opponent's stomach. The man doubled over, grunting. Carlos drew his right fist down and all the way back. The uppercut crashed under the man's chin, sending him back a few feet. He fell splashing into the mud, where he lay, unable to get up.

Carlos looked around. No one moved. He glanced behind him at the two men holding down Julio. Carlos stepped toward them, and they released his friend. Carlos helped Julio up, and the workmen cleared a path as they walked to Carlos's pickup.

Carlos rubbed the knuckles of his right hand. "I couldn't help it, Julio. I couldn't take it anymore."

"I know. But I don't think anyone was hurt too badly, so there probably won't be trouble for you."

"I hope not."

He glanced back at the worksite and noticed a rain-spattered crimson Cadillac Escalade parked about thirty feet from where the fight happened—close enough for the tall, thin man in the expensive leather jacket behind the wheel to see Carlos easily beat three men. At first suspicious, Carlos gave it no further thought after he and Julio climbed into his pickup and drove away.

Halfway home, Carlos stopped at a fast-food restaurant, ordered a Coke with extra ice. He drank some of the soda, then spilled out the rest. He folded the ice into his handkerchief and wrapped it around the knuckles of his right hand, hoping to reduce the swelling in case Marisol saw it.

For Carlos, the fight was over and done. Most likely, Juan would leave him alone now—unless he and his friends decided on revenge with weapons. He stopped at a hardware store where he and Julio each bought a ten-inch piece of pipe and duct tape. When their wives were asleep, they made blackjacks. And before he left for work the next morning, Carlos secretly went into the top drawer of their bedroom dresser, moved aside some socks, and took out a black, .38-caliber caliber snub-nosed revolver.

Chapter Twenty

Carlos and Julio left work the next day relieved that no one had bothered them. When they approached Carlos's pickup, the crimson Escalade pulled up next to them, and the tall, thin man with the expensive leather jacket got out and walked to Carlos.

"Como se la mano?" he asked, pointing to Carlos's right hand.

"It's a little stiff," Carlos said in English. The swelling had subsided somewhat, but the knuckles were bruised and painful to the touch. He'd managed to hide it from Marisol, but if she'd seen it, he would have said that a heavy piece of drywall had fallen on it at work.

"It's been quite a while since I saw a fight like that," the thin man said, now in English. Carlos sized him up. Six foot, long black hair, and dark brown eyes. His facial features were thin, almost delicate, but had, nonetheless, a sinister look. Carlos noticed the jacket, the expensive shirt and slacks, and the highly polished black loafers.

"You ever box?" the man asked. "I mean professionally, or the Gloves?"

"No," Carlos said as Julio watched from behind the hood of the pickup. "Just got lucky, I suppose."

"That was more than luck," the man said and held out his hand toward Carlos's left hand. "Don't want to put any pressure on that one," he said, motioning to the bruised hand.

As Carlos grasped the man's hand, he noticed the diamond-studded ring on his fourth finger.

"My name's Dominic Juarez," he said. "Have you heard of me?"

Carlos shook his head. "No. Should I?"

"Many people who are here illegally know me."

Carlos hesitated, unsure of how to reply without giving himself away. For all he knew, this guy was a cop. "Why do you think I'm here illegally?"

"I know people," Dominic said, stepping closer to Carlos. "I did some checking. I'd like to talk to you about something. Can we step over here?" He gestured forward as he put his hand on Carlos's shoulder and led him a few feet away from the pickup.

Dominic stopped and faced Carlos. "I'll be quick. I was very impressed with you in that fight yesterday. I wouldn't want to tangle ass with you, boxer or not."

"What's this about?" Carlos asked. "What do you want?"

"I want you to make some money for yourself."

"How?" Carlos asked with a sideward glance. "Doing what?"

"It's very simple. Tomorrow at work, ask about me. Check me out. You'll find that for years I've been supplying false identification to illegal workers. They're excellent documents. The best. The cops can't even tell they're phonies."

"And you want to sell some to me and my friend?" Carlos asked.

Dominic laughed. "No, no. I want to give them to you. And I want you to help me sell them."

"I don't think I want to get involved in anything like that."

"You don't need extra money?" Dominic asked. Before Carlos responded, he added, "There's plenty of money in this business, and it comes fast and easy." He pointed to his Escalade. "How long would you have to work to be able to buy something like that? Three years, four? Work with me, and you could pay cash for it in less than a year."

He paused for a second, watching Carlos. "Should I keep talking?"

Carlos was quiet. Something inside him screamed, "Get out of here! Now!" But he could use the extra money. "Go ahead," he said. "But tell me exactly what I have to do to make that kind of money."

Dominic smiled. "You check around with the people you work with. If they're illegals without papers or have bad papers—I'll show you how to know that—sell them mine. Go to other places where there are illegals and do the same thing."

Carlos scratched his forehead. "How much money are you talking about?"

"Depends on how many you sell and for how much," Dominic answered. "You get one-third of what you sell. Usually, they go for eight hundred or a thousand dollars, but some of my guys have sold them for fifteen hundred or even two thousand."

Carlos's eyes widened.

"Do the math," Dominic said. "If you sold just three of my fakes a week, for a grand each, you get one-third of three thousand dollars, a grand a week."

Carlos shoved his hands into his pockets and stared down at the asphalt street. "There's a catch here somewhere," he said, looking up at Dominic. "There has to be for that kind of money. And why me?"

"Okay," Dominic said. "It's a good question, and I was just about to tell you. You'd find out anyway so be assured what I say is true."

Carlos glanced behind him at Julio, whose hands were spread open and his eyebrows raised, silently asking what was going on.

"This is my situation," Dominic said in a soft voice as he leaned his head closer to Carlos. "There's a lot of money in this business and that draws competition. People are trying to muzzle in. There have been fights, and a few of my guys were roughed up."

He pointed to Carlos. "That's why I want you. I saw what you can do yesterday. And word gets around. I don't think too many of my competitors are going to mess with you, especially if I've got a few of my other guys with you."

Carlos put his hands on his hips and looked away, shaking his head. "I don't know about that. I've got a pregnant wife and three kids. Gangs might get involved, and then there's going to be shootings and killings. I can't risk that."

"That's understandable. But don't worry about the gangs. I pay them to stay away."

"Why not have them sell the papers? Why not have them keep the competition away?"

"Two reasons," Dominic responded, holding up two well-manicured fingers. "First, they're watched too closely by the cops. Some of the gangs have been infiltrated. And there's more money for them in drugs and whores."

"I'd still want to keep my job, just in case."

"Sure. Go ahead. But I think once you start making big money, you'll want to do this full time."

Carlos tugged his earlobe. "I've got to think about it."

"Good idea," Dominic said. He pulled a folded piece of paper from his shirt pocket and handed it to Carlos. "Here's my phone number. Call when you've made up your mind. And remember, check me out when you go to work tomorrow."

They shook hands, and Carlos and Julio got into the pickup.

"You aren't really thinking of doing this, are you?" Julio asked after Carlos told him about the offer. "Even if you don't get beaten up or shot, you could get arrested. Then you're gone, deported."

Carlos looked away. "I don't know, Julio. I just don't know what to do. That's a lot of money. A grand a week. Four thousand a month. I could have almost twenty-five thousand in six months, maybe more. That goes a long way to building the nest egg we were talking about. You know how much that would buy us if we have to go back to Mexico? We could sell the building here, empty our savings, and with the extra twenty-five grand, we'd be set. We could start a business or buy a farm or an apartment building and rent it out." He squeezed the steering wheel. "The more I think about it, the more I think I'll take the chance. I don't have to do it forever. Six months. Maybe a year."

Julio said nothing, just propped his elbow on the bottom of the open window and stared outside.

"Please, Julio," Carlos said. "I know I don't have to tell you, but nothing about this to Marisol or Carmella."

The next day, Carlos discreetly talked to other workers about Dominic. He was well known and well respected. And he took care of his people. "If you're going to do this," one worker said, "this is the man to work for. But be careful. It's a dangerous business, or I'd be doing it myself."

Carlos thought about it the rest of the day. It would only be temporary, just until he got the money he needed. Whatever happened, his family would at least be financially stable if they had to move.

He called Dominic just after leaving work and made plans for dinner. They met at an expensive Italian restaurant where Dominic explained everything to him. It wasn't just green-card counterfeits that he'd sell. It was drivers' licenses, insurance papers, passports, and Social Security cards.

When Dominic finished talking and answering questions, Carlos stared down at the table and took a deep breath. He needed this money, and you don't make that kind of cash without taking a chance. He looked at Dominic. "Okay, I'm in. I'll do it."

Dominic smiled and held out his hand. "You won't regret it." Carlos shook Dominic's hand, but his stomach was queasy wondering if he would.

Chapter Twenty-One

When he returned from his meeting with Dominic, Carlos waited until Marisol went to sleep, then walked quietly out on the back porch. His yard was small but well maintained, the grass neatly clipped. A wooden fence ran along the back of his property, separating the yard from a narrow alley. Chain-link fences lined both sides.

He sat on a bench parallel to the outside kitchen wall, massaged his temples, and reached into his shirt pocket for a cigarillo. Lighting it, he took a drag and slowly exhaled, watching the smoke form a blue cloud in the cool night air, then slowly dissipate. There were no streetlights in the alley and only the moon lit the yard.

Voices came from the alley to his right. Dogs barked. The neighbor on the second floor of the building next door stepped out on the porch holding a flashlight. He switched it on, and the beam passed slowly along his fence, a search light across a dark prison wall.

The voices stopped, and the dogs settled down. The neighbor shut the flashlight and went back inside, slamming the door behind him. Carlos took another drag from the cigarillo. The haunting thought of being constantly alert for immigration agents and police, perhaps even being hunted by them, made his skin crawl. And the prospect of moving his family to another state was more than worrisome, it was terrifying. Return to Mexico? Disastrous.

Things had been going well for so long. The job, the building, his family. After years of uncertainty he'd finally begun feeling secure. How could this be happening? He'd put so much at stake, risked his life to get here.

Carlos came to America illegally eleven years earlier. In Mexico, he started working as a farm hand at ten years old. At sixteen, he moved to Mexico City, where he found work on the assembly line of an old, swelteringly hot auto parts factory, then in the oil fields.

He married Marisol at nineteen and at twenty-one had two sons. Work in the oil fields paid reasonably well compared to most other jobs in Mexico, but when Marisol became pregnant again two years after their second son, he had to earn more. An oil field worker knew a few "coyotes," who took people across the border, for a fee.

He'd heard rumors about the coyotes being ruthless and merciless, that some people had died at their hands. But he discounted that as propaganda put out by Americans trying to discourage Mexicans from entering their country. Besides, he was young, healthy, and strong. He'd handle whatever happened.

He didn't like leaving his wife and children, but he could make far more money in the United States. Marisol and his sons would stay with her parents, who lived in the outskirts of Mexico City, where she could find work at one of the many hotels after she had the baby. He'd send her money once he planted roots and found steady work.

A week later, he and four others were led on foot in the dark across the border into Arizona just east of Nogales. They crouched in a gulch waiting to be picked up and taken just north of Los Angeles, where farm hands were needed. Like the others, Carlos had a cloth sack filled with some clothes, a half dozen bottles of water, beef jerky, and some hard candy. In his wallet were the names, addresses, and phone numbers of three relatives of friends who went to America five years earlier and now lived in Los Angeles.

He tried to conceal his growing foreboding from the others but several times had to wipe away the perspiration that stung his eyes as it dripped from his forehead. Half an hour later, a trailer truck pulled in front of them. Their guide stepped forward and greeted two fellow coyotes as they jumped down from the cab of the truck. They waved the illegals forward and opened the trailer doors.

Carlos's nose crinkled from the stale, dank odor in the trailer as he and the others climbed in and saw six other men looking tired and bedraggled. Two small lanterns in the front of the trailer provided minimal light, barely enough to cast vague, quivering shadows on the trailer walls. The trailer doors squeaked and clanged shut, and Carlos felt as if he were in a tomb.

Their destination was about 300 miles from Nogales, but to avoid being caught, the coyotes took a poorly patrolled, but much longer route through the desert. After daybreak, the blistering desert sun beat down, and before long the trailer simmered, and the air inside was suffocating. His water was soon gone and, like the others, he lay motionless on the metal floor, sweating heavily and trying to remain calm.

Five hours into the journey, a few of the men stopped perspiring, and their skin went dry and pale. Carlos had seen it before in the factory where he'd worked.

Heat stroke.

If they weren't given water and put in a cool place soon, they could die. One of them struggled to his knees, then went down on all fours. He screamed and slammed his fists on the floor. Carlos and another man grabbed him and laid him back on the floor, telling him to control himself, that they'd be in Los Angeles soon. It was a lie and Carlos knew it. There were still hours to go.

Two of the men shouted and pounded on the front wall of the trailer. "They can't hear you," Carlos shouted, "with this trailer bouncing around and the engine in the cab roaring."

Another man rolled back and forth on the floor. He started shaking as if in an epileptic fit. One of the men tried to comfort him as he moaned and prayed, but he pushed him aside and vomited. Earlier in the trip, some of the men urinated into a heap of rags in the front of the trailer and the putrid smell permeated the air. Now, mixed with the foul smell of vomit and body odor, the stench was overwhelming. Two others succumbed to it, and also threw up, and the vomit swirled across the trailer floor as the truck bounced and swayed from side to side.

Carlos felt his stomach roll. The bitter taste of vomit came to the back of his throat and he squeezed his neck muscles tight, put his hand over his nose, and breathed through his mouth, keeping the vile stink from his nostrils. Gradually, he took a breath or two through his nose until he acclimated to the foul odor.

A man next to Carlos tossed his head from side to side, mumbling and gurgling. He gasped and his eyes opened wide. He started to say something, but his body shuddered, then went limp and his head rolled back. His eyes glazed over, and the pupils slid upward. Carlos stared at him and knew he was dead. Carlos laid him gently on the floor. He emptied the man's sack and put it over the dead man's head.

"Is that how we all end up?" someone yelled.

"Be calm, be calm," Carlos said and lay back on the floor. But he was far from calm. He cursed himself. *Tonto! Idiota!* He should have listened to the warnings about the coyotes. If he didn't survive this, Marisol would never know what happened to him, forever wondering about his fate.

Dios hace. God's will. He closed his eyes, trying to sleep and keep the dead body next to him out of his mind. Eventually, he and the others dozed into fitful slumber until the truck abruptly stopped, jolting its passengers awake. Voices approached the rear of the trailer. Then, the doors creaked open.

Fresh air filled the trailer as the men inside looked out to a tree-covered hill about fifty yards away. Carlos and the others covered their eyes from the light cascading into the dark trailer. Momentary relief. Then, anger coursed through him, and he pushed himself into a wobbly stance.

"*Animalas! Bastardos!*" he shouted. "You should burn in hell with your mothers!"

He stepped forward as the other men struggled to their feet, also shouting at the men outside.

That's when Carlos saw it.

The shotgun.

The coyote raised the weapon, pumped a shell into the chamber, and yelled at them to shut up and get off the truck. He stood aside as they stumbled out.

Carlos motioned with his head to the trailer. "There's a dead man in there."

"Don't worry about it," the man said. "We'll take care of it."

"How?" someone asked.

"None of your business!" the scowling coyote snapped.

"Can we have some water?" another man pleaded.

The coyote with the shotgun pointed behind him. "Over the hill. There are people waiting for you. They have water." He motioned them to go.

They staggered to the hill. In the shade of the trees, a light breeze cooled Carlos's sweat-soaked body. His breathing settled, and he felt better.

Atop the hill, Carlos looked down on two dark-blue mini-vans and a rusting green pickup truck at the side of a narrow gravel road running along a high, red clay ridge. Five men stood near the vehicles. One held a shotgun.

The others with him started down the hill, but Carlos hesitated. He was wary and considered making a break from the group. But to where? He didn't even know where he was.

Reluctantly, he plodded down the hill. Two of the illegals broke into a run yelling, "Water! They said you had water."

One of the coyotes reached into the back of a van and pulled out a case of bottled water. As the men approached, he handed the bottles out.

"Slowly," he said. "Drink slowly. Don't gulp it all down or you could die."

What? Carlos was surprised. Sympathy? Concern?

Then, the man said, "They don't pay us for dead wetbacks."

When they finished drinking, they were ordered into the vans and pickup. Carlos climbed into the back of the pickup so he'd be out in the air and wind. Leaning back against the side wall of the truck bed, he glanced at his watch. Almost three o'clock. He'd been in the trailer for ten hours.

Uneasy and unsure, he nonetheless managed to doze off, waking occasionally when the truck hit a bump or made a sharp turn. An hour later, the small caravan pulled into a farm and up to a man standing in front of a red and white barn. Tall and husky, he wore a Stetson, cowboy boots, jeans, and a red flannel shirt. He motioned the men to get out of the vehicles.

"My name is Sam," he said in reasonably good Spanish. "I own this farm, and I'll direct operations here and on other farms nearby." He turned and walked toward the barn, telling them to follow.

The barn was cooler than outside, and a breeze wafted through it. As his eyes adjusted to the dimmer light, Carlos could see a dirt floor and cots lined up along both sides of the barn, each with a footlocker in front of it. Then, his eyes riveted on a long metal folding table covered with a red plastic table cloth in the middle of the barn. On it were two large platters of sandwich halves and two dozen sweating water bottles.

"Thought you guys might be a little hungry," Sam said with a smile. "Go ahead and chow down. I'll be back in an hour to get things organized. Feel free to take a nap. If you need to, there's a shack behind the barn. It's an outhouse with six commodes."

He pointed to his right. "About twenty yards out we rigged up a shower of sorts. It's a slab of concrete surrounded by a wooden fence and with four hoses hanging over it. Go ahead now, help yourselves to the food."

The men rushed to the table and grabbed the sandwiches and water, brushing away flies circling the platters. Carlos thought he'd never enjoyed a meal as much as this one. He devoured the first half sandwich, but slowed down to relish the second, taking sips of water between bites.

"Maybe it will be all right now," Carlos said to the man next to him. "This looks like a good place. The owner seems to have a heart."

"I hope so," the other man said, his cheeks bulging with food. "I thought my life was over in that trailer."

Carlos was correct. They were treated well, but they were also supervised carefully and pushed hard as they worked the fields. After breakfast each day, they worked Sam's fields or were driven to farms in the area and labored in the scorching sun from 6:00 a.m. until 6:00 p.m. Lunch came about noon, and they had forty-five minutes to eat and relax. They were paid six dollars an hour, about $420 a week, a lot of money in Mexico. Carlos estimated 50,000 pesos. And every week he sent his wife $350.

They worked Sunday through Friday. On Saturdays, they were on their own, free to stay on the farm and relax or be driven to a town ten miles away to attend Saturday evening mass, shop, and eat at one of the restaurants. There were several banks where they could wire money to their families or mail checks from the post office. They were not, however, permitted to drink in bars.

Carlos remained on the farm through the harvesting season, then hitchhiked to Los Angeles, where he stayed in a cheap motel. The next morning he called the people on his list.

On the first call, an automated voice said the phone was disconnected. His head dropped and he gritted his teeth as he dialed the next number. The phone rang eight times. No answer. His stomach tightened as he dialed the last number. It rang four times before someone picked it up. "*Bueno*," a voice said, and Carlos almost screamed with joy.

He stayed with these friends for two days before finding a small apartment and furnished it with only a sofa bed, a small table and chairs, a television, and radio. It was stark, but it was cheap, and he wanted to spend as little money as possible so he could save and send for his family.

Two days later, Carlos found a job busing tables and washing dishes, then at a meat packing plant. On most weekends, he worked at a car wash, which netted him eighty to one hundred dollars a day, depending on tips. And like clockwork, Carlos mailed half of his wages to Marisol.

For two years, Carlos worked and saved, spending only for basic necessities, although occasionally treating himself to some fast food, a movie, or a few beers at a nearby tavern. When he'd saved almost $15,000, he rented a two-bedroom apartment and sent for his family.

Now, looking into the night, Carlos sighed. The experience seemed unreal. And he greatly feared it might all have been for nothing. He put out his cigarillo, stood, and stretched. Then, he went into the kitchen, opened a cabinet above the refrigerator, and took down a bottle of tequila. Carlos wasn't a drinker, but tonight a few shots might help him sleep.

Chapter Twenty-Two

Mike flicked on the news as he prepared to leave for the day and heard that small crowds were gathering in East Los Angeles and other heavily Hispanic parts of the city. It wasn't a riot—at least not yet. But rocks and bricks were being thrown into storefront windows, and police were cordoning off the areas.

He called Josephine to say he'd be late, perhaps even do an all-nighter, because of the disturbances. She wasn't happy about it, but didn't press him. He contacted National Guard commanders in and around Los Angeles and had them put their troops on alert. Then he got Los Angeles Mayor Dawkins on the phone. "Can you get this under control?"

"Eventually, but it's progressing quickly," Dawkins answered. "Police on the spot tell me about two hundred or so rioters are headed downtown. But there could be a bigger problem. There are roving bands that look like they're heading into non-Hispanic middle-class neighborhoods. That's dangerous. Those people will protect their homes. I'm sure some of them must have guns. This could turn into a nightmare."

"I have National Guard units close to you on alert. I'll activate them and put them under your control," Mike said. "They'll report to their armories soon and will be available in three hours or so."

"Good. Right now, just about every cop on the force is moving into the area, which leaves us thin in other parts of the city."

"Okay," Mike said. "I'll keep abreast of things and—"

"You know what set this off, don't you, Governor," Dawkins cut in. "You know what some of those rioters were yelling? 'Fuck DiGrasso, Obey the court, DiGrasso is a criminal.' This was your doing. This has been simmering since you banned our sanctuaries. And then you ignore the Supreme Court. What did you expect? I could have told you this was going to happen. I could have—"

Mike's grip on the phone tightened. "You knew! Then why the hell didn't you prepare for it?"

"Don't tell me how to run my city! Don't tell me what I should have done!"

Mike took the phone from his ear and looked away. This was not the way to handle the situation. He breathed in deeply and put the phone back to his ear. "All right. I'm not telling you what you should have done."

"It sure sounded like—"

"Hold on, Dave. We're both pissed off, and that won't get us anywhere. Let's calm down and talk about this in a few days."

Dawkins was quiet for a few moments. "Okay. I'll keep you posted," he said and hung up.

Mike called the Sacramento police chief, who told him the capitol city was quiet. "But I ordered extra cars out on the street," the chief said, "and I'll put other officers on alert. If something happens, we'll be on top of it right away."

He then contacted the police chiefs in four other major California cities. No signs of riots there yet either. He hoped Los Angeles would quiet down. If it exploded, the riots might spread to other cities. It had to be stopped, and quickly.

An hour later, however, there was no denying that Los Angeles was in the midst of a riot. Mike watched as helicopter film crews provided aerial views of small crowds coalescing into larger groups of hundreds raging through neighborhoods, some heading for downtown.

The cameras panned the eerie, fearsome scene. Burning buildings, smoke swirling into the night sky, overturned cars, looters running with televisions, radios, clothing, and anything else they could carry. Occasional gunshots pierced the wail of fire engines and squad cars speeding to the area.

By late afternoon the next day the riots were quelled. The damage was extensive and there were four dead and dozens injured. Some of the worst carnage occurred when the rioters moved into middle-class non-Hispanic areas. Dawkins had been right. The people there did defend their property, many of them with guns. Two of the rioters and one homeowner were killed and many more hurt. A few houses were set afire and dozens of others damaged.

But the most frightening incident occurred just before the National Guard arrived to help police restore order. Nearly 200 rioters carrying sticks, baseball bats, bricks, and other weapons approached a high-end area of downtown Los Angeles. In front of them were fifty police officers in riot gear. Mike watched, mesmerized, as the mob neared the police lines, ignoring the bullhorn orders from the police to stop and disperse.

The police fired tear gas, but it landed in the rear of the crowd and those in front charged forward. Now, it seemed nothing could stop them—as if this thin blue line couldn't hold. The mob was fifty yards from the police line when the officers drew their sidearms.

Mike's throat locked, and his mouth went dry. Good God, don't let it come to this. He stared trancelike at the TV as the police raised their weapons to their shoulders, pointed straight up. But the rioters continued toward them. Mike almost squeezed his eyes shut as the police pointed their guns at the crowd. They took aim, but the crowd kept coming. Police shouted orders.

Then gunshots. Two volleys.

Above the rioters' heads.

The crowd stopped. Again, police on bullhorns told them to disperse. For a few tense minutes, the rioters mingled, seeming confused and unsure what to do. Then, gradually, the crowd began breaking up. Mike's head dropped, and he let out a deep sign of relief.

When the Guardsmen arrived, the mayhem subsided. Pockets of violence remained and fires still burned, but it appeared authorities were taking control. Mike went home at four in the morning and slept until nine, then cleaned up, had breakfast, and got back to his office at 11:00 a.m., and called Mayor Dawkins.

"It looks like the worst is over," Mike said.

"Seems like it, but I'd like the Guard to stick around for a while. These things can re-ignite for no apparent reason."

"You've got it. And I'll send some people there to assess the damage and see how we can help. I'll restore the state funds I cut off from you. And as far as the costs from the riot, you've got a blank check."

Dawkins was silent for a moment. "Thanks. But I still think you'd be better off lifting that ban, Governor. It could help ease the tension a little bit."

"I'll give it some more thought. But let's discuss that after you start putting your city back together. If there's anything I can do, just pick up the phone."

Mike spent the day clearing up last minute business and left at 6:30. Josephine was at a Rotary Club dinner so Mike had his driver take him to a small restaurant in a low-income neighborhood. It was on a busy street across from a closed factory and an empty lot.

There were six tables with chairs, and three booths with worn-down vinyl seats. A counter with stools formed a U shape around the grill, where the smell of cooking oil filled the room. In short, a greasy spoon. But Mike liked it. It reminded him of his youth when he worked part time as a short-order cook, and he enjoyed being around the blue-collar patrons.

Just as he finished his meatloaf with mashed potatoes and gravy, an elderly man walked in and sat at the counter. Mike guessed he was in his mid or late seventies. His clothes were clean and well pressed, and his shoes had a glossy shine. He was about five-foot-ten and slender, but his posture and frame made Mike imagine he'd been strong and well-built as a young man. Brown liver spots splattered his arms and hands, the fingers of which were gnarled from arthritis. His face was wrinkled but his bright blue-green eyes offered an almost youthful appearance. He took off his cap and smoothed his sparse gray hair straight back.

Something about him reached out to Mike—a quiet dignity or an inner peace. But it took a few moments before he realized what it was.

His father.

The old guy reminded him of his father. That was probably how he would have looked had he lived that long. Mike approached the man.

"How are you today?"

The old man looked up at him. "I'm doing fine, young man. How are you?"

"Very well. Mind if I join you for a minute?"

"Do I know you?"

"That depends. Do you watch TV news a lot?"

"No. I still like reading the newspaper and listening to the radio. Why? You some kind of bigwig?"

"No," Mike said. "I just play one on TV."

"Well, okay, sonny. Have a seat, and tell me what I can do for you."

Mike sat on the stool next to the man. "Oh, I don't want you to do anything for me. But I had to say hello because . . . well, because you remind me of my father."

"I see," the man responded. "You two were close, huh?"

Mike nodded and tears came to his eyes. "Yes. Very."

"You know, sometimes it's good to see tears in a man's eyes. Shows he's enough of a man to have strong feelings and not be afraid to show them. I'm guessing your father isn't alive."

Mike nodded. "That's right. He died a long time ago. He was still relatively young. Sixty-four."

"That's too bad. I'm sorry. What did he do?"

"Just a laborer. Used to load and unload trailers and box cars. Strong as a bull."

"Maybe he unloaded some of my cargo. I was an over-the-road trucker. Had my own rig. A Mack."

Mike laughed. "Maybe. It's possible. What are you planning to eat?"

"Roast pork," the man answered and smiled as he leaned to Mike and whispered, "It's cheap."

Sadness swept over Mike. He didn't feel sorry for the old man, but there was an empathic connection with him. "Listen. I'd like you do me a favor."

"What's that, sonny?"

"Let me buy you a nice big steak. Believe it or not, they have very good ones here—porterhouse, strips, rib eyes. I've had them."

"No, no," the man said, waving his hand. "I don't want to impose or take charity." He stopped. "Do you think I need charity?"

"No, but you brought back pleasant memories, and I'd like to pay you back."

The man's eyes widened. "Well, to be honest, I haven't had a steak in a while."

"Great. Then you'll let me buy it for you?"

The man thought it over. "That's very kind of you. Okay, I'll have it."

Mike called over the cook. "Danny. Give this man a steak." He looked at the old-timer. "What kind?"

The man pursed his lips. "The porterhouse. That's the biggest." He paused. "Don't know if I can finish it, though."

"That's why God created doggie bags," Mike said and turned to the cook. "A porterhouse, Dan. A big one."

"Sure thing," Dan said and went into the refrigerator next to the grill.

Mike reached into his pocket and took out two fifties. He handed them to the cook. "That's for this meal. Take a tip for yourself and keep the rest for another few dinners for him."

Mike held out his hand. "It's been a pleasure talking to you."

The man shook Mike's hand. "Thanks very much. You're a good man. What's your name?"

"Mike. Yours?"

"Joe."

Mike smiled. "How do you like that? Joe was my father's name."

Chapter Twenty-Three

The next day, Mike met with his attorney general to get one of his periodic updates on how effectively the new immigration law was being enforced. The latest report was the best yet.

The immigration law established a California border patrol and permitted it to deputize citizen volunteers after a thorough background check and training.

Three hundred recruits had completed four months of training and were in the field. And more than 500 citizens had been sworn in as part-time deputies.

Equally good news was that twenty-four companies had been fined for noncompliance with the law, and some had had their business licenses threatened. The message was clear and business owners began meticulously screening the people they hired and reporting those they suspected of being illegals. Realtors and landlords also saw the writing on the wall and were cooperating.

The result: a tripling of illegal immigrants turned over to federal immigration authorities and a notable drop in people trying to cross the border illegally into California. Although only a rumor at this point, it appeared that many illegals were already beginning to move out of the state.

After the attorney general left, Mike wondered if federal immigration people would be able to process so many deportations. That had been a problem in the past and with the growing number of illegals now being caught, it could only get worse.

He called both of California's U.S. senators to express his concern. They told him they were aware of the situation and were working on appropriating funds to increase federal immigration personnel in the state. He considered calling Ballard, but decided against it. No need to get him involved yet.

Stone called Mike the following day. "Stern is mustering her forces. She wants an immigration bill that'll make it past any judicial test."

"We expected that. Can she do it?"

"Don't know for sure," Stone said. "But there's a good chance. She knows how to work the system, and she's got a bag full of bargaining chips. Can't say how many she'll draw from our side, but there might be just enough. I haven't talked to all of our people yet. Still, I've got to tell you, quite a few of them aren't comfortable with what you're doing. If I had to guess, I'd say she'll get the bill she wants."

Mike rubbed his chin. "Won't be worth much if it doesn't include the provisions that make it effective."

"Doesn't have to be. She's grandstanding. She wants to embarrass us. Wants us to look like we're creating an unnecessary crisis and that she's stepping in to save the day. She's got most of the local press in her pocket, and the national media are making you out to be an anarchist. If this bill goes through and you veto it, they're going to make you look like the grinch who stole Christmas."

"All right, John," Mike said. "You and Manny do another head count to see where we stand and who we might lose to her. And tell our chairpersons on the judiciary committees that when they get the bill, I'd appreciate them bottling it up for a while."

"That's already on my list."

Chapter Twenty-Four

Mike was elated that his three daughters were there together for Sunday dinner. They had cocktails on the deck before dinner, and everyone appeared in good spirits because the girls were rarely all in town at the same time. His oldest, Rose, was a teacher and lived in San Francisco. The middle child, Rebecca, still lived in Sacramento but her sales job kept her away quite often. The youngest, Patti, was working on her master's degree at Berkeley and resided on campus.

As they talked and joked, Mike beamed with a deep fraternal love and pride in the girls. They were doing well on their own. And all were beautiful. Rose was virtually a carbon copy of Josephine, Becky reminded him of Catherine Zeta Jones, and Patti stood out among the rest because of her blue eyes and light brown hair, which she bleached to blonde. Those genes she got from his father, who was also blue-eyed with a light complexion.

They laughed as they sat down to dinner. Patti waited to drop the bomb as Mike took his second helping of roast beef.

She leaned toward Mike, her long blonde hair tumbling across her shoulders. "Dad," she said sweetly, all but fluttering her eyelids, a technique that had worked more than once. "Why are you doing this with the Supreme Court?"

Mike finished loading his plate. "Let's not talk about that, Patti. This is something I strongly believe in and need to do. Let's leave it at that, okay, sweetheart?"

Rose spoke up. "I think Patti is right, Dad. Can't you just rethink it?"

Before Mike could answer, Becky said, "I agree." She ran her fingers through her short brown hair. "This can't do any good, and Mom is really nervous about it. So are all of us."

He looked at Josephine, his eyebrows pressed down. "You put them up to this?"

She shook her head. "I knew nothing about it. But I think you should hear what they have to say with an open mind. I'll stay out of it. You already know what I think."

"Mom's telling the truth," Patti said. "She didn't do anything. We talked with her when we heard what you were doing. But she didn't tell us to talk to you like this."

He held up his hands. "I've made up my mind. So, let's drop this, okay? Please."

"Why not just pass a bill that's not so harsh?" Patti asked. "Why are you being so tough on the illegals? They're people, too, with families and friends."

"Patti, please don't lecture me on compassion. I'm being tough on them, as you call it, because they're breaking the law. They're a drain on this state—and the whole country. They don't belong here. I sympathize with their predicament. I honestly do. But I'm not going to sit here and recite chapter and verse about why this has to be done." He cut into a piece of beef. "Now, can we just eat and talk about something else?"

Patti's jaw muscles flexed. "For God's sake, Dad. Just hear us out."

Mike's face flushed. "You're not listening to me. I'm going to follow through on this. And I don't want to debate it."

"You're just closing your mind on this," Patti shot back. "What are you afraid of?"

"Watch your tone with me," he said, his voice rising.

Becky gasped. She touched her father's hand. "Take it easy, Dad. We only want to have a say in this. We're not little girls any more. Just hear what we have to say. Don't shut us out."

"I'm not shutting you out. It's just that I've made up my mind, and there's no point in discussing it any more."

"Just hear us out, Dad," Becky said. "We're worried."

He put down his knife and fork. "Well, don't be. I've given this a lot of thought. I'm ready for whatever happens."

"What if you go to jail?" Rose asked. "What do you think that'll do to us? If you don't care about yourself, at least think about your family."

"I'll deal with that when and if I have to. I've gone through all this with your mother. She'll get through it. And so will you. Becky said it herself. You're not little girls anymore."

From the corner of his eye, he saw Josephine sit forward and begin to speak, then apparently change her mind and lean back. Becky and Rose slumped in their chairs. But Patti sat straight, peering into his eyes. Mike knew she'd only just begun to fight. He wasn't surprised. She'd always been spunky. Mike sometimes thought that because she was the youngest, he and Josephine may have spoiled her a bit.

"You're just being stubborn!" Patti shouted and threw her napkin on the table. "You're just thinking about yourself! How do you say it?" She pointed to her head. "*Testa Dura*. Hard head. You can't—"

Mike pointed his finger at her. "I told you to watch how you talk to me! This discussion is over! Period!"

Patti stood. "This is such bullshit! Why the fuck—"

Mike jumped to his feet. "You mind that mouth of yours! I'm not going to tell you again! I swear if you keep this up, I'll paddle your little ass."

Patti put her hands on her hips. "Is that supposed to scare me?"

"It had better!" Mike shouted and began walking around the table toward her.

Becky and Rose jumped in front of him and held their hands against his chest. "Come on, Dad," Rose pleaded. "Don't do that. Please."

Josephine went to Patti and put an arm around her. "Calm down, Mike. Please, calm down."

Mike's chest heaved. He stood still and forced himself to breathe deeply. They were silent for a moment. Then, Mike pointed at Patti again. "You'd better show me some respect. Don't ever come into this house again with that . . . that attitude, or whatever. And leave that foul mouth of yours at the door, too."

Patti's face was beet red and her lips were sucked tightly into her teeth. She began to speak, then stopped, whirled around and walked out, slamming the door behind her.

Mike threw his hands into the air. "Dammit! This was supposed to be a nice, pleasant family dinner. I've been looking forward to it all week."

"We're sorry, Dad," Rose said. "We didn't think this would happen."

He sat back at the table and they joined him. They were quiet; then, Mike cocked his head and squinted. "Now, what put the bug up her butt? There something going on with her?"

Rose and Becky looked at each other suspiciously.

Mike noticed. "So? What is it?"

"She's got a boyfriend," Becky said, her brown eyes looking down.

"They're really serious," she added. "His name is Marco Martinez. She loves him, and he's just googly-eyed around her. I wouldn't be surprised if they got engaged pretty soon."

"Well, what the hell does that have to do with this?"

"He's Mexican," Rose said.

"I gathered that from his name. So bloody what?" Mike said, then looked upward with a wry smile. "Ahh. I got it. He's illegal, right?"

"No," Rose said. "But his family is. He was born here, but his parents and two older brothers weren't. They've got good jobs. They're afraid they'll get found out and lose them and be deported back to Mexico. If that happens, her boyfriend would probably go with them. It's a very close family. Then Patti's got a big decision to make."

Mike exhaled heavily. "Oh, for God's sake. Did she know this before she got entangled with him?"

Rose nodded. "Yes."

"How old is he?"

"Same as Patti, twenty-two."

Mike shook his head. "So his family has been here for at least twenty-two years and still haven't gotten legal status?"

"I guess," Rose answered.

"Have you met him?"

Rose nodded. "Yeah. He's very nice. Good-looking, too. And smart. He's an accountant for a good company."

"How come I never heard about this?"

"It's only been a month," Becky explained. "It just happened. Love at first sight, I suppose. She was planning to bring him over to meet you and Mom, but she didn't want to do it today because she wanted to talk to you about the immigration law and didn't want him around when she did."

Mike leaned back and sighed. "You know, I should be happy. My daughter is in love and may get married. I might be a grandfather soon. But her boyfriend's family being here illegally muddies things up a bit, doesn't it. Shit!"

Becky touched Mike's arm. "Dad, can I ask a question, a favor maybe?"

"What?"

"Well, Patti . . . actually all three of us, were wondering if you could do something about it. I mean her boyfriend's family."

Mike spread his hands. "What can I do? They've got to get themselves legal status. If not, they might be deported."

"Can't you give them some kind of dispensation . . . a pardon?" Rose asked.

"I can't do that."

Rose looked as if she'd been slapped. "But you're the governor."

"Yeah, but I can't just pass out pardons and dispensation willy nilly. I'm the governor, not the Pope."

"Well," Rose responded, "how about having them apply for citizenship and you kind of pushing it through fast without a lot of questions asked?"

"No, honey. I won't do that. It's not right. They have to get in line like all the others. I don't play games like that, and you know it."

"And," Josephine added, "what if it comes out that the governor, who made illegal immigration his crusade, is cheating for a family whose son his daughter is in love with? The hypocrisy would stink to high heaven."

Becky pursed her lips. "Well, I guess that's it. Sorry about the blow-up."

"Ah," Mike said and smiled. "What family doesn't have its little spats now and then?"

They laughed and when the girls left Mike and Josephine sat on the deck.

"Jo, did you—"

"I already told you. I didn't know anything about this. I was as surprised as you."

"All right. And thanks for not piling on. The three of them were enough. Hell, *Patti* was enough."

"They're scared, Mike. Especially Patti, because of her boyfriend."

"I know. But it's too late to back off now."

"I figured. Especially after your press conference and those interviews. You won't give an inch. I'd like to be in your corner. So would the girls. But—"

"I know. And I understand. I don't expect you all to be cheerleaders for me, but I really don't want to go through anything like this again. If you can't stand by me, at least don't stand against me."

He sat in a lounge chair. "That girl. I swear she's always got to me more than the other two combined."

Josephine sat next to him. "What if her boyfriend's family goes to Mexico? You think she'd go with them?"

Mike's lowered his head. "Let's hope that doesn't happen."

Chapter Twenty-Five

Shortly after Mike announced that he'd defy the court decision, Stern sat in her office awaiting Griswold, House Minority Whip, Thad McMasters, and Senate Minority Whip, Dan Campbell. Griswold and McMasters came in together. Stern greeted them and motioned to the conference table to the left of the door. "Is Campbell going to be late again?" she asked as they stepped to the table.

"No," Griswold said. "He's tied up. The public works bill he's trying to get through is running into trouble."

He unbuttoned his suit coat and sat at the table. McMasters pulled up a seat next to him. "It's a big issue for him," Griswold said, "and he wanted to be in on the fight. Besides, he's sick. May be the flu. If that bill wasn't so important to him, he'd probably have gone home."

"You let him get away with that?" Stern asked, pressing her lips tight.

"What was I supposed to do?" Griswold shot back. "Drag him here in handcuffs?"

"All right, all right," she said, waving a hand as she sat at the head of the table. She positioned her chair exactly in the middle of the table's edges. "Let him know what we cover today. I'll want to meet with him as soon as he's able."

She looked at each of them. "Before we talk about the new bill, Thad, what reactions did you get to impeachment hearings?"

"What!" Griswold said. "Impeachment hearings?"

"Nothing solid yet," Stern said. "Just putting out feelers."

Griswold's face flushed. "Don't you think you should have talked to me about that? I'm the House minority leader, for crisssake. Why did you go around me?"

Stern held her palms up. "You've got your hands full on the new immigration bill. Thad's the whip. He's the go-to guy for something like this. It wasn't meant as an insult."

Griswold stared into her eyes. "I should have been told, Liz. Period!"

"I'm telling you now, Tom. I'm not trying to keep you out of the loop. I just wanted Thad to delicately ask around to see if there was any possibility of doing it."

"That's going too far too fast," Griswold replied.

"No, I don't think so, Tom. All I want is an overview of the landscape, that's all. Just want to see where we stand, if there's a chance."

"What makes you think we could pull that off? And even if we get impeachment hearings, the Senate's not going to kick him out of office."

"We don't know that," Stern said and bent toward Griswold as if she were about to whisper a secret. "Look, Tom, it doesn't matter if the Senate sends him packing. The idea is to keep putting on the pressure, load him down with more and more problems."

"How the hell does that help us pass the damn new immigration bill? We're taking our eye off the ball."

She grinned. "No. It's just a new ball. I can keep my eye on more than one, and I know you can, too. I just want the gov in the hot seat—a real hot seat—hot enough for him to maybe back off a bit."

She tapped Griswold's hand. "Look how this is playing out for the people. DiGrasso has already ignored the Supreme Court, we're going to hit him with a restraining order and he'll ignore that, too. And then, the riots. There was a lot of damage in L.A. and everyone knows what sparked those riots. It was the sanctuary ban and then his defiance of the Supreme Court. He's beginning to look like the renegade that he is.

We'll leak something about impeachment to the press, and that will send a signal that we're trying to rein in a guy who's gone over the edge."

She stopped and held up her index finger. "And there's something else. I'd bet a bundle that the Supreme Court holds him in contempt. They've got to. I'm stunned they haven't already. So, there's more icing on the cake."

Griswold fingered the edges of his mouth. "You may have something there. All right, let's get on with this."

She turned to McMasters. "So, what did you find out about impeachment?"

"I talked to a dozen of our people. Two of them jumped at the idea. Most of the others were very tentative, kind of a wait-and-see attitude. Three said they weren't up for it."

"Well," Stern said, "that's not too bad considering we're still in the first inning. Keep it up, okay?"

McMasters nodded.

"All right," Stern said, "let's get on to the new immigration bill. We're in a fight, gentlemen. I'm not going to let that smug son-of-a-bitch get away with this. I need you to get your people in line. I don't want to lose one vote on our side. Be sure they know that this is a party line issue, and discipline will be enforced. Anyone who flips will regret it."

Griswold sat back in his chair and crossed his legs. "I've got to tell you, Liz, I'm getting a sour taste in my mouth. This is sounding a little personal. I mean impeachment, strict party discipline, making the governor look like a criminal. If we're going to use that kind of muscle, there ought to be a good reason. Maybe we should just sit tight and let the game play out."

That was about it for Stern. She was tired of his reticence. "I don't *like* playing games, Tom. But when I *do*, I thought the objective was to win."

Griswold sat erect. "Win what! This is personal, and laws shouldn't be made on that basis. What the hell do you expect to gain from this?"

"Integrity! That's what. What DiGrasso's doing is wrong, and I won't just lie down and let it happen. He's ignoring a Supreme Court ruling, for God's sake. That's not just upsetting the applecart, it's burning down the whole damn orchard! I gave him a way out, Tom, remember? I wanted to work with him on a new bill. And he wouldn't even consider it."

As Griswold began to speak, Stern held up her hands and lowered her head. "Sorry for talking to you like that, Tom. I shouldn't have. I was out of line and I apologize. This situation has upset me quite a bit."

Griswold was silent for a few moments, eying Stern. "Okay. Apology accepted. Forget about it. We're all a little keyed up. It's okay."

"Thanks," she said. "And to tell you the truth, it *is* partly personal. I don't like the governor. I'm simply not bowled over by his charm. But that's not the main reason. I don't think either of you believe I'd go after him for that. This is about principle. I'm not going to let him mug our justice system."

McMasters looked at Griswold. "She's right, Tom. Unlike Liz, I happen to like the governor, but he's wrong on this, and we have a duty to try to stop him. He said he wanted a tough immigration bill and we gave him one. We all knew it could be challenged and he probably did, too. So, when the court struck it down, he should have accepted it like the rest of us. I'm with Liz."

He put his hand on Griswold's shoulder. "I know you're just trying to avert a collision course. But Liz makes a good point. DiGrasso is playing chicken with the judicial and executive branches, and that's a dangerous move. What happens down the line? If he gets away with this, the system will never be the same."

Griswold shook his head. "But we all know this is a waste of time. He's just going to veto the damn bill, and we won't be able to override and we'll look like jackasses. We'll lose credibility."

"No, we won't," Stern said. "We'll roast him. We'll be all over the news. He's created an unneeded crisis, won't compromise, put his personal politics ahead of what's best for the state. We'll make this a political disaster for him. And, frankly, I'm kind of looking forward to it."

Griswold looked away for a moment. "You're set on this?"

"We can't just let him roll over us, Tom," Stern said.

"Besides," McMasters added, "I'm not altogether sure we won't be able to override his veto." He turned to Stern. "I'm picking up word that a lot of his own people aren't exactly thrilled with what he's doing.

They're nervous about him taking such a drastic step. They feel like he's putting them in a pretty nasty situation."

"Yeah, there's been some cloakroom talk about that in the Senate, too," Stern said. She looked at Griswold. "Are you picking up anything?"

"Just some scuttlebutt. I haven't had a chance to look into it. I'll get on that today."

Stern put her palms on the table. "And there's more, guys. I talked to some of the sanctuary city mayors, and they're going to lean on their representatives. Five of those representatives are in the governor's party. All the mayors want is for us not to include the sanctuary ban in our bill."

"So, there you go, Tom," McMasters said. "It's not hopeless after all." He smiled. "Now, are you going to suit up and join the team on the field?"

Griswold slumped back in his chair. He steepled his fingers and brought them against his lips. Stern knew he was in a bind. She could tell from his hesitation that he thought this was fruitless. But she'd have the leadership, and the rank and file, behind her, making him the odd man out and that wouldn't be forgotten. Besides, many people in the legislature were his personal friends and he wouldn't just turn his back on them.

"Okay," he said, "I was hoping there might be another way to handle the situation. But I guess not. So, I'm in."

"Thanks, Tom," Stern said. "It would have been twice as tough to do this without you."

She stood and went to the refrigerator in the kitchenette in the rear of the office and returned with three bottles of water. "All right," she continued as she passed them out, "are there any on our side that we might not be able to count on?"

"I've got one or two in the House," McMasters said. "But I think you're solid in the Senate. Right, Liz?"

Stern stepped back into the kitchenette to make sure the refrigerator door was completely shut. "Yeah, but I'll double check. Don't want any last-minute surprises. Thad, pigeonhole anyone you suspect won't toe the line. Tell them this is serious business and anyone who defects will not be looked upon kindly. I'll hold a press conference in a few days to announce we're writing a new bill. I want to get out ahead of this before we introduce the bill."

"They'll tie it up in committee," Griswold said, screwing off the cap of the water bottle, "and debate it to death when it hits the Senate and House floors."

Taking a sip of water, Stern paced in front of the table, four paces forward and four paces back. "That's why I want to put the issue out in the open right away. Let the media play it up and maybe get a few more of DiGrasso's people behind our bill. I want to go on the offensive and raise the heat on the governor."

Stern paused and scratched her forehead. "We've got to pull some votes from the opposition. That shouldn't be too hard, all things considered. There are two in the Senate I'm pretty sure I can turn. One is a young guy, got into the Senate a few years ago. Nice kid, reasonable. He was the opposition, but I liked him and helped him learn the ropes. He was very appreciative."

She looked at the ceiling. "And there's another one. We've gone head-to-head on some things and he always came up short. I think he's afraid of me. Sweet, little ol' me. Can you imagine that?"

They laughed. "No, Liz. I can't imagine that all," McMasters said.

"Great," Stern continued. "We've got a good chance here. Do whatever you can to bring his people in with us. Reason with them, call in some favors, give out some promises. And a few subtle, diplomatic threats might be in order. Remember, the more of the opposition we get to vote with us now, the better the chance we'll override the veto. It might even make DiGrasso reconsider vetoing the bill."

Chapter Twenty-Six

The next morning, Stern called the young senator she'd befriended and asked him to stop by after lunch. Then, she made an appointment with the senator she rankled so much. She munched on a sandwich, quietly thinking about how she'd approach the young senator. Not that she needed to think about it too much. It came naturally to her. She read people well and quickly found their strengths and weaknesses. She would put that talent to use very well today.

At 1:30, the young senator was shown into her office. He'd been elected when he was twenty-eight years old. He was bright and affable, but also green and vulnerable. He'd virtually memorized the Senate's parliamentary rules and thought he was ready for everything. But you can't always fix a car by reading a manual. Experienced technicians know the tricks and short cuts and pass them on to younger mechanics. For this senator, the mentor was Elizabeth Stern. She wasn't always a cold-hearted person. That's why she'd helped him. But she was almost always a calculating one. Someday she might need the young man, and she saw him as a person who wouldn't forget or ignore her kindness.

Stern greeted him with a hug, and they sat on the sofa together. She started with small talk, occasionally dropping a subtle reminder of her past assistance. Then, she got to the point. "What's your take on a new immigration bill?"

"I've got mixed feelings. I'm not sure what the governor's doing is right. But I wouldn't want to go against my party. I haven't thought it out."

"Well, I'd like you to please start thinking about it," she said pleasantly. "And don't worry about breaking with your party. It's not that unusual. Don't concern yourself about it. I'll look out for you. I have in the past, haven't I?"

"Yes, you have, Liz, and I appreciate it."

Perfect. Time to play the trump card. She touched his arm. "I need you to show some of that appreciation now. This is a big issue for me, and I need your help. Can I count on you?"

"You need my vote for the new immigration bill?"

Stern sensed his nervousness. "Don't be so edgy. Your career is just starting, and this vote isn't going to affect it much one way or another. I do need your help. I'm sure of all of my people, but we need a few from your side to come with us."

He hesitated. "I need to think about this."

"I can understand that. But things are moving quickly. There's not a lot of time. I need a commitment from you."

"Today? Right now?"

Stern rarely felt uncomfortable cajoling and conniving. But she did today. She really did like the young guy. Still, she had to keep on the pressure. "Yes. I don't like putting you in this kind of spot. I think you know I'm not that kind of person. But we've got to act fast. I've got to know if I can rely on you. Are you with me?"

"This is a tough call, Liz. How would you feel if I refused?"

She sat back into the sofa and looked away from him. Time for the closer. "How would you feel if the situation were reversed? If you'd taken me under your wing and I turned down a favor you asked for. I wouldn't hate you, of course, but I'd have to rethink our friendship and perhaps my opinion of you. I don't think a little reciprocity is too much to ask. And remember that there may be times when I can help you again in the future."

He rubbed the back of his neck. "Okay. I'll vote with you. It's the least I can do."

She smiled. "You won't regret it. I promise."

He stared down for a moment, and Stern thought he'd realized what she'd just done. His eyes narrowed and he ran a finger across his lips. "Listen, Liz, I'm happy to help you out on this. But that doesn't mean you can count on me every time. As I said, I'm at odds with myself on this immigration thing, so I'll go along with you on it. But I won't on something that's really important to me."

"I know. And I wouldn't ask you to. This will be the exception to the rule for you and me." She put her hand on her heart. "I promise."

He seemed to be soothed, so she chatted with him for a few more minutes, then looked at her watch. "Oops, I've got another meeting coming soon, and I need to bone up for it."

She thanked him again, took his arm, and led him to the door. "Let me know if you ever need anything."

She returned to her desk to recap the conversation and began planning her next move. This one would be easier for her emotionally—none of the mild remorse she'd had with the young senator. She didn't think much of the senator she'd meet next, considered him a weakling. She'd exploited that more than once. She intimidated him and she knew it.

She tugged her right ear three times as she thought, then the left one, also three times. Maybe she'd take a different tack this time, maybe use the carrot instead of the stick. She'd had her staff find any legislation he was interested in, especially regarding appropriations. Now, she studied that material.

Any general knows that surprise, the unexpected, is worth a mountain of ammunition. When Stern walked into the senator's office, her greeting and pleasant demeanor were different from anything she'd shown him before.

"Thanks for taking the time to meet with me," she said. "I appreciate it very much, especially since you and I haven't seen eye-to-eye on a whole lot." She took a seat in front of his desk, which was cluttered with disorganized stacks of papers.

And it wasn't just his desk. More stacks of paper, two empty coffee cups, and some candy wrappers covered the conference table to her left, two boxes filled with who-knows-what were on the floor under the window behind him, and his suit coat lay crumpled on the couch behind her. Being an OCD neat freak, the messy surroundings sent a shiver through her.

"I'm always willing to talk," he said.

"I think it would be good for both of us to make amends and work together on a few things," Stern said. "Bumping heads all the time doesn't help either of us, don't you agree?"

"Sure. It'd be an interesting change of pace to be on the same side now and then. But we're so far apart on so many issues, I'm not altogether sure we can find common ground."

"Money. Money is common ground. I have pet projects and so do you. We could work together there. I know you want funding for a private airport just outside of Los Angeles, and you know I'm trying to get more money for the state's healthcare program. We can work on those things together. I know you're not crazy about pouring more money into state healthcare and, frankly, I don't think we need another private airfield for corporations and rich guys. But I could buy into the airport if you can buy into more money for healthcare."

"This state's healthcare system is a disaster. I don't see how throwing good money after bad is going to help."

"It would help us. It's a start. A chance to deal with each other in a way that we both get something. Here's another thing. You want to keep senatorial staffers at their current level. But some of my people want to increase them. I'm minority leader and I think if I talk to them, I could change their minds."

"I'm sure you could. But why would you?"

He took a deep breath, and she could see suspicion in his narrowed eyes and slightly tilted head. "As I told you," Stern said, "it's a start. I just think we'd both be better off if we settled some of our differences and tried to work in tandem once in a while. I don't want you to compromise your principles. But I don't think a few trade-offs here and there means you're losing your integrity."

She paused, trying to imagine what was going on in his mind. "And there's another way I can help. Word is you're trying to move from the Transportation Committee to Ways and Means. I have influence to help you there."

He began clicking the ball point pen in his hand. "That all sounds very nice. But I've got to tell you, Liz, I'm not sure what this is all about. You and I have been at each other's throats for years. Why the sudden turnaround? Get down to brass tacks. What is it that you really want?" he asked leaning forward. "It's the immigration bill, isn't it? You need votes from the opposition, and you came to me. And I don't know if I want to break with my party."

Stern sat back. It was time to go back to the stick. "Okay, I'm not as good at being friendly as I am at being a conniving bitch. I thought you'd like it better this way rather than the way things were in the past. Now, I'm not so sure. So, I'll level with you."

She leaned across his desk, her fingers locked. "Yes, I want your vote on that bill. And I'm willing to pay for it. Forget siding with me on healthcare." She figured she could probably get that through without him. "But I want that immigration bill to pass. So I'll side with you on everything I just mentioned if you stand with me on this. What do you think? Do we work together or do we fight?"

He folded his arms in front of him and stared at Stern. She could read his mind. This might be a chance to square some of the things she'd done to him in the past. But she was making one hell of an offer. That airport would mean some heavy corporate campaign contributions. And he'd wanted that move to Ways and Means for a long time.

"Let me think about it," he said. "I'm not used to this generosity from you."

"I think you could warm up to it. All right, think about it. But I need to know soon. I hope this works. Who knows, this may be the start of a beautiful friendship."

She stood up and shook hands with him. "It's a good offer. You should take it. Now, I'll get out of your way."

Stern smiled when she entered the corridor. He'd cave. Walking back to her office, she reflected again on something she'd considered for days. Despite increasingly good prospects for getting the bill she wanted passed, she wasn't fully convinced she could get it past the governor's veto. This had to be a lead pipe cinch. And the only way to be sure of that was for the governor not to veto her bill. Stern really didn't want to, had a sick feeling about it. She was a tough, tooth-and-claw fighter, but didn't see herself as an evil woman. Still, she had to take the fight as far as necessary. She glanced at her watch and put the matter out of her head. It was just after 5:00 p.m., and she was meeting her daughter for dinner at 6:30.

Chapter Twenty-Seven

The following morning, Stern called Mike. "Governor, I think we should meet. There's something I think you'll want to know."

"What is it?"

"It's not something to be discussed on the phone. We should be in your office, or maybe even outside the capitol building."

Mike's forehead furrowed. What the hell was she up to?

"All right. Come to my office this afternoon, about one."

"I'll be there."

"What's this about, Liz?" Mike asked before she could hang up.

"Not on the phone. I'll see you at one."

Mike stood. This couldn't be good. Stepping slowly back and forth in front of his desk, he opened and closed his fingers into fists several times as he tried to guess what Stern was up to.

He stopped. He put his hands on the desk to steady himself, then bent over and shook his head. "No! No, it can't be that!"

How could she possibly know about that? It was sixteen years ago. His breathing quickened. He sat back at his desk, trying to control his feelings. He looked at budget proposals, but it was no use. This time he couldn't compartmentalize, couldn't concentrate. He looked at his watch. Only 10:30.

He couldn't just sit around waiting, so he went to the gym and worked out hard until almost half-past noon, cleaned up, and returned to his office at a quarter to one. Taking a bottle of water from the refrigerator in the kitchenette, he paced behind his desk. Finally, he sat, shirt sleeves rolled up, and waited.

He stood when Stern entered. "Have a seat, Liz," he said, gesturing to the chairs in front of his desk and hoping his face didn't reflect his worry.

"Thank you," she said.

Mike sat and noted Stern rolling a ring on her right hand, then with another on her left hand.

"So, what's the big mystery, the big surprise?" he asked.

Stern rubbed her palms on her skirt. "Governor, this is not something I like doing, and that's the truth. I've never done anything like it before and hope I never have to again. But I need you *not* to veto a new immigration bill."

"Let's have it," Mike said flatly, but his pulse was racing.

She gave him a sideward glance. "Does the name Karina Sanchez mean anything to you?"

Mike's stomach rolled. Then, his fear turned to anger. "Not even you would go that far."

"I'm afraid I would."

He stood and walked around his desk. "You're as low as they come, Liz! You're a night crawler."

Stern pushed herself out of the chair and stepped back, saying nothing, just gawking at Mike with wide unblinking eyes.

He stood straight, chest puffed out. His voice was a growl and his fists were clenched, except when he pointed a menacing finger at her. "You would bring up a one-month affair I had sixteen years ago? You'd threaten my marriage over a meaningless fling. You're scraping the bottom of the barrel, Senator, or maybe you just live there."

Stern took another step back, keeping the chair between them. "It's not something I want to do. I told you that. But I want a new bill passed. I want you to comply with the Supreme Court decision. This doesn't have to come out. I'm the only one who knows, and I can keep a secret."

He advanced toward her, his jaw muscles flexing. "That's outright blackmail. If you let this out, I swear I'll spend the rest of my life bringing you down. I will be merciless! Relentless! You can make book on that. I'll do whatever I have to."

"I expect you would," she said, turning her gaze away, then back to Mike. "Don't make me do this, Governor."

Mike didn't take his eyes off hers. Maybe she really didn't like what she was doing. But that didn't matter. Like it or not, she'd follow through. And the effect on his already strained marriage could be devastating.

"Obey the court ruling and don't veto the new bill," she said. "Say that after more thought, you decided it wouldn't be worth the cost, something like that."

He turned and walked behind his desk. "How did you find out about this?"

"She called me the day after you announced you wouldn't obey the court and I met with her. Did you know that most of her family is here illegally? She resented your immigration law, thought it was anti-Mexican and a slap in her family's face."

"Then why did she wait so long to contact you?"

"She said she wanted to see if the law would be tested in court. She figured it would be struck down. But after you refused to comply with the decision, she felt compelled to come out with it. Besides that, you should know that your breakup wasn't as amiable as she let on. She took it bad and she's harbored a grudge against you ever since."

"Okay," Mike said calmly and sat. "You've made your case. You've twisted your knife into me. I don't think there's any more to talk about."

Stern walked to the door but turned to Mike before she opened it. "I hope you accept this, Governor," she said and left.

Mike put his elbows on his desk and rested his face in this palms. Now what? His heart was pounding, and his hands were shaky. He went into the bathroom and splashed cold water on his face, dried off, and went back to his desk. He couldn't back off, couldn't stop the whole process. "I've got to follow through," he said aloud. "Too much depends on it."

Unable to get his mind off of the problem, he called Stone and asked him to meet for a drink. Stone's consistently calm demeanor and objectivity might help settle him down. Mike once told him that his name should have been "Stonewall" instead of Stone.

They met in the cocktail lounge of an off-the-beaten-track restaurant. It was small and dimly lit, with only six empty stools and four tables, also empty. Glittering lights around the mirror behind the bar reflected in Mike's brandy as he swirled it in its snifter and related his meeting with Stern. Stone listened patiently, occasionally taking a sip of his scotch and soda. Mike finished talking, then bent forward with his forearms on the bar, staring straight ahead. Stone turned in his stool toward him.

"I'm not one for giving advice on romance," Stone said, his index finger over his mustache. "I thought maybe you just wanted to get it off your chest. But I do have an opinion of what you should do if you want to hear it, although I think you already know what needs to be done."

Mike nodded, still staring straight ahead. "Yeah. I've got to tell Jo."

"I agree. It's all you can do unless you want to give in to Stern—the low-life bitch."

"I can't give in, John. It's just too damned important."

The ice in Stone's glass clinked as he swirled his drink with a swizzle stick. "Then you've got to level with Jo."

"I know. But maybe I should think about it more. Maybe there's a solution I haven't thought of. I could locate Karina and talk her out of admitting we had the affair."

Stone shook his head. "She might lie to you. Or, she might agree not to and then change her mind. No, buddy. I think there's no better solution than telling Josephine." He put his hand on Mike's forearm. "You'll come to that conclusion eventually. So you may as well do it now. Besides, Stern could use this against you again. You've got to diffuse the situation, or it'll forever be the Sword of Damocles over your head."

Mike took a deep breath and rolled his head back. He let out a long sigh and nodded. "You're right. You're absolutely right." He patted Stone's shoulder. "Thanks, John."

"My pleasure. Are you planning to tell Jo tonight?"

"Yeah. May as well get it over with."

Stone got off the stool. "Okay. I hope I helped a little."

"You always do. Thanks again. I appreciate it."

Stone waved his hand. "Glad to do it. That's what friends are for. If there's anything else, just pick up the phone."

"I'll do that."

On the way home, Mike considered how to tell Josephine, but realized that there was no good way. The affair had been a foolish thing, a tryst. She worked for Sacramento's mayor, and he'd met her several times. She was astonishingly beautiful.

It began at a cocktail party. The chemistry was there immediately, and both of them sensed it. They met the next night. That was the beginning. Her sensuality and sexual prowess enhanced his yearning for her. Each time they met, he could hardly wait to see her again. But eventually guilt overcame him. He had strong feelings for her but wasn't in love, although he suspected she was. He'd never lied to her. She knew he was married, and he told her that their affair wouldn't last forever. Someday, it would have to end. And he ended it as kindly as he could, a month later.

She could never compete with Josephine. He could never love anyone as much as his wife. They were more than just married. They were interlocked spirits, soul mates.

He got home just before 6:00. He was weak as he walked into the kitchen, where Josephine watched television as she got ready to prepare dinner. She smiled.

"Hi, Mike," she said, then cocked her head. "You don't look well. Not feeling good?"

"No," he said in a low voice. He paused for a few seconds, looking down, his arms hanging limply at his sides. "I've got to talk to you about something. Let's sit in the living room."

"Something wrong, Mike?" She stared at him. "There is. I can see it. What's going on?"

They walked into the living room. Mike went to the bar and poured a brandy. He turned to Josephine. "Want something?"

"From the way you're acting, maybe I should. A brandy."

He poured it and handed it to her as they sat on the couch. The room was lit only by the faint sunlight from the windows. Mike stared down at the floor and bent forward, elbows on his knees. Josephine took a sip of brandy but said nothing, just looked at him, her eyes blinking rapidly.

He took a large gulp of brandy.

"Jo, I did something a long time ago . . ." His voice broke, and he cleared his throat. "I did something a long time ago. Something stupid and foolish." He sat up straight, but couldn't face her. "And I've regretted it ever since. Never forgave myself."

Josephine sat erect, staring at her husband. She took a sip of brandy, then put the glass on the coffee table. "The affair?"

Mike's head snapped toward her, his face twisted in disbelief, as if a giant king cobra had appeared in front of him. "You *knew*?"

"A woman can tell. I sensed it right away. I just lived with it all these years."

"Why didn't you say something?"

She looked away and swallowed hard. A tear rolled down her cheek. "I'm not sure. I think I wanted to let it play itself out. I didn't want to confront you. Thought maybe that we could get back to the way we were. I didn't want it to break up our marriage. We had three girls to raise."

Mike bowed his head and sighed. "It only lasted a month, and there was no emotional connection between us. And it was sixteen years ago. I've never done anything like that again," he said, raising his right palm. "I swear on my father's grave. Never."

Josephine squeezed her lips into her teeth, and looked down.

"I'm sorry, honey," he said and reached for her hand. She pulled away. "I'm sorry," he said. "I would never want to hurt you." Mike put down his drink, then reached to put his arms around her.

Again, she pulled away. Tears ran down her cheeks. "It hurts, Mike. Even though it's long over with, it still hurts hearing it now."

"I'm sorry, Jo. I've never felt so rotten about anything in my life. Can you forgive me? Can we put this behind us?"

She didn't answer, just wiped away the tears with her fingers. Then, she looked at him. "Why are you telling me this now?"

Mike sighed. "Blackmail. Stern found out. Said she'd let it out if I vetoed her immigration bill and didn't obey the court order."

"The conniving whore," Josephine said, and Mike could see that even now, in her sadness and anger, she despised anyone who would do that to her husband.

"You've got to know I still love you, intensely," he said. "Always have and always will. Whatever I have to do to make up for this and get our marriage back to normal I'll do. I swear to you."

Josephine suddenly slapped him hard on his right cheek. "How could you do that?" she shouted and slapped him again. Then, she put her face in her hands and sobbed.

Mike just sat there at a loss for what to do or say. Finally, he took her hand.

"We can still save our marriage. We can go to a counselor or something. We've got to try. We've been through so much together all these years. You know I love you and I know you still love me, even though you're angry. We can make it work. We've got to."

"I've lived with it this long," she said and stood, smoothing out her slacks. "I think I'm actually glad that it's out in the open. Seems to soften the blow a little. I don't have to deal with it quietly by myself anymore. But with everything else that's going on . . . I mean, ignoring the court, the problem with Patti . . . it's getting to be too much. And now, this." She shook her head and rubbed her temples. "I've got to be away from you. I've got to think and let this settle in my mind. I'm going to stay with my sister for a while and sort things out. Then, we'll see what happens."

She turned and went upstairs to the bedroom to pack. Mike called to her, but she ignored him.

After Josephine left, Mike poured another drink and sat in the dark. He was jittery and perspiring. Was she going to leave him after all these years? He felt as if some fate had designed the whole thing, that it was some kind of supernatural punishment for what he'd done. Who could know that defying the court would, in some twisted, convoluted way, lead to this disastrous outcome? Would he have started this thing if he'd known it might lead to losing Josephine?

"You self-righteous fool," he said out loud. He sat out on his deck and watched night fall. Then, he went inside, guzzled down another brandy and went to bed. But hours passed before he finally dozed off.

Chapter Twenty-Eight

Two days after her blackmail attempt on Mike, Stern and Griswold were at the Senate press room's podium. Griswold looked tired, the lids of his blood-shot eyes drooping slightly. Stern, however, appeared rested and ready for action.

Both were used to the commotion of a press conference and were at ease in front of the lights, cameras, and clamoring reporters. Stern adjusted the podium microphone first with her right hand and then her left, cupping it in precisely the same manner each time. After preliminary remarks, she announced that a new immigration bill was being drafted.

"The legislation we soon plan to have will be more realistic than the first one and far more likely to pass judicial scrutiny. We believe it will do the job the people want. It isn't necessary to go as far as the first bill did to get a handle on immigration. We'll take your questions, now," she said and pointed to a reporter in the first row.

He glanced at his notebook. "The governor's party holds both Houses. How do you expect to get the new bill passed?"

"They've only got us by three seats in the Senate," Stern responded. "I'm pretty sure we'll pull enough of the opposition to get the bill passed. We're still tallying up in the House."

Griswold leaned toward the microphone. "We're in pretty good shape. There are members of the governor's party who are concerned about what he's doing. We'll probably get quite a few to break ranks."

Stern added, "The people are taking note of all this—the arrogant defiance of the court, the confrontational attitude regarding sanctuary cities, the riots—and they're realizing that the governor is not the man they thought they voted for. I think there's some buyers' remorse among voters, and that will nudge their representatives to reject the governor and vote for our bill."

She motioned with her head to another reporter—young, with eagerness framing his expression.

"Why announce this now?" he asked. "The bill hasn't even been introduced."

"Good question," Stern said. "We want to let the people know that we're taking action to avert a confrontation that the governor seems intent on having."

"What if the governor vetoes it?" the same reporter asked.

Stern hesitated, thinking back to her meeting with Mike and tried to keep any giveaway expression from her face. "Maybe he won't. He could change his mind. If he doesn't, we may be able to override it. The sanctuary city mayors are working with us to change a few minds in Congress. If the governor sees a lot of defections in his party, he may reconsider the veto. If not, we've still got to try. There's a lot at stake. We want to steer us away from a needless showdown created by the governor's personal dislike of what he sees as the judiciary abridging legislative power. He's stated that clearly."

Stern next called on the comely strawberry blond from the *Sacramento Bee*. "What kind of showdown are you talking about?"

"Well, one possibility is that the federal government might act to back the court's decision. The president has no authority over local and state police, but he could federalize the National Guard to prevent enforcement of the immigration law. It's been done before. In 1963, for instance, President Kennedy used the Guard in Alabama to make sure two black students could enter an all-white university. And there have been similar presidential actions. This is certainly a different situation, but what I'm saying is that there is precedent. It could happen and we'd like to avoid it."

"But the president is a friend of the governor," another reporter blurted out.

"That won't matter," Griswold said. "The president isn't going to let that prevent him from doing his duty. He'd get a worse black eye than the governor."

He pointed to the reporter from one of the local TV stations, a Robert Redford look-alike, with a thick mass of curly light-red hair. "Pardon me, but this sounds like an exercise in futility. What's to gain from doing this?"

Stern put her hands on top of the podium. "I am not exaggerating when I say that this is an attack on our judicial system," she said in a solemn voice, as if giving a funeral sermon. "The people need to know what's happening and how dangerous it is. We want to be on record as having done everything we could to put things right. Maybe the governor will budge a little when he sees how hard we plan to fight. And maybe a drop in his poll numbers might give him pause."

"DiGrasso's not a poll watcher," the reporter said.

Griswold chuckled. "Don't kid yourself. Every politician is a poll watcher, some more than others, but we're all susceptible to them to one degree or another."

He signaled to a reporter in the rear of the room, who straightened his tie as he stood. "How is this bill going to be different than the one that was struck down?"

"I can't give you all the details because it's not finished yet," Griswold said. "It will be quite similar to the original bill but without provisions that might cause the Supreme Court to rule against it."

They took questions for another fifteen minutes and ended the conference.

"I think that went well," Stern said to Griswold as they walked away.

"Me, too. I think the governor is shortly going to be juggling a very hot potato."

"Yeah, but I doubt that he'll bend. Got a head like a rock." She checked her watch. "I have appointments with a few more senators I think I can flip."

"All right. McMasters and I will work the house."

"Okay, Tom. Let's meet tomorrow and take stock of the situation."

Stern was in a cheerful mood the next day, having gotten two more votes from Mike's party the previous day. She greeted Griswold with a big smile when he arrived just before noon. "Hello, Tom. Have a seat. How are you?"

Griswold took off his gray suit coat and wrapped it around the back of a chair in front of Stern's desk and sat down. His limp seemed exaggerated this morning.

"Hip acting up?" Stern asked.

"A bit. I've been on my feet a lot the past few days. But I'm fine. I have good news."

"That's nice to hear." She put her elbows on the desk and rested her chin in the heels of her palms in a schoolgirl pose. "Let's have it."

"I talked to McMasters this morning. He told me we got five votes from the other side in the House so far."

"Wow!" Stern jumped up and pumped her hands in the air as she spun around once. "I got two more in the Senate. Looks like Mr. DiGrasso is going to get his head handed to him. The bill passes with a solid majority."

Griswold smiled. "Actually, it's better than that. We picked up three more in the Senate besides yours."

Stern's jaw dropped. "Good Lord. I thought it was going to be tougher than this."

"Me, too. This is a big embarrassment for the gov."

"And it means overriding the veto is possible."

"Maybe. Just maybe."

"Feeling better about this now?"

"Yes, I am," he said and stood, grimacing slightly and grabbing the back of the chair to push himself up. He threw his suit coat over his shoulder. "I've got to run. I just wanted to give you the news in person."

As he limped to the door, Stern called out. "Great. And Tom—" He looked back, and she said, "Why don't you get off your feet for a while? I think we can live without you for a day or two. Go home and put a heating pad or something on your hip."

"Maybe I will."

Stern sat with her arms limp at her sides and looked up at the ceiling. She smiled and shook her head. Couldn't have gone much better. They were gathering so many votes that the governor's veto might be useless. She washed her hands, applied moisturizer, and walked to the Senate Judiciary Committee conference room. When she reached the hall outside, she walked back to her office to be sure the lights were out and the door locked.

Half an hour later Mike got a call from the SJC chair, Nancy Granger.

"What's up, Nance?"

"I just spent ten endearing minutes talking with Lizzie Borden," Granger said.

Mike snickered. "How bad was it?"

"She didn't waste time or try to sugarcoat anything. Right after hello, how are you, she got right to the point. Told me she expected delays when the bill came to my committee, but insisted that I don't drag it out. Said I shouldn't be an obstructionist, that she could help me on certain matters and made some veiled threats about fighting me on every piece of legislation or appropriation I'll ever want.

"She had specifics. Then, she said we wouldn't be in the majority forever and when they had the chair back, there'd be hell to pay. Pushy bitch. I can't stand her."

"Yeah, sometimes she's her own worst enemy," Mike said.

"Not while I'm alive she isn't."

Mike laughed.

"Here's something else," Granger said. "She sounded awful cocky, Mike. Like maybe she's got a big last-minute surprise for us."

"Maybe," Mike said, and as soon as he hung up called Stone, who had no good news for him. "They're getting a lot of our people, more than I expected. She's going to get that bill passed, and in pretty short order. Those sanctuary mayors are taking a toll, putting a lot of pressure on our guys. I don't know for sure at the moment, but she just may well be able to get it past your veto."

Mike drummed his fingers on the desk. He'd known there would be defections, but this was worse than he'd anticipated, much worse. "Okay, John. Do what you can to keep our people in line."

The situation was developing fast. He rubbed his chin. Somehow he *had* to get ahead of things again.

Chapter Twenty-Nine

"Maybe there is hope after all," Julio said after he and Carmella watched the news reports of Stern's press conference with Carlos and Marisol.

"We can pray," Carmella responded to Julio. *"De su boca a los oidos de Dios.* From your mouth to God's ears."

When the news ended, Carlos led the others into the kitchen for dinner. Their children had eaten earlier and were in Julio's apartment doing homework or watching television. Marisol had given birth to a girl, Alexis, and the baby slept peacefully in her crib in the master bedroom.

The fluorescent light in the kitchen gleamed on the turquoise tiles on the walls as Marisol ladled out one of her specialties, *meneudo,* tripe soup. Finely diced onions and slices of lime accompanied the soup, and the room was filled with a rich, sweet fragrance from the pork stew simmering in a kettle on the stove. And just a whiff of freshly peeled jalapeno peppers was almost strong enough to make their eyes water.

Walking into the kitchen, Carlos thought back to the night of the Supreme Court decision. He and Marisol had gone out with their friends for dinner to celebrate. Along the streets on their way to the restaurant people were in a festive mood, gathering in groups, laughing and cheering. The atmosphere in the restaurant was equally jubilant. They stayed out late, even though Carlos and Julio had to work the next day. A huge weight was off their shoulders. For the first time in months, they relaxed and enjoyed themselves without feeling engulfed in a dark shroud of worry.

Then, listening to the radio as he drove home from work a few days later, Carlos heard the governor say he'd disobey the court decision. Stunned, as soon as he walked into his apartment, Carlos turned on the television to get more information. There was plenty. DiGrasso's decision was on every channel. Regular programming was halted to cover the news.

He watched for a few minutes, then went to check on the kids. His oldest, Christian, was doing his homework on the kitchen table. Carlos ruffled the boy's hair. "How are things at school?"

"Good. I'm studying for a math test."

"Be sure you say a few prayers before you take it."

The other boys—Jorge, the middle child, and Ernesto, the youngest—were also doing homework at a small table in their bedroom. Marisol had taken the baby to the doctor for a check-up.

Carlos grabbed a can of beer and some leftover meatloaf and green beans from the refrigerator and took them into the living room. Putting the food on the coffee table, he snapped open the beer and took a long pull. He lowered the volume on the TV so that only he could hear it. He and Marisol had tried to keep what was happening from the boys. But the news was all around school. They couldn't keep the boys in the dark so they explained the situation as simply as possible, but always telling them that there was nothing to worry about.

He picked up a piece of the meatloaf with his fingers and took a few bites, then pushed the plate away. Sitting on the sofa with the beer in hand, he put his feet on the coffee table. Only the light from the kitchen and the street lights outside dimly lit the living room. He sat there for almost an hour, switching from channel to channel, trying to find something that might alleviate his concern. It didn't happen. And all the jubilation he'd felt just days earlier transformed into fear, and sadness smothered his joy.

Now, as they sat at the table and said grace, he wondered if even the love of God could help them.

"If this Senator Stern gets a new law," Julio said, "it might not be as drastic as the one we have now."

"Getting a new law will not be so easy to do," Marisol said. She often studied her children's social studies books or read history and civics books from the library. "Her party is the minority, and the governor will veto the bill. I don't want to be pessimistic, but it will be very difficult to override the veto."

"But we have Mexicans in Congress," Carlos said and dipped his spoon into the soup. "We have people with influence. And we have many voters."

"That didn't matter in the last election," Julio said and swallowed a spoonful of soup. "Oh," he said, closing his eyes and turning his head upward, "*delicioso*, Marisol. As always. Perhaps the demonstration next month will make a difference. There will be thousands."

"Oh, it will make a *difference* all right," Carlos said, sarcasm dripping from his tongue. This was one of the few things he and Julio disagreed on and, therefore, rarely discussed. "It will make the Americans angrier with us than they already are. Fools! Idiots! Out there waving Mexican flags! Do you know what that did to public opinion?"

"There were very few Mexican flags at the last rally. Mostly American flags. And there were so many of us."

Carlos didn't want to take this further, but couldn't help himself. "Yes, but the Mexican flags were there before. Do you think the Americans have forgotten, that they'll be fooled by this phony display of their flag?" He hesitated and took another spoon of soup. "No, *mi amigo*. They will not. They'll see right through it. These demonstrations don't help us. They hurt us. And this one will hurt us the most, because it's coming so soon after the riots. That's still in the minds of the people in this city and probably all across the country. *Tenga cuidado*. Be careful out there. You've had hecklers in the past but I bet there will be a lot more this time. And they will be a lot more unfriendly than before."

Carlos raised his hands in the air and rolled his eyes upward. "And then you have those crazy *Reconquistas*. They want to take back the territory lost to the Americans in the Mexican-American War. Lunatics!"

He stopped and looked at Carmella and Julio. "I'm sorry. I know Roberto is one of them. But how do they expect to do that? Guerilla warfare? Do they really think they can get away with that? And as more Americans learn what they want, you'll see a backlash that'll make the governor's law look like charity."

Carlos knew that Carmella and Julio investigated the *Reconquistas* when their son Roberto was recruited in high school. They didn't like it but couldn't prevent him staying in the movement. Even their daughter Erika tried to reason with her brother, to no avail. He was too ardent, and rather than continually bickering with him, they finally accepted it.

"They're not beyond guerilla war if it comes to that," Carmella said. "But the main thing they want is to operate politically, to dominate state governments with their followers, take governorships and state legislatures. Then they'd declare the state independent and have Mexico recognize it."

Carlos closed his eyes and shook his head slowly. "How can anyone believe something like that? Do they honestly think the Americans would tolerate it?"

"They're true believers," Carmella said. "Some of them are ready to die for the cause. It's an impassioned movement. Very emotional."

Carlos grimaced. "Ready to die? Well, if they push things too far, some of them just might. Better they keep quiet. This kind of attitude will only make things worse for us."

Marisol put her hands on the table. "I think Carlos is right. And I can't blame the Americans for the way they feel. We come to their country, and we act as if we deserve everything they do as citizens. How do you think Mexicans would react if the situation were reversed?"

Carmella sat erect. "But, Marisol, we had no choice. How can you say that? We came here for a better life. To give our children better lives. What's wrong with that? It was the same with you and Carlos."

Julio dipped his spoon into his bowl. "Everyone in this country came from someplace else. They were welcomed. Why not us?"

"Because they came legally," Marisol said, "when America was expanding. They went through Ellis Island and other immigrant processing centers and got medical examinations and had their documents checked. They did all the paperwork and took the tests for citizenship."

"Why so easy for them?" Carmella asked. "Because they came from Europe, that's why."

"No, Carmella," Marisol said. "It was different then. America was growing quickly, and they needed more and more immigrants to do the manual labor needed to build the country as it grew. It's not like that now. The need for manual labor isn't as great. And what there is, the Americans believe should go to them."

Julio brought the soup bowl to his mouth and swallowed the remaining *meneudo*. "I don't agree. Most Mexicans here do the work that Americans will not, or do it for less money."

Carlos also lifted his bowl and drank the rest of the soup. "We're getting off the subject," he said, wiping his mouth with his napkin. "We can't assume this new law will be passed. If it does, we might be okay. If not, then we're back where we started. And we have to expect the worst and be prepared."

Carmella put the empty soup bowls into the sink, and Marisol set plates on the table. She placed the kettle of stew in the middle of the table, then a plate of warmed tortillas and a bowl of jalapenos next to it. Carlos filled everyone's plate, then tore off a piece of tortilla, folded it into a scoop shape and shoveled out a large mouthful of the stew. As he chewed, he gave Marisol the okay sign with his fingers.

"Carlos," Julio said. "You should join the rally next month. The more of us out there, the more effect we have. We've got do everything we can."

Carlos shook his head as he scooped out another mouthful of stew. "No, I won't do it, Julio. Better we work on ways to get around this law or make plans to move."

Carmella pushed away her plate. "I'm not very hungry. All this talk about what's going on—"

Julio put his hand on hers. "Take just a few bites. You need to eat."

Carmella took a small mouthful and chewed it slowly, looking down at her plate. They were silent for a few moments, then Carlos said, "I'm thinking of working at the car wash on weekends again." He wasn't, but he wanted to change the subject. "Seventy or eighty bucks a day. Not near as much as the construction work, but it'll come in handy."

They finished dinner without saying more about the immigration law. Carlos and Julio went into the living room, each with a fresh can of beer. Marisol and Carmella washed the dishes and joined them, Carmella with a glass of wine and Marisol with a large beer glass filled with ice water. The ladies sat on the sofa, Carlos and Julio on the chairs.

"How's the baby?" Carmella asked Marisol.

"Fine. Hardly any trouble at all."

Carmella smiled, but her demeanor showed Carlos her concern. Apparently, Marisol also noticed it. "Don't worry about me, Carmella," she said. "Everything will work out."

"This must be even worse for you," Carmella said. "Good Lord, to have an infant with all this going on. I should be comforting you, not the other way around."

"Marisol's right," Julio said and leaned to his wife. "Everything will work out. Don't worry. There is still time."

Carmella buried her head in her hands and cried. "I don't know. I don't know. Can this really be happening?"

Julio squatted in front of her. He cupped her face in his hands. "I promise you by the love of God, Carmella, whatever happens, we'll be fine, no matter what it takes. But now you've got to be strong. You have to think clearly." He brushed away her tears and kissed her.

Marisol hugged her friend. "Julio's right, Carmella. Whatever happens, we'll stay together and work our way through it." She stood, took Carmella's hands, and pulled her to her feet. "Let's you and I sit on the porch." She put her arm around Carmella and led her forward.

Julio sat and exhaled deeply. "This is the worst part for me. Watching her like this. She's been this way ever since the governor mentioned the new law. She normally doesn't show it in front of others. But when we're alone she breaks down like this once or twice a week. And it rips me up inside."

"It won't be like this forever."

"I don't know. She hardly ever smiles. It's like this is all she thinks about. She went back to the psychologist, but it hasn't made things any better."

"Marisol will help her. And we'll find a way out of this. Don't worry. We will."

Julio tried to smile. "Yes, we will. It's just the not knowing what's ahead. That's what weighs on you. I don't know if Carmella will hold up."

"I know, I know," Carlos said and stood. "Want something stronger to drink, some whiskey or tequila?"

"Good idea. Whiskey. I can use it," Julio said.

"Be right back," Carlos said and walked into the kitchen. He opened the cabinet and moved a few bottles around until he saw the whiskey and grabbed it. Taking two glasses and the bottle, he returned to the living room and poured a drink for both of them.

Julio took a sip. "How can the governor do this? Is this legal? Cannot anyone stop him? I thought you had to obey the court. Isn't he breaking the law?"

"I don't know. He must know more about the law than we do. So, maybe he can."

Carlos drank some whiskey. "I don't think we need to put the building up for sale just now. But we might have to think about it soon. I *do* know that we have to start making and saving more money. Moving will be expensive, and we'll need money to settle somewhere else, maybe buy another place like this. And we'll really need it if we have to go back to Mexico. If we save enough money, we'll be able to live fairly well there. I'm going to take some time off the construction job so I can sell more of those counterfeit papers. I'll talk to the foreman tomorrow to see if I can take a few months off to settle some family business in Mexico. Others guys have done it."

Chapter Thirty

Carlos found he had a talent for salesmanship and a knack for spotting potential customers. Even selling the counterfeit papers part time, he made $4,000 the first month. The next month, $5,000. And it had been easy, although he twice had to fight off Dominic's competitors and make up some creative stories for Marisol when he came home with bruises and cuts. Selling those papers full time, he could make maybe $8,000 a month. At that rate, he could stop doing this in five months or so.

So Marisol wouldn't find out about the money, and how he got it, Carlos rented a safe deposit box to store it, then every month sent money from the safe deposit to relatives in Mexico to put into a savings account there. When he'd made the money he wanted and was ready to quit, he'd explain everything to Marisol.

The foreman let him take the time off, probably because Carlos worked hard, never complained, and rarely missed a day of work. "But," he told Carlos, "be back on time or you're gone."

Working full time, he pulled down almost $8,000 in the first three weeks.

But nothing good lasts forever.

Carlos and two of Dominic's other people were approaching workers leaving a block-long factory surrounded by a chain-link fence that was known for employing illegal immigrants. Dark had fallen. As he talked to two of the workers at the factory gate, he heard someone yell and saw workers scatter, scrambling over the fence or trying to get into cars in the parking lot. He knew what was happening before he saw the state police and ICE cars approaching from both sides of the block.

Carlos tried to remain calm and think clearly. He stepped to the other side of the street, then walked past the apartment buildings across from the factory. He had good documents on him—driver's license, green card, and insurance papers in the glove compartment of his pickup. Still, he hoped he wouldn't have to use them.

The revolving lights on the police cruisers rolled intermittently along the buildings on his right as he reached the end of the block and turned right. He could see his pickup about halfway up the next block in front of him.

He relaxed as he approached the end of the block—until a police cruiser pulled in front of him and stopped. When two officers got out of the car, Carlos considered running back into the alley he'd just passed, but he knew that one of the policemen would follow on foot while the other got back into the patrol car to pursue. Besides, even if he could outrun them, he couldn't outrun their radios. Other police would be around him in minutes. He continued to walk, pretending nothing was wrong.

It didn't work.

The policemen approached, and he stopped. "Something wrong, officers?"

"Just some identification," one of the policemen said.

Carlos was scared, but kept telling himself Dominic's papers were foolproof.

Wrong.

The officer stared at the driver's license closely, holding it above him in the light of a street lamp. He handed it to the other officer, who did the same, then nodded to his partner. The officer put the license in his shirt pocket and looked at Carlos. "You'll have to come with us. Turn around and put your hands behind your back."

The cuffs locked tightly around his wrists. After reading him his rights, the police took him by his arms and put him in the back seat of the patrol car. In near panic, Carlos's face flushed, and he was covered in sweat. How would Marisol react?

At the county jail, he was put in a holding cell with a dozen others, but was allowed to make a call. An hour later, Dominic arrived with a lawyer to bail Carlos out.

"How you doing?" Dominic asked as they walked to his Escalade.

"I guess I'm all right. Still kind of shaky. And my wrists hurt. They put those cuffs on tight."

"I know. It's a scary experience. I remember the first time I got pinched. Damn near pissed my pants."

When Carlos got into Dominic's Escalade, he called Marisol to tell her he was all right and would be home soon. Then, he asked Dominic, "What happens now?"

"Stay off the streets. Don't sell any papers for a while. There's a big backlog of illegals, but sooner or later they'll most likely take you before an immigration judge because you were carrying counterfeit documents. He'll decide if you're deported. That could be a few weeks or a month or two. It's hard to say. It's always different. If that happens, you're going to have to go on the lam. So be prepared. You may have to get out fast. I'll warn you if I hear anything. If they catch you, the lawyer with me tonight is very good. But he's expensive."

"How expensive?"

"Again, it depends. You were only caught with the fake IDs, not *selling* them." He looked at Carlos. "Have you been arrested before?"

"No. Not even a traffic ticket."

"You should be okay. They've got big-time criminals to deal with. Next to them, you're small potatoes. You might get off with a fine, but you could still be deported. The lawyer will be there if they take you in front of the immigration judge. Even though you're an illegal, you still have rights. And, like I said, this guy is very good."

"How expensive?" Carlos asked again.

"Figure on eight, maybe ten thousand."

"*Ten thousand!* My God. That's a lot of money for me."

"Don't worry. The way you've been selling those documents you'll make it up in three or four weeks."

Carlos looked away. Not a chance. He was out of this.

But he didn't say anything. If Dominic knew he wanted to quit, he might not help. "But not right away," he said. "You told me to stop for a while."

"That's right. I'll work you someplace else. Maybe another state. You can quit the construction job after that. Keep working full time for me and you'll be pulling down eight or ten grand a month."

Again, Carlos looked away. No, he wouldn't. But, once more, he kept it to himself. "What do I tell my wife?"

"That's up to you. Make up a good story, or tell her the truth."

"I don't understand what happened. I thought the documents were perfect. How could they have caught me?"

Dominic nibbled his lower lip. "I've been asking myself that since you called me tonight. I'll check it out first thing in the morning."

"Take it easy," Dominic said when he dropped Carlos off at his pickup. "Relax. This will work out. Stay in touch."

When he entered his apartment, Marisol was sitting on the sofa in a house dress reading a magazine. The children were playing video games in their room.

"I hope you've got a good explanation for this," she said as he sat down in the chair across from her. "Something is going on and whatever it is, it's not good. You've been coming home late almost every night, and your excuses are getting worse and worse. And the bruises and cuts. You can't be having that many accidents at work."

He bowed his head. He'd thought about this all the way home and knew he had to tell her. He was out of it now. No more phony papers. No more Dominic. No more police. No more lies.

"For a while," she said, "I thought it was another woman. But you'd have been more discreet. Not almost every night. You're smarter than that."

"No. It's nothing like that."

And he explained everything to her.

The next day, Carlos told Julio what happened. Cloudy, gloomy weather heightened Carlos's depression.

"How much do you trust this Dominic?" Julio asked.

"He was right there for me yesterday. Bailed me out an hour after I called him. But I'm not going to work for him any more." He ran a hand through his hair. "If I'm deported, what happens to Marisol? They'll investigate and find out she's an illegal. And the baby. She was born here; she's a citizen. Who knows?" He looked at Julio. "They might come after you, because we own the building together."

"I've been thinking about that from the very beginning."

"I'm sorry."

Julio put his hand on Carlos's shoulder. "You don't have to be sorry."

Carlos sighed. "I'm not sure what to do. There are so many ways this can work out."

"Take it easy. We need to take things one step at a time and try to think of solutions for anything that happens."

Carlos nodded. "The one thing we have going for us is the extra money I made before I got caught. Almost sixteen thousand in my Mexican bank, and we've got about fifteen thousand in our bank here. And there's about forty thousand in equity in the building."

"Carmella and I have about twenty-five thousand in savings. That's almost a hundred grand between us. So, we'll be okay wherever we go."

"With your relatives in Texas, maybe," Carlos said.

"That's possible. But we should stay together. We've been in this with each other for a long time. The work, the house, the closeness of our families. We're like brothers, and I don't want us to separate. Same with Carmella and Marisol. Let's see what happens in the next few weeks. But we should think about selling the building and finding someplace else to live."

Carlos nodded. "It makes us able to move quickly if we have to."

Chapter Thirty-One

Mike was in his office with John Stone when Mendoza called.

"Hello, Manny, what's up?" he asked.

"I want to talk to you, Mike. You going to be there for a while?"

"Sure, I'll be here. But what's the problem?"

"I'd rather explain personally."

"All right. Come over as soon as you can."

Mike's eyebrows raised as he looked at Stone. "Manny's uptight about something."

"What?" Stone asked.

"He didn't say. Said he wanted to talk to me personally. He should be here soon. Want to stick around? I think anything he wants to tell me he'd want to tell you, too."

"That's fine with me. If he's got a problem, maybe I can help."

Mendoza arrived half an hour later. Mike and Stone greeted him at the door. "How you doing?"

Mendoza looked away. His eye twitched. "Not so hot."

"Want me to leave?" Stone asked. "Or, I can stick around if you like."

"Yeah. Stick around, John. You should be in on this, too."

"What's the problem?" Mike asked.

"I've got to tell you guys a few things."

Mike gave him a sideward glance. "Sit down and let us know what's going on."

Mendoza slouched into the sofa, and Mike and Stone sat in chairs facing him.

Mendoza sighed deeply and said, "There's no easy way to say this. I'll keep it short. I'm a criminal, a crook."

"What!" Stone and Mike said simultaneously.

"I'm a crook. Been on the take."

Mike frowned. "What do you mean, on the take?"

"I mean bribes. I've taken bribes from lobbyists to push or block legislation that affected their companies."

Mike's head dropped. Stone's face went white.

"Manny," Mike said, "that doesn't make sense. You're as honest as they come."

Mendoza shook his head. "Not anymore. I gave up my pride. I gave up my integrity." He hesitated. "But I won't go on living like this, despising myself, living in fear I'll be found out."

"What brought this on, Manny?" Mike asked. "Why are you telling us now?"

"Raymond Diaz."

"The guy who owns *La Palabra?*" Mike asked. "The Spanish language newspaper?"

"Yeah. And a radio station, too."

"What about him?"

"He wanted to talk to me over lunch. I had to go. He's in my district, and he's a wealthy and influential man. So, I met him for lunch today. When I got there he was friendly and gracious. Then, he lowered the boom. Told me that he'd found out about the bribes and tried to put the muscle on me."

"How did he learn about the bribes?" Stone asked.

"He said that in his business, they make a lot of contacts and learn a lot things. Said his reporters are always digging."

Stone sat forward. "What did he want, Manny?"

"He wanted me to do what I could to inconspicuously get this new immigration bill passed. He had me over a barrel. If I didn't do what he wanted, he'd splatter my bribe-taking all over the papers."

"Why was he so concerned about the immigration bill?" Stone asked.

"He said he was concerned about the terrible effect the immigration law was having on Mexicans in the state. Then, he said he was angry about you not obeying the Supreme Court order. Can you believe that shit?"

"No," Mike said. "The son-of-a-bitch wants the new law passed for the same reason Stern does—because it puts me between a rock and a hard place."

Mendoza held his hand up. "That's not all. Here's some news for you. The opposition is quietly trying to begin impeachment hearings on you."

"What!" Mike said and turned to Stone. "I've heard nothing about that, have you, John?"

Stone shook his head, and Mike looked back at Mendoza. "How did you find out? Diaz again?"

"Yeah. It's like he told me, he's got a lot of contacts and his reporters are always looking for information. He wanted me to help move the impeachment along or at least do nothing to stop it."

"Why?" Mike asked.

"He said if you're impeached, Stern's bill has a better chance of passing. But then he also said he didn't much like you and your smooth-talking bullshit. He told me he'll do whatever he can to bring you down. And he's not alone. He said there are plenty of non-Hispanics who are upset and gunning for you. I told him I'd think about it, but I knew I wouldn't have anything to do with it. That's when I called you."

"You did the right thing," Mike said.

"What you did was wrong," Stone said. "No question. But you've been clean as a hound's tooth as a lawmaker and as a cop. You're not a bad man."

Mike agreed. But taking bribes was criminal. It stuck in his throat, and he was sure Stone felt the same way, despite his kind words. Still, this wasn't the right moment to press the issue.

"In a way," Mendoza said, "I'm glad Diaz did this. It forced me to come to terms with it all. I'm going to the attorney general and square all this away. I'll tell him everything. I'll cooperate. I'll wear a wire. I'll do whatever I have to."

"That's it, Manny," Stone said. "Now you're talking like the incredible hulk I've known for all these years."

"Coming out like this is going to help you," Mike said. "Turning yourself in and working with the investigation will go a long way. You'll surely see some leniency."

"You know, I really don't care what they do to me. I mean it. I deserve whatever I get. I'm glad it's over. I'm just worried about Arianna and the kids." He shook his head. "What a disgrace. To do what I did. To stoop that low. I was a cop, for Pete's sake. I never took a bribe in my life. I prided myself on that. But that's not what the people will see when this comes out. That's not what my family and friends will see. They'll see a discredited politician, a crook." He buried his face in his hands.

Stone sat next to Mendoza on the couch. "We're your friends, Manny. And we don't see anything like that."

"He's got that right, buddy," Mike said. "I see a guy with a conscience and the courage to admit his mistakes and make up for them. There's that pride and integrity you thought you'd lost."

No one spoke. Then, Mike bent forward. "Listen, Manny, you don't have to say a word about it if you don't want to, but this just doesn't fit. Why did you do it?"

Mendoza closed his eyes and rolled his head slowly from side to side. "It was Arianna. She was a gambling addict. Has been for a couple of years. Lost almost everything we had."

Mike's jaw dropped. Stone bowed his head and stepped to the window.

"She lost *all* of it?" Mike asked.

"Just about. With the equity in the house we've got a little more than a hundred thousand. Not much at my age. The worst part was my mother. I had to . . . well, you know, Mike. She has the heart condition, and her dementia was getting worse. I had to put her in a nursing home. And I can tell you, even with Medicare, that costs plenty." He looked down. "So, I went in the tank."

"And you knew nothing about this?" Mike asked.

Mendoza shook his head. "She handled all the banking and bill paying, so I wasn't aware that she was draining our savings. I knew she gambled, but not that she was hooked."

Mike rubbed his forehead. "I'd never figure Arianna to do something like that. She's so level headed."

"I know. That's why I never suspected. It's still hard to fathom."

Stone approached Mendoza. "It happens so fast, you don't know what hit you. It can happen to anyone. It doesn't make her a bad or a weak person."

Mike looked at him. "You know something about this?"

Stone nodded. "I'm sure I can trust you both to keep this quiet," he said, glancing at each of them.

"I'm almost afraid to hear this," Mike said. "But, yeah. Whatever you say stays here."

"Me, too," Mendoza said.

"Have you two ever noticed that I don't bet on anything, not even an office football pool? I don't even play the stock market anymore. It's not allowed. Too much like gambling. You can get hooked on it just like getting hooked on craps or blackjack or slot machines. And that's what happened to me about thirty-five years ago."

Mike's eyes bulged. "Wow! This is a big day for surprises." It was the last thing he expected from a man he respected so much for his intellect and logical mind.

"It starts innocently enough," Stone continued. "You take a few big losses and to win your money back you gamble more often and make higher bets. It's what I call 'chip inflation.' Once you've played with twenty-five and one-hundred dollar chips, sometimes even five-hundred dollar chips, going back to five-dollar bets are not only boring, but won't get your money back."

He put his hands in his pockets and looked at Mendoza. "So, before you know it, you're playing for bigger and bigger bucks, telling yourself that sooner or later you're going to run into a hot streak, and with the size of your bets now, you'll get your money back. You think you're due to win, that you can't just keep on losing. It's quicksand, and by the time you realize it, you're already in it up to your chin."

"That's what Arianna told me," Mendoza said. "She said she thought she could win it back. Said her luck had to change."

"Typical," Stone replied.

Mendoza sat up. "How did you—"

"Diana fortunately caught on early," Stone said. "She sensed something, probably because I was gambling more frequently. She checked our financial statements and saw I'd gone through twenty grand. I guess that would be something like two-hundred grand or so in today's dollars. It was about half of everything we had back then. She almost walked out on me."

"I know the feeling," Mendoza said. "I almost did, too."

"I wouldn't have blamed her if she had," Stone said. "But we worked it out, and I went into Gamblers Anonymous. We're supposed to tell everyone we know, just like with AA. But I chose not to. Diana knowing was enough.

"So there's my deep, dark secret. In a way, it was probably a good thing. Really put me on track. I disciplined myself, set goals, and looked at life—and people—differently. That's when I got my J.D."

Stone looked at Mendoza. "Anyway, I just wanted you to know that Arianna isn't stupid or evil. She just got caught up in a whirlwind and couldn't come out of it on her own." He hesitated. "Well, I've pulled us off the real subject here, haven't I? But please remember, this is between us."

Mike chuckled. "You can bet on it."

Chapter Thirty-Two

Two days after Carlos's arrest, Dominic met with him. And for the first time, Carlos began questioning Dominic's credibility, wondering if his cocky attitude on the night of the arrest had been as phony as his counterfeit papers.

Dominic was a street guy, and now he told Carlos that for weeks he'd been picking up information that worried him. He said the street talk was that things had changed since the new immigration law. Police and ICE officers were following through on illegals caught with false papers, and judges were under pressure to get tough with them. Undocumented immigrants were being rounded up by the busload and sent back to Mexico or any other country of origin. In short, this crackdown was for real.

What bothered Dominic most, he said, was Carlos being arrested with what he thought were foolproof counterfeit documents. He knew people in the Los Angeles and state police departments as well as in ICE. Some owed Dominic favors, and those who didn't knew he paid well for good information, so they kept their eyes and ears open.

"I checked with my contacts the day after you were arrested and found out that state police were being trained to spot the fake papers," he told Carlos. "But only a small percentage of the force, mainly those going on raids with ICE. They're going to train more, but my suppliers can make necessary adjustments, or I'll find other suppliers. Just the same, you might be in danger, so pick up new papers and think of finding other places to live for a while. The papers will hold up anywhere outside of California."

Carlos knew Dominic had a well-deserved reputation for taking care of his people. But he also knew it was more financial than altruistic. It made his people loyal. In Carlos's case, money was a prime motivator. Carlos was very good at selling the counterfeit documents and a damn good enforcer. He knew that if Dominic kept him from being deported and out of jail, he'd relocate him, probably in another state where he'd set up shop and recruit others. Like a franchise. And that could double Dominic's take.

Carlos picked up his new papers that same night, then met Julio at a small local tavern. They sat in the rear, away from the half dozen other men in the tavern.

"This is it," Carlos said. "We've got to act."

"I know. It's time to sell the building and decide where we go. Tomorrow I'll call the real estate agent who sold it to us."

"We're going to have to sell it fast, so we won't get as much as we want for it."

Julio nodded. "Probably not. But we'll still have a good bankroll for wherever we end up."

But the next night Dominic called Carlos. "I just got word that you'll soon be visited by the ICE picks," as Dominic referred to the immigration officers. "You'd better get moving."

Carlos sweated. He thought he'd at least be able to sell the building before he had to leave. And Marisol, alone with the four kids. It made him ill.

"How soon will they come after me?" Carlos asked.

"Don't know for sure. But maybe in a day or two."

"When do you think I should leave?"

"As soon as possible."

"All right. I'll go tomorrow."

"Now, listen. I don't know if the ICE picks or police will chase after you," Dominic said. "I doubt it, because they've got so many people to track down. But act as if they will. Act as if they're hot on your trail, breathing down your neck. Take nothing for granted. Don't stay in one place for too long, four maybe five days at the most."

He paused. "Now, this is going to be tough for you. But you've got to do it. Don't call your wife too often. Me either. Your phone records can help them find you. And don't tell your wife where you're going. She could slip up if she's questioned. Got it?"

Carlos said he did. But he didn't like it.

That night, Carlos and Marisol met with Julio and Carmella to explain what he had to do. He watched Marisol as he spoke, remembering how strong she'd been through it all, trying to steel herself for something like this. But now that it was a reality, she must be mortified.

They went over their plans. Julio would sell the building as quickly as possible and look for someplace else to live, most likely near Julio's relatives in Texas. They would take only valuables and their best clothing and leave the furniture behind. It was old and not worth the effort of lugging it along. And then, once again, Carmella broke into tears.

When Julio and Carmella left, Carlos sat on the couch with Marisol. "It won't be for long. Until you sell the house with Julio. Carmella and Julio are right upstairs, and we have other friends in the neighborhood you can depend on."

"I know," she said softly, starring at the floor. "I'll pray for you every day."

He took her hand. "I'll do the same for you. Don't worry too much. This will all be over soon."

He knew she wasn't consoled, but pretended she was. He felt helpless knowing that all of this was happening so fast that it unnerved her, and that she didn't know what to expect next. And he knew that she did not like being away from him, even for just a few weeks.

The next morning, Carlos withdrew $3,000 from the bank for himself and $3,000 for Marisol in case she needed cash quickly. He left his revolver with Marisol, hoping it might make her feel more secure.

They told the children he was going away for a while to work at a job in Southern California that paid much more than the one he had here.

Dominic had given Carlos the names and phone numbers of men in Bull Head City, Kingman, and Flagstaff, Arizona. They would either put him up in their homes or find him a secure place to stay. Arriving in Bull Head City in the early afternoon, he immediately called one of them, who took him to a motel just outside of town.

"The owner has worked with us in the past," the man said. "He was an illegal and was deported years ago. But he got real papers in Mexico and then came back here and became an American citizen. He still remembers what it was like to be here illegally, and he helps us when he can."

Carlos stayed in Bull Head City for three days before going to Kingman. He missed Marisol and the kids badly and worried about them. He knew he shouldn't call because he hadn't been gone long enough, but couldn't help himself. As he left Bull Head City for Kingman, he phoned her. She sounded well. But that was Marisol's way. She'd hide her feelings so he wouldn't worry. Still, he relaxed a little just talking to her and felt better when he hung up. But even so, he couldn't shake a haunting anxiety that awful things were about to happen.

Chapter Thirty-Three

Julio saw fear in Carmella's face when she returned from visiting Marisol. "Ernesto is having headaches and has a sore, stiff neck," she said. "He can't concentrate on his homework, and his temperature is 103 degrees."

"When did that start?"

"He said it was bothering him all day. Marisol is going to take him to the doctor. I'll watch the baby and the other boys. Drive her to the doctor and stay with her. I've got a bad feeling about this."

"All right," he said, then went downstairs to Marisol. She was sitting next to Ernesto, who was lying in bed with a cold compress on his forehead.

"How are you feeling?" he asked the boy.

"Not so good," Ernesto answered.

Marisol ran her fingers through her son's hair. "You'll be all right soon. We're going to take you to the doctor. Ready to go?"

The boy nodded and got up. They took him to Julio's car and were at the doctor's office in fifteen minutes. As the doctor examined Ernesto, Julio saw Marisol clasping her hands together so tightly that her knuckles were white. The doctor stepped back and put his hands on his hips. He told the boy to sit in the waiting room.

"I'm afraid it's serious," he said when Ernesto left.

"No!" Marisol gasped, bringing her hands over her mouth. "How serious?"

The doctor sat next to her and put his hand on her shoulder. "It's meningitis."

Tears rolled down her cheeks. *"Oh, querido Dios. Por favor.* Help him, God. Make him well. Please."

"How serious is it?" Julio asked as he took Marisol's hands and squeezed them. "Could he die?"

"Not necessarily. But we've got to get him to the hospital. They'll run tests to see if it's a bacterial or viral infection. Both can be treated with medications. Ernesto is young and otherwise healthy, and that's a plus."

Less than an hour later, the boy was in an isolation ward and Marisol and Julio, wearing protective clothing, sat next to him. Julio stayed until 10:00 p.m., but Marisol said she wanted to stay for the night.

Driving home, Julio was consumed by sadness and fear. He thought of the Castellano boys as his nephews. They even called him and Carmella uncle and aunt. If anything happened to Ernesto, he'd be heartbroken. And who knew how Carmella would react. What's more, Ernesto's illness was also another serious complication if they had to leave quickly. Marisol would never go, as long as her son was in the hospital.

As Julio was getting ready to go to work the next morning, Marisol came home and went to see him and Carmella.

"How's Ernesto?" Julio asked her anxiously as he buttoned his shirt. She looked drained. Her face was pale, her eyes bloodshot, and her clothing disheveled.

"The doctor said the infection was bacterial, not viral. He said bacterial meningitis is less serious and easier to treat. And he told me that Ernesto's brain hadn't been affected."

"Oh, that *is* good news," Carmella said. *"Gracias a Dios.* What a relief."

"How long will he be in the hospital?" Julio asked.

"The doctor didn't know for sure, but probably about a week, maybe more."

"How is he feeling?" Carmella asked.

"He's in good spirits. He doesn't mind the hospital as much as I thought he would."

"Then you won't have to spend all your time there," Carmella said. "Julio and I will take turns staying with him. I told the Garcias what happened, and they said they'll stay with him any time you like."

But the good news was only a short respite from their troubles. Julio and Marisol were meeting at her kitchen table with their real estate agent the next day when two ICE officers arrived. They presented their identification when Marisol opened the door.

"Mrs. Castellano?" one of them asked. "Marisol Castellano?"

"Yes."

"May we come in?"

Marisol stepped back. "Have a seat," she said, motioning to the chairs in the living room.

"No, thank you. This won't take long," one of them replied as they stepped into the living room. He was tall, perhaps six-foot-four.

The real estate agent left, and Julio walked into the living room.

"Mr. Castellano?" the tall one asked Julio.

"No. Just a friend," he said, trying to keep the nervousness out of his voice.

The agents were polite, but Julio could almost hear Marisol's heart pounding as they questioned her.

"We're following up on your husband Carlos," the tall one said. "He was caught with counterfeit identification, and we have an arrest warrant for him. We know he's here illegally. Is he home by any chance?"

Marisol appeared in control of herself, almost calm. Julio knew she'd expected this would happen sooner or later, but that probably hadn't softened the impact, especially when they told her about the arrest warrant.

"No," Marisol said. "He's out of town. He found some good-paying work downstate."

"Do you know where?" the other agent asked.

"He moves from job site to job site, so it's hard to keep track of where he is at any time."

"We'll find him eventually. If you cooperate, things will go easier for both of you. We can offer certain accommodations that'll make deportation less of a problem, maybe give you more time to plan and make arrangements in Mexico."

"I can't help you," she said. "I really don't know where he is."

"Mrs. Castellano, if he's here illegally, we'll naturally investigate your status as well. Do you have identification?"

She stared at them for a moment, not knowing what to say. Before leaving, Carlos had her destroy the counterfeit papers he'd given her, fearing that she might get caught with them.

Thinking quickly, Julio said, "Her purse was stolen the other day. All her identification was in it."

Marisol picked up on his lead. "I can get new identification, but I'm tied down with the baby and can't find my birth certificate. My son is in the hospital with meningitis, and we're trying to sell the building. That lady who just left was our real estate agent."

"I'm sorry about your son," the shorter one said. "But you're going to have to produce new identification soon. We can help with that. Come down to our office. If not, you'll have to appear before an immigration judge, and we'll start deportation proceedings."

"I understand. I'll start doing that in a few days. Is that okay?"

"That'll be fine."

Marisol sank into the couch when they left. "Now what? Things are catching up to us quickly."

Julio rubbed his chin. "We've got to sell the building and move as soon as Ernesto is out of the hospital. We can drop the price four or five thousand dollars. Once it's sold we can get out of here. I talked to my cousin in Texas yesterday. They're going to look for a place for us and try to find me and Carlos a construction job. Have you heard from Carlos?"

"Not since he called a few days ago. I'll probably hear from him in a day or so. I don't know if I should tell him about everything that's happening, especially about Ernesto. He'd worry, maybe come home, and that would be bad. He might get caught and sent to jail because of the arrest warrant. And he'd almost surely be deported."

"It might be a good idea to tell him about the ICE agents and the arrest warrant. But I think you're right about Ernesto."

Carmella came home from work, and they told her what happened. She sat on the couch next to Marisol, her face twisted in sympathy. "You're being very brave about all this. I wish I could be, too. But this eats away at me. I pray for Ernesto all the time."

Marisol leaned toward her friend, but Carmella smiled and put up her hand. "Don't worry. I promise not to cry."

Chapter Thirty-Four

On February 24 at 4:48 p.m., the call came. It was Josephine. Mike's heart fluttered. Was she coming home? Or, was this it for them?

Her voice quivered. "Did you hear, Mike? Did you hear the news? I mean about John."

"What news? What about John?"

"He's dead, Mike," she said and burst into tears.

"What! Did you say John is dead?"

"Yes."

"Are you sure?"

"Yes. Absolutely."

"How? What happened?"

"Heart attack. He . . . he died in the emergency room."

Mike's head dropped. His lips trembled. He rested his forehead in the palm of his hand. "Oh, good God. I can't believe it. I don't want to believe it."

He took a deep breath. He was limp. The phone shook in his hand.

"Are you there, Mike? Are you okay?"

He rubbed his forehead. "Yeah. Yeah, I'm all right. This is just awful hard to take."

"I know, Mike. I know. I'm heartbroken, too."

"Did you talk to Diana?"

"For a few minutes. I was just about to go see her."

"Okay. You do that. I'll finish up here and meet you there in an hour."

As he left, Mike told his staff about Stone, and many broke into tears. He ordered flags to half staff, then left for Stone's home. He and Josephine stayed with Diana as family and other friends arrived. They left at 8:00 p.m..

At home, Mike poured a cognac for both of them. They sat on the living room sofa with just the flickering light of the fireplace. The tranquil ambience ordinarily soothed Mike. He often sat here by himself just like this after a hectic day and let the tension evaporate. But not tonight. Tonight, the placid atmosphere afforded no peace.

"How you holding up?" Josephine asked.

"I'm not sure. In shock I suppose. Disbelief. Denial. I guess it's the suddenness. I mean . . . I mean I talked to him just yesterday. And now . . . now he's gone. It doesn't seem real. I'm having a hard time accepting it."

"It's a bad time, Mike. But you'll deal with it."

Mike rubbed his temples. "Right now, Jo, there's nothing to deal with. After the initial shock, I'm numb. I don't feel anything. And that bothers me. I'm ashamed of it. How can that be? I loved that guy."

"It's natural, Mike. One of the stages of grief."

"Maybe. But there's nothing inside me. I *want* to feel the grief and the pain and the loss and the loneliness. But I don't. My heart and soul are anesthetized. How do I handle that?"

"You'll get past it."

"Yeah, but when?"

"Give it time, Mike. Just give it time."

They sat quietly, then Josephine shifted toward him. "I don't know if this is the right time to say it, or if it will help. But I've got to tell you I'm sorry for walking out the way I did." She leaned toward him and put her arm around him, then pressed her face against his.

Mike felt her tears against his cheek. He slipped his arm around her and squeezed. "It's okay, babe. Forget it ever happened. I'm just glad you're here with me."

"It was such a stupid, emotional thing to do."

"Well, I can't blame you. What I did was pretty stupid, too."

She smiled and caressed his face. "It was terrible for me. I missed you. When I heard about John . . ."

"Listen," Mike said, "maybe this is the one good thing that came out of John's death. At least it brought you back."

"I suppose. Is it okay between us now?"

"It is for me if it is for you."

"It is," she said and kissed him. "I'm glad it's over."

"Me, too."

He swallowed the rest of his drink and walked to the bar. "I'm going to have another one of these," he said, pouring more cognac into his glass. "Want another splash?"

She shook her head. "No. I'm drained. I think I'm just going to go up to bed. Do you mind? I don't want to leave you alone right now if you want my company."

"No. That's fine. Go ahead. I could probably use some time by myself."

She leaned over and kissed him on the cheek. "I love you."

"Love you, too."

When Josephine left, he leaned his head back and rolled it from side to side. He closed his eyes remembering his first day in the Senate. Stone walked into his office that morning and held out his hand. "I'm John Stone. Welcome to the sausage factory."

Mike chuckled and shook his hand. "Pleased to meet you. I've seen you on TV a few times."

"Really. Well, as you can see, I'm much better looking in person."

"I noticed that right away."

Stone smiled. "I can see we're going to get along just fine."

"I think so, too."

"If you've got some time, I'll show you around and introduce you to some people. Then we can grab lunch."

"Sure thing. And thanks. I appreciate it."

"You're welcome. And if there's any way I can help in the future, just pick up the phone."

"I'll do that."

As usual, he was true to his word. Whenever Mike had a dilemma or needed advice, Stone was his go-to guy. And it wasn't just politics. He thought back on Stone sitting quietly as Mike told him about Stern's blackmail attempt, then giving him the advice and moral support he badly needed. He recalled Stone confessing his gambling habit. It must have been a terrible embarrassment for him but he did it anyway to show Mendoza that his wife wasn't a terrible or weak person because she gambled away most of their savings.

And what a pleasure to be with. Mike pictured him stroking that John Barrymore mustache and talking history and law. He took it seriously, really seriously. But not so much that he didn't enjoy it, kind of like a literary agent engrossed in a great novel or a movie critic relishing a great movie. But he was never so immersed that he couldn't find some humor in it all.

Mike was dog-tired, exhausted, hollow. It was as though if he felt for his pulse, there wouldn't be any. He dreaded lying in bed tonight. Even more, he dreaded waking up the next morning, and the next and the next, with the horrible reality that his friend was dead. There'd be no more of those deep, spirited, uplifting conversations about history, philosophy, ethics, politics, society, or for that matter art and literature. A true Renaissance man. If a vacancy had opened in the state Supreme, Stone would have been Mike's pick. A spark of anger flashed though him because Stone's life ended too soon, far from completely fulfilled. There was so much more he could have done.

He gulped his drink, then plodded to bed. And that's when it hit. That's when the sorrow closed in—deep and almost physically painful. Mike's highly emotional nature usually manifested itself in his temper. But it was equally intense in sadness. Normally, he hid it. But this was different. His sorrow was visceral. A chapter in his life had closed. And with a terrible ending.

As he climbed into bed, he said, "You know, Jo, until now, even I didn't realize how close I was to John."

Chapter Thirty-Five

A week later, it was on the front page of newspapers across the country and the lead story on TV news. Mike figured it must have been Stern who leaked it, and that meant she thought she had the votes to impeach him. For a fraction of a second, he expected Stone to call to offer encouragement. A rush of sadness swept over him.

He called Mendoza. "How bad is it? We must have had a lot of our guys go with Stern."

"Sure did," Mendoza replied. "It got pretty heated, and I swear it almost came to blows. Stern and her boys must have called in a lot of favors and made a lot of promises. I kind of figured we'd lose some of our people, but I didn't want to tell you until I could be specific."

"And Stern leaked it before you had a chance."

"That's right. I'll stay on top of this. Maybe I can pull some of our people back. We might get enough to take the wind out of her sails. But I wouldn't count on it."

"I guess this means you're on board with me," Mike said.

"Yeah. I still have reservations, but after hearing you and John go over this, I think you're doing the right thing. How are you holding up, I mean with John's death? I liked John a lot. A brilliant guy. But I know you two were very close."

"It's hard, Manny. There's an emptiness inside me. It would be like something happening to you. I was just thinking about him before I called you. But I'll get past it."

Two days later, Stern and Griswold held a press conference to announce that impeachment hearings would begin the following month. They kept it short and allowed only a few questions.

"We've decided that the governor's actions warrant impeachment," Griswold said, gripping the sides of the podium. "Defying a Supreme Court decision reflects badly on our entire legislature, our entire state. It's a rogue and lawless move that endangers our judicial system. And Governor DiGrasso deserves more than a slap on the wrist."

He pointed to a reporter, who stood and asked, "What will the charges be?"

Stern stepped to the podium. "There are a number of them. Abuse of power is one. He's certainly acting like he thinks he's a king instead of a governor. Failure to comply with a Supreme Court order. Failure to abide by the Constitution. And how about just disgracing the office of governor? There are others, but we think these will do."

She called on a reporter from a local TV station. "Even if you impeach the governor, that doesn't mean the Senate will remove him from office. Do you think you have the votes to do that?"

Stern bent closer to the microphone. "We're still tabulating that. Even if we don't, this is at least more than just a reprimand. The legislature is showing its severe disapproval of what the governor is doing. And it's more than just ignoring the court. Look how he handled the sanctuary ban. He just dug in his heels without even an attempt at a bipartisan solution. And I think it's simply hypocrisy for him to take legal action against those cities and then refuse to comply with a Supreme Court decision."

She almost smiled, knowing that DiGrasso would be watching and hearing her call him a hypocrite again. She gestured with her head to another reporter, who said, "The governor is making a pretty good case for what he's doing."

"Yes," Stern said. "Governor DiGrasso is very good at obfuscating the primary issue. He can be very convincing. But the fact is, he's acting foolishly and dangerously. Congressman Griswold was right. This is a threat to our entire judicial system."

She and Griswold fielded two more questions, then ended the conference.

Chapter Thirty-Six

Julio arrived early for the immigrant rally with his son Roberto who, much to his father's disapproval, chose to march with the *Reconquista* contingent of the demonstration. They'd argued vehemently the previous night, but it did no good. Roberto was passionate about the *Reconquista* cause. More than just a member of the group, he was one of its leaders in Los Angeles.

It was Saturday, just five days since Carlos left, and around him Julio could see 10,000-plus people gathering with American flags and posters reading: "America Is A Nation Of Immigrants," "All We Want Is A Better Life," "DiGrasso's Law Is Unconstitutional," "Mexicans Vote Too, Governor."

The march in downtown Los Angeles began at 9:00 a.m., and Julio was relieved to see that it was proceeding peacefully, even though counter-protesters lined the streets behind the police barricades. Their posters read: "Get Legal," "We Like Your Burritos But Not You," "Fix Mexico, Don't Ruin USA." Almost 200 police on foot, horseback, and in patrol cars accompanied the marchers, whose column stretched for miles.

Half an hour after the march began, Julio heard shouting a few blocks behind him. He'd expected hecklers, so he thought nothing of it. As he trudged along, however, the shouting intensified.

Initially, he inched toward the commotion out of curiosity. But for no apparent reason, he became nervous.

Then, the gunshot and the screams.

People ran from the area and sirens blared in the distance.

He walked faster, pushing and twisting his way through the crowd.

When he arrived at the scene, police had restored order. He heard that a man had been arrested and an ambulance called. Julio recognized a friend of Roberto's, a *Reconquista,* and ran to him. "Roberto. Roberto Perez," he said. "Where is he?"

The *Reconquista* lowered his head. "He was shot."

"What! Roberto got shot? Oh, dear God. Are you sure?" he asked, grabbing the man by the shoulders. "Are you absolutely sure it was Roberto?"

The *Reconquista* nodded.

"How bad was he hurt?"

"I don't know. They just took him away in an ambulance a minute ago."

Julio put his head in his hands, then ran his fingers through his hair. He went to one of the policemen questioning witnesses. "My son Roberto was the one who was shot. How is he? Where did they take him?"

"I can't say for sure. He was unconscious when they took him away. I'll have you driven to the hospital," the officer said and radioed for a squad car.

"How did it happen?" Julio asked.

The policeman shrugged. "I got here after he was shot. I don't know."

A middle-aged woman standing nearby stepped toward Julio. "I'm very sorry about your son, but the *Reconquistas* brought this on. They instigated it." She pointed to *Reconquista* signs and banners lying in the street: "You stole this land from us," "We're not illegal, you are," "We'll take our land back."

She told him the *Reconquistas* began shouting insults at hecklers. Roberto was at the front of the group, walking close to the barricades and laughing at and taunting the people behind them. Roberto raised his middle finger, she said, and shoved it at one of the counter-protesters and shouted, "Fuck you, Gringo son-of-a-bitch," and the fight was on. Roberto was knocked to the ground, and two men began kicking him. He took a gun out of the inside pocket of his jacket, but one of the men grabbed his hand. They wrestled and the gun went off.

The squad car arrived and ten minutes later Julio was at the emergency room where Roberto had been taken. Weak and wobbly, he walked into the waiting room and approached the nurse's station. About half of the plastic chairs in the center of the room and along the walls were occupied with people whose faces expressed their concern. Some were crying.

Julio trembled as he asked one of the nurses at the desk about his son. She picked up the phone and called for a doctor. "Take a seat please," she said. "A doctor will be out in a few minutes."

"Can you tell me nothing?" Julio pleaded. "Is he alive?"

The nurse tilted her head and looked at him sympathetically. "I'm sorry, Sir. I wish I could help but I can't. The doctor will be here shortly. Please take a seat and try to be patient."

Julio stared at her for a moment, then sat in a chair by the wall. He tried to be calm, telling himself that just because his son had been shot didn't mean he was dead or seriously injured. He put his elbows on his knees and rested his head in his hands. Oh, Lord, what would this do to Carmella?

A doctor in surgical scrubs arrived a few minutes later. Julio stood. "My son. My son, Roberto. The one that was shot. How is he?"

The doctor bowed his head and before he said anything, Julio knew. He sat down, bent over, and sobbed.

The doctor sat next to him. "I'm very sorry," he said, and waved a nurse over. "There was nothing we could do. He was shot in the heart, and he was dead when he got here. Are you on any kind of medications?" the doctor asked Julio as the nurse approached. "Blood pressure, cholesterol, anti-depressants. Anything like that?"

Julio said no, and the doctor turned to the nurse. "Get an Alprazolam. Two milligrams, and bring some water." He looked at Julio. "That's a sedative. It'll calm you down a little. I'll write you a full prescription before you go."

Julio looked up, tears still welling in his eyes.

"Thank you. What is it I do now?"

"Just relax here for a while, then we'll get you home. The next thing is to contact a funeral home. They'll take it from there."

The nurse returned with a pill and a paper cup of water. The doctor handed them to Julio. "This will help."

A hospital security guard drove Julio to his car. He went to Marisol first. He wanted her with him when he told Carmella.

"Hello, Julio," she said, smiling when she opened the door. But as she looked at him, the smile disappeared and near panic formed on her face. Her mouth opened and she looked at him with a sideward glance.

"What's the matter, Julio?" She gestured to the couch. "Sit down. Tell me what's wrong."

Julio flopped on the couch and began crying. "It's Roberto," he said, his voice shaking. "Roberto is dead. He got shot in a fight at the rally."

"Ah, *Dios no! No!* Oh, my God, please, no!" Marisol shouted as she too collapsed onto the sofa, dropped her head, and cried. She put her arms around him. "Oh, Julio, Julio. I'm so sorry. He was like a son to me and Carlos." She hesitated, her eyes widening. "Carmella. Good Lord. What will this do to her?"

Julio shook his head. "I don't know. I thought about it on the way here. I don't know how to break this to her. I want you to come with me, okay?"

"Of course. But first we have to calm down. Have you told Erika?"

He shook his head.

"We should do that first. Then all three of us will tell Carmella. I'm going to check on the baby. The boys are in the backyard playing with their friends. I'll send them to the Garcia's. Why don't you call Erika, and the funeral home?"

Julio rushed to Erika when she arrived half an hour later, and they embraced tightly and cried together. Marisol wept with them. Father and daughter spoke for a few minutes, then Erika said, "Okay, let's do this now and get it over with."

Julio and Marisol nodded. Marisol cradled the baby in her arms. Julio put his arm around his daughter and pulled her close as they walked out the kitchen door to the porch where stairs led to his apartment.

Carmella was at the kitchen table sewing one of Julio's work shirts. She got up with a wide smile and hugged Erika. "What a nice surprise," she said, then abruptly stepped back. "What's wrong?" she asked, looking at each of them. "I can see it on your faces. Something is wrong."

Julio put his arms around her. "Sit down."

She pulled away. "Tell me what's going on!"

Erika began to cry, and Julio put his arms around Carmella again. "It's Roberto."

She jerked her head back. "What about him?"

Julio hung his head, and Carmella sucked in a deep breath.

Julio held her tighter. "Roberto is dead. There was a fight at the march and he was shot."

Carmella looked at him in horror. "*Que! Mijo!* Oh, no. Oh, please God, no. Not Roberto. Please!"

She broke away from Julio and paced, shaking her head violently back and forth, pulling her hair. She raised her hands into the air and screamed, "No! This can't be!" Then she crumpled into a chair. She put her head in her arms on the table, and her body shuddered as she sobbed.

Marisol's lips were pressed firmly together as tears streamed down her face. She pulled a chair next to Carmella, held the baby in one arm and put the other around her friend. "Go ahead, cry, cry. Get it out of you."

Erika sat next to her mother and hugged her, and their bodies convulsed as they cried together. Then, Carmella jumped up. She'd stopped crying and stared forward, motionless.

"Are you all right?" Marisol asked, standing up. Carmella said nothing. Staring straight ahead with unblinking eyes and her arms hanging limply at her sides, she walked trancelike down the hallway toward the living room.

Then, she turned back to them. She began to laugh and twirl around with her arms held out. They stared at her, dumbstruck. Julio didn't know what was happening or what to do. Carmella laughed loudly as she twirled faster and faster. Julio rushed toward her, but she collapsed before he reached her.

"Carmella!" he shouted as he knelt down next to her. He put his left arm behind her upper back, pulled her up, and ran his other hand across her face and hair as her head rested motionless on his chest. Marisol and Erika squatted next to him.

"Carmella," he pleaded. "Carmella. Please. Can you hear me?"

Marisol stood. "I'll call 911. Erika, put some ice in dish rags and hold them on her forehead and wrists."

Marisol reached for the phone on the wall as Carmella's eyelids fluttered and opened. She looked around as if she didn't know where she was.

"Carmella," Julio said, running his fingers along her face. She looked up, seeming surprised to see him. Then she put her arm around his neck, leaned her head on his chest, and wept quietly. He looked helplessly at Marisol and Erika.

Marisol hung up the phone and stepped forward. "Let's get her to bed."

Erika helped her father pick up Carmella and took her to the bedroom down the hall from the kitchen. They laid her on the bed, beneath the large crucifix hanging above the headboard. She was perfectly still, saying nothing, just staring at the ceiling, her eyes reddened and puffy. Julio sat on the bed next to her and held her hand. Erika sat on the opposite side of the bed and squeezed her mother's other hand.

"Try to rest," Julio said, stroking her forehead. "Try to sleep. I'll be right here." He motioned for Erika and Marisol to leave. They walked into the kitchen, closing the bedroom door behind them.

Carmella awoke at 6:00 that evening. Julio was lying next to her with his arm around her. "How are you?" he asked.

She slowly pushed herself up with her head hanging down on her chest. "I'm all right now," she whispered.

He helped her up and walked her into the kitchen to sit with Erika and Marisol's baby.

"Marisol took the prescription to the drugstore," Erika said. "She should be back soon."

Erika made chicken broth, and tea mixed with honey. Carmella picked up the spoon next to the soup bowl and looked at it. "It's a little dirty," she said, then dropped it into the sink and reached for another one from the cabinet drawer.

Marisol returned and gave Carmella a tranquilizer. She and Erika tried to converse with her as she slowly sipped the tea and spooned some broth into her mouth. She occasionally said something but was for the most part quiet.

Finally, she pushed away the soup and tea, then smiled at Marisol and Erika. She took their hands. "Thank you. Thank you so much for being here."

"We'll always be here, Mom," Erika said, hugging her mother.

"Whatever you need," Marisol added.

Carmella stood up slowly. "I need to take a shower and change clothes. No, a bath. A nice hot bath."

"That's a good idea," Julio said. "I've got to go to the funeral home. Marisol, will you stay with Erika?"

Marisol nodded.

Erika walked her mother to the bathroom.

"Why don't you two relax?" Carmella said with a weak smile. "Lie down. Maybe you'll get some sleep like I did."

"Yes, I can use some rest," Marisol said.

"Me, too," Erika agreed. "Call if you need anything."

Carmella nodded and closed the door. Julio heard the water running in the tub as he put on clean clothes. "You two try to rest if you can," he said and left for the funeral home.

"We will," Marisol answered.

Making the funeral arrangements pushed Julio into an even deeper depression. There was such a finality to it, the last act of a play in which his son dies. He entered his dimly lit apartment quietly and checked on Marisol and Erika. Both were asleep, Erika in the second bedroom and Marisol on the living room couch with the baby. He looked into the master bedroom, hoping Carmella was also sleeping, but she wasn't there. He noticed light at the bottom of the bathroom door.

She was still in the tub?

Then, "Oh, no!" he shouted as he grabbed and turned the bathroom door knob. Locked.

"Carmella!" he shouted and pounded the door with his fist. "Carmella, open the door!" He slammed his shoulder into the heavy wooden door but it wouldn't give.

Marisol and Erika ran to him. "What is it?" Marisol asked.

"I don't know for sure. But we've got to get this door open. Erika, my tool box is on the porch. Get me a screwdriver and the crowbar," he said and again slammed himself into the door. "Hurry!" he shouted as he tried kicking the door open.

When Erika returned, he first tried to pry the door open with the screwdriver.

No good.

So, he shoved the curved tip of the crowbar between the edge of the door and its jamb, just above the knob. He pulled hard three times, and the door flew open.

"No!" he shouted, and rushed to the bathtub. "No. Oh, Carmella, Carmella," he sobbed as he reached for her.

Marisol's legs buckled as she gasped loudly and covered her mouth with her hands. She fell to her knees and turned her head away as Erika screamed and ran to the bathtub.

Carmella's naked body lay in the tub, her head rolled to the left, her glazed eyes open. Her arms were at her sides. Both of her wrists were slashed open and floating palms up in the blood-red water. On the floor next to the tub, Julio saw the sharply honed, blood-streaked paring knife she'd managed to secretly get into her pocket when she'd gone for another spoon.

Chapter Thirty-Seven

It must have been paranormal brain activity, because Mike was apprehensive for no reason when Josephine called him at his office.

"Can you come home, Mike?" she asked.

"Why? Something wrong?"

"It's Patti. She went to Mexico with her boyfriend and his family."

Mike stood. "What?"

"She's gone. She went to Mexico with them."

"When?"

"She called Becky this morning."

"Do you know where in Mexico?"

"She didn't say, but I guess we can find out."

"All right. I'll be home in an hour."

"What are we going to do, Mike?"

"I don't know yet, Jo. We'll figure something out."

"Okay. But I'm scared, Mike. I'm worried about her."

"I know. Me, too. But try to stay calm."

As he was driven home, his concern morphed into anger. How the hell could she do this? Could she have changed so gradually over the years that he and Josephine didn't notice?

When he walked in, Josephine and Becky were sitting on the living room sofa, their eyes damp and reddened. Mike sat next to Josephine and put his arm around her. "Come on, babe. Don't worry yourself to death. Does Rose know about this?"

Josephine nodded. "I called her just after I talked to you. She said she'll fly in tonight if it would help. I told her not to, because Becky was in town and was coming over."

"Good," Mike said to Josephine. "No need for her to be here."

She just nodded and wiped away the tears with the crumpled tissues clasped in her hand.

Mike looked to Becky. "Okay. What's the story? What happened?"

"The company where Marco's father and brother work did a check on all of their employees, because a week ago it was raided and some illegals were found. There was a big fine, and the owner was afraid if they got caught again they'd get an even bigger fine or maybe even lose their business license. So, they had all their employees document that they were here legally. Marco's father and brother obviously couldn't. They were deported, and Marco went with them. Patti went with Marco."

Mike put his hands over his eyes and rubbed his forehead. "Son-of-a-bitch. I can't believe she pulled this stunt."

"But she did," Josephine said. "So, now what?"

"I'm not sure. Can you get hold of her?" he asked Becky. "Can you find out where she is?"

"She has her cell phone."

Mike stood. He put his hands on his hips and paced. "Give her a call and find out where she is. Maybe I'll go down there and see if I get her to come back."

"I don't think she will, Dad. She's in love with Marco. I mean she's *really* in love. And she won't be happy to see you. She's still mad about you and the immigration law."

"Well, give her a call anyway. Maybe if I see her face-to-face I can talk some sense into her."

"Okay," Becky said and walked out to the deck to make the call.

Mike fumed. "You know, I've got a mind to just let her stay down there."

Josephine's face flushed. "No! Mike, you wouldn't. You couldn't. She's your daughter. What's the matter with you?"

"What the matter with *me?* What about *her?* Just leaving her family like that," he said, snapping his fingers. "She didn't care about us. Why should we care about her? She just writes me off as if I was some kind of cruel stepfather who beat her and kept her in rags. I don't deserve this! We don't deserve this! None of us."

"Stop it!" Josephine shouted. "I won't listen to this! Are you crazy? She's your daughter, and you'd just let her go without trying to get her back? You do something or I will."

Mike sat back on the sofa. Josephine began to speak but Mike beat her to it. "All right. All right. I'll do something. Let's find out where she is, and we'll go down to see her."

Minutes later, Becky walked back into the living room. "She's in Del Lago. It's a town a few miles from Durango. Marco's family got them a small apartment close to where they live. But Dad, she doesn't want you to go there. She doesn't want to see you. She says she's not coming home and you shouldn't try to make her. She doesn't even want to talk to you. She just hung up on me the second I said you wanted to go get her."

Mike jumped from the sofa. "Why that stupid little . . . What's wrong with her? I feel like going down there and dragging her back here."

"Oh, that's *brilliant*, Mike," Josephine huffed. "Just brilliant. I can see the Mexican police throwing you in jail. Great photo op. Will you calm down and think clearly?"

Mike breathed in deeply and exhaled heavily. "Okay. All right. Listen, Jo, you call her. She'll probably talk to you. I guess it's just me she suddenly decided to hate. See if you can talk her into coming home. Maybe she'll let *you* go to see her."

Josephine took Becky's phone and called. "Hello, Marco. Yes, this is Patti's mother. How are things there for you?"

Mike could vaguely hear Marco's voice but couldn't make out what he was saying. He signaled Josephine to put the phone on speaker, but she waved him off.

"I see," Josephine said. "Well, at least that's good. Is Patti there? I'd like to talk to her." She looked at Mike and covered the speaker of the phone.

"He said they're doing all right. Patti's coming to the phone. Mike, do me a favor and go out on the deck or something. It'll be easier if I talk to her in private. Please, Mike. Let me handle this. If she even thinks you're here, she might just hang up again."

Mike bit the edge of his fist. But then he nodded and walked out on the deck. Becky went with him.

"Mom will straighten things out," Becky said. "This is all emotion. When Patti settles down, she'll see things clearly and do what's right."

"Ah. I'm telling you, Becky, she'd better. Of all the nerve. Just picking up and leaving all of us hanging like this. What the hell did I do to warrant this? That law needed to be passed and enforced. It's not my fault that his family didn't become citizens, or at least get worker visas or something."

"I know, Dad. She was wrong. She's my sister and I love her, but she's wrong to do this."

Mike paced. Becky sat on one of the patio chairs. "I think Mom will get through to her."

"I'll say it again, Becky. She'd better, because I'm about ready to write that girl off."

"Don't say that, Dad," Becky pleaded, and tears formed in her eyes. "Please, don't talk like that."

Mike stepped to her and cupped her chin in his hands. "All right, sweetheart. Don't worry about it. I'll get a hold of myself." He wiped her tears away. "I'm just very angry with her. But this will work out. Mom will take care of it." He sighed. "Do me a favor and go inside. Maybe if you talk to her, too, she'll come around."

Becky left and Mike sat and tried to relax. His anger toward his daughter was overcoming his instinctive fatherly love. She had no reason to do this. No right to hurt her family. He had to fight off the urge to just disown her, never see her again.

Then, the guilt came. Despite her antics, she *was* his daughter and he *did* love her. He shouldn't feel the way he did. And he hadn't even patched things up with her about the argument they'd had over dinner. His anger dissipated, and sadness took its place.

Josephine stepped out on the deck. "She won't come home. She said they're planning to get married down there."

"Huh. Am I invited?"

Josephine sat down next to him. "Oh, stop it. This is no time for jokes. I think I'll go see her. I've got to do something. If I talk to her personally, maybe I can get her to reconsider."

"Maybe. Take Becky with you. Or, better yet, I'll go with you but won't go to see her. I'll stay at a hotel."

"No. I'll go by myself. I think it's better if you stay out of this altogether."

"That's up to you. I'll make a few calls and see if I can get some government official down there to meet you at the airport and get you a good hotel and take you to Patti. Get a flight out tomorrow. I don't want to use the governor's jet for personal business like this. We've got some airline miles, so upgrade to first class."

"I'll do that now."

She left and Mike sat quietly, impugning himself once more. The law. The damned immigration law again. More problems. More family discord. The damned law. Was it worth it? Was it too late to back down?

Mike picked up Josephine at the airport. She didn't have to say a word. He could see it. Her head hung down, she walked in slow, short steps, oblivious to the people around her. He wrapped his arms around her. "No good, huh?"

She shook her head. "She won't come back."

"*Damn* that girl!" he said and led Josephine to the waiting limo.

"I may have made things worse," she said as they climbed into the back seat.

"How's that?"

"I smacked her, Mike."

"What?"

"I slapped her."

"Why? What happened?"

"She really pissed me off. I kept getting angrier as we spoke. She was so hard-headed. Unreasonable. Obstinate. Outright disrespectful.

I couldn't believe it was our daughter. Finally, she said they would get married next month and before I could say anything, she said everyone was welcome except you. That was too much for me. So, I slapped her. And I was going to do it again, but Marco stood between us."

Mike laughed. "And I thought I was the only one who could irritate you that much."

"I couldn't help it. I did it before I knew I did it."

He put his arm around her. "That's all right, babe. I'm sure you two will make amends. I don't know where that leaves me, but you two will be okay after the dust settles."

"I hope so. I don't want to be estranged from my daughter."

"How was it down there?"

"I was treated very well. The mayor picked me up in a limo at the airport with six motorcycle policemen. He got me into a very nice hotel, and when I cleaned up he took me to see Patti. But it's awful there, Mike. The business area around the hotel was all right. But when you got away from that the poverty is all around you. Dilapidated homes, broken windows, garbage in the streets. Some of the streets aren't even paved. They're gravel or just plain dirt."

"What about where Patti is?"

"Not too bad. They have an apartment. It's small but it's clean, and Marco's family lives about a mile away. It's not a real bad part of town. She made me mad, but I worry about her. Marco said he's sure to find a job soon. But I don't know. And . . . I'm afraid."

Mike squeezed her. "Don't worry. Things will work out."

But that wasn't what he felt inside. He didn't see how things could ever be the same for his family again.

Chapter Thirty-Eight

Mike didn't see it coming, but Mendoza most likely did, which probably saved the governor's life. Mendoza had earned ten citations for bravery and extraordinary police work in his twelve years on the LAPD. Highly professional, he'd trained himself to be aware of everything around him, developing a sixth sense of sorts—so he may well have anticipated what was about to happen.

Mike and Mendoza walked through the domed rotunda of the capitol building, heading for a meeting on a new education bill, occasionally stopping to chat with someone. About forty feet to their right, two clean-shaven men in business suits sat on a bench with laptop computers resting on their thighs. Nothing was particularly unusual about them, but Mike noticed Mendoza watching them from the corner of his eye.

The men reached inside their laptop cases.

Mendoza's head snapped toward them—as they each pulled out two semi-automatic hand guns.

"Look out, Mike! Look out!" Mendoza shouted and pushed Mike forward.

Gunshots echoed thunderously through the rotunda.

Screams. More gunfire exploded.

People ran. Some dove to the floor. Others ducked, looking for somewhere to hide. Mike and Mendoza crouched and sprinted for cover behind a staircase about thirty feet ahead.

"*Reconquistas!*" the gunmen shouted repeatedly as they fired.

Mendoza grunted. He stiffened, then went limp and collapsed, face down, to the floor. Mike grabbed one of Mendoza's arms and dragged him toward the staircase.

Then, the sledge hammer impact of a bullet just above Mike's right knee. He crumbled to all fours, groaning, but crawled for cover, pulling Mendoza with him.

The two gunmen moved toward him.

Shit! He wasn't a bystander.

He was the target!

And the staircase was ten miles away.

White-hot pain streaked down the center of his lower back as a bullet skimmed across it, ripping a deep gash. He winced and stopped crawling.

Capitol police returned fire. Two of Mike's bodyguards appeared in front of him, firing their weapons. One of them abruptly whipped left, as if shoved, then bent to one knee, continuing to fire. A capitol policeman groaned, bent over, and fell heavily down to his side.

One of the attackers spun backward, hands flung into the air, and fell face forward. The other slumped to his knees, head hanging down on his chest, and slowly slipped sideways onto the floor.

Pools of dark red blood formed on the white marble floor beneath the gunmen as two capitol policemen cautiously approached them, sidearms pointed. Other policemen ran to Mike, his fallen bodyguard, and Mendoza. Another called for help on his radio as he tended to the wounded officer.

Mike's unwounded bodyguard turned to him. "You okay, Governor?"

"I don't know," Mike said, clenching his teeth. "How's Congressman Mendoza? How's Bill?"

"Don't know about the congressman," the body guard replied, taking off his belt and wrapping it delicately around Mike's leg, just above the wound. "But Bill was hit in the shoulder."

Mike tilted his head toward Mendoza as capitol policemen slowly turned the congressman on his back. One of them put his fingers on Mendoza's carotid artery.

"Is he alive?" Mike shouted.

"He's got a pulse," the policeman said. "It's weak, but it's a pulse. Paramedics are coming."

"Manny!" Mike shouted. "Manny, can you hear me?"

No answer.

His bodyguard slowly pulled the belt tight around his leg.

"My back," Mike said. "I'm hit in the back, too."

"I'll take a look. Can you sit up so I can get off your suit coat and shirt?"

"I'll try," Mike said, and his bodyguard helped him up.

The bodyguard took off Mike's suit coat and Mike pulled off his necktie. After removing Mike's shirt, he lowered Mike to his side, then folded the shirt, put it over the back wound and pressed hard. Mike grimaced, and the bodyguard lowered him on to his back again.

Mike looked around him. The shooting had been a blur, and only adrenalin and autonomic physical reaction had governed Mike. But now it hit him. He turned to a capitol policeman. "How the hell did they get past security with those guns?"

The officer raised his hands and shrugged. "I don't know, Governor. I just don't know. But somebody's going to fry."

The capitol policemen gingerly unbuttoned Mendoza's blood-soaked shirt and gently pulled it down on his sides. A dozen more police, weapons drawn, ran into the rotunda. Sirens blared outside, and minutes later four paramedics pushing gurneys rushed in. One knelt beside Mendoza; another squatted next to Mike. The others tended to the wounded bodyguard and policeman.

"How you doing, Governor?" the paramedic asked, as he cleaned and bandaged Mike's back.

"Hard to say," Mike said. "How does it look to you?"

"It's a pretty deep gash, about a foot long, from the lower middle of your back to your buttocks. But I should be able to stop the bleeding. Then I'll bandage up your leg."

"Okay," Mike said and looked at the paramedic working on Mendoza. "How is he?"

The paramedic continued working without looking up. "He's been hit three times. In the abdomen, chest, and in the shoulder."

"How you holding up, Bill?"

The bodyguard rolled his head toward Mike. "Okay . . . I think. Never been shot before. I didn't feel the pain very much at first, but now it hurts like hell."

"He seems all right," the paramedic said. "Looks like the bullet hit just the soft tissue of his shoulder."

Mike's paramedic taped down a bandage on Mike's back, then carefully rolled him on his side and worked on the leg wound. "Went right through your calf, but I don't think it hit the femoral artery."

"That's strange," Mike said.

"What's that?"

"My legs are cold. Like they're frozen."

"Stay calm. You'll be at the hospital in twenty minutes."

Two doctors and three nurses wearing surgical frocks and masks awaited Mike in the emergency operating room. An anesthesiologist walked in as one of the nurses took off Mike's clothes and put him in a hospital gown. Mike felt weak and limp as another nurse put a blood-pressure cuff on his arm and stuck an electrical-disk monitor to his chest.

"How are you, Governor?" one of the doctors asked.

"I was just about to ask you that question," Mike said.

The doctor, a middle-aged man with a weathered face, smiled. "We'll find out right now," he said and began scrutinizing the wounds. "I'm going to give you a local in the back and leg so I can inspect these wounds thoroughly," the doctor said. "Then I'll see if we need to put you out under general anesthesia."

Minutes later, needles went into Mike's right leg and lower back. Light glinted from the stainless-steel instruments as the doctor probed the wounds. Metallic rattling sounded as one of the nurses pulled an intravenous pole to the operating table. Hanging from it, two fluid-filled plastic bags with clear plastic tubing swayed slightly from side to side. The third nurse finished inserting minicatheter needles into his arm, then pressed in the IV needles.

The heart monitor beeped and the blood-pressure cuff swished, inflating and deflating every few minutes. Instruments clinked occasionally as the doctor placed one on a tray and a nurse handed him another.

Mike was breathing heavily. How bad were the wounds? Did Josephine know what happened? Was she on the way?

He looked at the doctor. "Why are my legs so cold?"

The doctor looked at him. "I'm going to put you out."

Mike nodded, and felt the anesthesiologist ease a needle into his right arm.

Chapter Thirty-Nine

The same two immigration agents were at Marisol's apartment a few days after the funeral for Roberto and Carmella. Julio saw them pull up in front of the building and went downstairs to be with Marisol. Again, the agents were courteous—but they meant business. When she couldn't produce proper identification, they said deportation papers would be drawn up. They told her to pack what she most needed, because if the immigration judge ruled against her, she'd immediately be sent to Tijuana.

"Contact your family or friends to pick you up," the tall agent told her. "I'm sorry. I don't enjoy doing this."

Tears formed in Marisol's eyes. Julio put his arm around her. "How can she leave? Her son is in the hospital. We don't know where her husband is, and she has an infant and two other children."

"And what about the building?" Marisol pleaded. "What if it's not sold? We need the money from the sale."

"I'm very sorry, Mrs. Castellano," the agent said. "But it's out of my hands. There's nothing that can be done. You won't go before the judge for a while, a few days, maybe a week or more, so that'll buy you some time. But sooner or later you'll be sent back to Mexico. The law is the law. You're here illegally."

When they left, Marisol plopped on the sofa, put her head in her hands and shook it back and forth. "I'm beginning to panic. I feel overwhelmed. I can't leave with Ernesto in the hospital. And the baby and the building . . ."

"Calm down," Julio said, trying to sound reassuring despite the anguish still tearing away at his heart from the loss of his wife and son. "One step at a time. There should be enough time to get things ready if we do it sensibly and plan carefully. Erika and I will help."

"Maybe I should call Carlos," she said. "If he's caught, so what? He'd want to be with me and the kids in Mexico anyway. No, no, that might help police find him. What if he's sent to jail? What if he doesn't call?"

"Of course, he'll call," Julio said. "It's been five days since the last time."

"Okay, Julio. I'll try to keep my head. But what about Ernesto? And where would I go?"

He squeezed her hand. "Once they release Ernesto, you can live with my family in Texas for a while. When the building is sold, Carlos and I will move down there, too. You can take the baby with you. Carmella and I . . ." He looked down and tears formed in his eyes. "I mean . . . I mean, Erika and I will look out for the boys until you're settled."

She put her arms around him. "Oh, Julio. How awful this is for you. I wish there was something I could do to make you feel better. I'm heartbroken, too. I can't believe she's gone. I keep expecting her to walk in. It must be so much worse for you."

Julio wiped the tears from his eyes. "How is Ernesto?"

"The doctor told me yesterday that he's improving, but he can't say exactly how much longer he'll be in the hospital."

"Everything will be fine when he comes home," Julio said. "Just fine."

Carlos called the next day. He heard first the joy in Marisol's voice—then the fear.

"What's wrong, Marisol?"

A brief silence. "I'm fine, Carlos. And so are the kids. But some terrible things have happened in the last few days."

Carlos tensed. "What terrible things? What things? Tell me what's going on."

Another pause and Carlos could feel her distress. "What happened?" he almost shouted.

He heard her begin to cry. "Roberto and Carmella are . . . they're dead."

"*Que! Muerto!*" Carlos shouted. "Did you say they were dead?"

"Yes."

He went weak and felt sick to his stomach. "*Ah, mi Dios!* What happened?"

She told him. His head dropped. "How is Julio?"

"He's still pretty bad. Relatives came in from Texas for the funeral but only stayed a day. Erika is living with him. That helps a little. But she's grieving, too. I do what I can, but how do you help someone overcome something like this?"

Then she told him about the immigration agents.

He clenched the phone firmly. "That's it. I'm coming home. I'm in Bull Head City, and I can be home in five hours, maybe less."

"No, Carlos. Wait. It's okay for now. It'll be a while before they come for me. No need for you to come now. There's an arrest warrant for you. You might go to jail. Let's hold on a little bit longer. Please."

"An arrest warrant?"

"That's right."

He was quiet for several seconds. "Okay. I'll stay put. But I'm going to call Dominic to see if he can do something. If he does, and I think he will, don't mention that I won't be selling those phony papers anymore. That's my ace in the hole. If he thinks I won't work for him, he might not help."

When they hung up, Carlos called Julio and they spoke for fifteen minutes. He was heartsick and angry that he could do nothing. Then, he called Dominic, who agreed to help. A day later, he got back Carlos.

"Everything's under control."

"What happened?" Carlos asked. "What did you do?"

"Do you remember some years ago in Chicago, an illegal Mexican woman and her son were going to be deported but a pastor at a local church took them in and declared that they had sanctuary?"

"Yeah, I do remember that. The police respected the sanctuary. They wouldn't go in to arrest her. Is that what you did?"

"Yes. There's a monsignor at a church not too far from your building who's sympathetic to illegals. I called him and he said to bring her and the children over. Said they'd be safe there. I dropped them off about an hour ago. And the monsignor said he'd have nuns look in on Ernesto."

"Ernesto!" Carlos snapped. "Why are they going to look in on him?"

Silence. Carlos assumed Dominic slipped up about something. "What's going on with Ernesto?"

"Yeah, I forgot. She didn't tell you. Didn't want to worry you. He's in the hospital. Has meningitis."

Carlos slouched and bowed his head. His hands trembled. "How is he? Is it serious?"

"He's doing well. The doctors told Marisol that he had a less serious form of the disease and that he was healing well. But they can't say for sure how long he'll be in the hospital. Maybe three or four more days."

Carlos let out a relieved sigh and slowly regained his composure.

"As soon as the boy is out of the hospital," Dominic said, "I'll slip your wife and kids out of the church and have them meet you in Arizona, probably Phoenix or Kingman. I've already got people there looking for a place for you."

"Thanks. This is a big load off my shoulders." Then, "Are you telling me the truth? Is Ernesto really going to be okay?"

"Absolutely," Dominic said, but as soon as they hung up, Carlos called Marisol. When she told him Ernesto was doing well, his concern dissipated. But now he made up his mind. To hell with Texas or Arizona. They were going back to Mexico. The money he and Julio had saved, and what they'd get for the building, would set them up nicely. Then this nightmare would be over.

But fear ate away at him. They weren't of the woods yet. And predators still lurked in those woods.

Chapter Forty

Mike was in the operating room for nearly two hours. He spent two more in recovery, then was put into a hospital room that looked more like a hotel suite—large and well decorated with an expansive picture window. After the nurses settled him in, Josephine and a doctor entered.

Although groggy, he could see Josephine was distressed. Her reddened eyes were moist, and her quivering lips were pressed together. She took his hand and started to speak, but couldn't. She cleared her throat and remained silent.

The doctor looked down at Mike. "I'm Doctor Holloway, Governor. I was part of the surgical team that worked on you. How are you feeling?"

"Why is my wife so upset?" Mike asked.

"I'm afraid I have some bad news," the doctor replied.

Mike clenched his teeth. "What is it?"

"The bullet that cut down the center of your back nicked your spinal cord. You're probably still too light-headed to realize it now, but your legs are numb."

Mike pushed himself up and reached to his thighs and squeezed. No feeling. Then, his calves. No feeling. He tried to move his legs. Nothing.

He lay back down and closed his eyes. And his mind screamed, No! It can't be.

His breathing was heavy and rapid. "Is there anything that can be done? Is this permanent?"

"We don't know, yet. The wound was badly swollen and inflamed. Once we saw the damage, we closed it. When the swelling eases, we'll have a neuro-surgical team look at it. But that won't be for three or four days."

"Three or four days? Why so long?"

"It's the inflammation. If we start poking around in there now, we might make things worse. I'm sorry, Governor, but you're going to have to try to be patient."

Mike looked up at Josephine. She bent over and wrapped her arms around him. "Oh, Mike. I can't believe this is happening. It's a nightmare. But I'll take care of you. No matter what. I love you."

Mike put his hand on hers. "I know you will, sweetheart. But it'll be all right. And maybe it's not as bad as it seems right now." He looked at the doctor. "What are the chances I'll come out of this all right, without being paralyzed?"

"It's impossible to say right now, Governor. I'm sorry. I know this must be a very trying time for you and your family. But we can't do anything except wait until the swelling subsides.

"Your leg wound is going to be fine. The bullet went right through but missed the femoral artery. Some blood vessels and muscle tissue were ripped up, but we sewed those up pretty fast. The bullet grazed the femur, the bone in your thigh, but not badly."

"Not that it makes much difference if I'm paralyzed."

"Try not to think like that," the doctor said. "I'm going to prescribe a sedative for you to ease your anxiety. You're already on heavy-duty pain killers. We have one nurse assigned exclusively to you, and I'll look in on you regularly. And a doctor will be on call twenty-four-seven. Any more questions?"

Mike said no, but as the doctor turned to walk away, he called to him. "Can you tell me anything about congressman Mendoza?"

The doctor looked down for a moment. "He's in critical condition. It could go either way. His aorta was punctured, and a chunk of his liver was severed. The liver can normally heal itself and function even with part of it gone. I'm sorry. I know he's a friend of yours. We'll keep you posted. Anything else?"

Mike shook his head. "No. Thank you, Doctor."

Mike looked at Josephine. "First John. Now Manny. And me, paralyzed. My God. What kind of curse has been thrown on us? What the hell did we do to deserve this?"

He pulled Josephine close to him. They were quiet for a few moments, then Mike swallowed hard. "Stay strong, babe. This is going to be tough. But we're going to have to bull our way through it. We'll work it out. We'll get past it."

"I know," she said, but Mike could feel her body tremble as she wept.

The phone rang and Josephine grabbed it. "Hello," she said and listened. Then, "Oh, that's very nice of you."

Mike could vaguely hear a voice on the phone. Josephine said, "Yes, he's awake. Here, I'll give you to him. And thanks for calling."

She handed Mike the phone. "It's Marty."

"Hello, Mr. President."

"I tried getting through earlier, Mike, but you were still under anesthesia. How are you?"

"Not so good," Mike said, and told him about the paralysis.

"Good Lord, Mike. This is awful. I can't believe it. How's Josephine?"

"She's scared, but she's holding up."

"Is there anything I can do?"

"Nothing I can think of. I'm just going to have to tough this out."

"If anyone can, it's you."

Minutes after the call, the phone rang again. This time, Mike answered it—and his heart went to his throat.

"Daddy? It's me, Patti. How are you?"

"I'm all right. There are some complications. But I'll live."

"What complications?"

Mike considered telling her, but didn't. "Nothing to worry about. I'll be fine. I'm not going to die on you. Ask your mother. She's right here."

He started to hand the phone to Josephine, but Patti spoke up. "No, Dad. That's okay. I was just scared when I heard about it." She was silent, and Mike was about to say something, but Patti said, "Dad. I'm sorry. I'm really sorry for leaving like that and talking to you and Mom the way I did. I don't know what got into me. I guess I inherited that famous temper of yours. I was wrong and I'm sorry."

"That's okay, sweetheart. It'll be fine now."

"Dad, Marco and I had a long talk. We're coming home. He can probably get his job back, and he'll send his family money. And they're going to try to get American citizenship."

Mike cleared his throat. "That's good news," he said, then turned to Josephine and mouthed, "Patti." Josephine expelled a sigh of relief.

"When will you be leaving?" Mike asked.

"In a few days."

"All right. Let us know and I'll have you picked up at the airport. Now, here, talk to your mother."

Josephine and Patti talked for a few minutes, then she hung up and looked at Mike. "That reminds me. Becky's driving in from San Francisco. Should be here soon. Rose is in Dallas and she'll fly in tomorrow."

"That's great. That'll help." He glanced at the clock. "Wow. Nine o'clock. Past visiting hours. You better go."

"No, Mike. I'm the governor's wife. I can stay as long as I want."

"Don't, Jo. You go home and try to get some sleep. Call Becky and tell her to meet you there when she gets here. I'll see you all tomorrow. I'd like to be alone and maybe fall asleep."

When Josephine left, Mike sat up. He grabbed his legs, squeezing tightly as he moved his hands from foot to thigh. Numb. He lay back and again tried to move his legs, grunting as he struggled and willed the legs to move. Nothing.

He rolled his head from side to side. What would the rest of his life be like? How would this affect his job? His family? His marriage?

He called for the nurse to give him the sedative. It helped, but he later needed a sleeping pill to help him doze off.

Chapter Forty-One

Carlos waited in the motel room. Waited nervously. Tensely. Waited sweating and fearful. He'd gone out for dinner, but barely eaten. He returned to the dark, quiet motel room, and tried to relax.

Impossible.

All he could do was wait.

For what? A call from Dominic? A call from Marisol? The police at his door?

Dominic had phoned two days ago and told him to get a motel room in Kingman and stay put. He said not to contact his wife, that she'd call him when the time was right.

"We're going into the final phase," Dominic said. "I don't want anything to go wrong. Until we're ready to move, you're the invisible man. You don't exist."

"I understand," Carlos said. But inside he ached with the need to just talk to Marisol.

"Things are falling into place," Dominic told him. "Julio sold the building. And, you'll be happy to know that your son is feeling fine and will be released from the hospital in a few days."

Carlos sighed in relief. "*De gracias de Dios.*"

"Julio will pick him up when he's released. I told him to start packing, but to take only a few sets of clothes and his most valuable possessions. Marisol will tell him what she wants him to take for her, but only necessities and valuables. They've got to move fast and travel light."

"What about Marisol? How is she? And how are the children, the baby?"

"I stopped at the church yesterday. Everyone is fine and in good spirits, all things considered. No need to worry about them. Julio will get your son as soon as he's released, then pick up your wife and children and they'll be on their way to you. I told Julio where you are and how to get there. I'll come to see you a few days after that and we'll find you a house or, temporarily, an apartment. Then we'll have you selling the counterfeit papers and making money again."

Carlos grimaced, fearing what Dominic would do if he learned about his plans for returning to Mexico permanently. "That'll be good," was all Carlos could say. "I can use the money."

And so, he waited.

Five long, solitary, agonizing days had passed since he last spoke to Marisol. His loneliness was so deep that it was nearly tangible, pulling him into a whirlpool of despair.

He slumped into a chair by the table next to the window and opened a can of beer, trying desperately to make himself believe that the horror of these past months was almost over. He switched on the television—but he saw nothing, heard nothing.

He jerked like a high-strung alley cat when his cell phone rang. Then, joy swept through him when he heard Marisol.

"Oh, Carlos. It is so good to hear your voice."

"I feel the same. I love you and miss you and the children so much, I couldn't begin to tell you."

"*Te adoro tambien.*"

"When will you come?"

"Tomorrow. Ernesto will be out of the hospital in the morning, and we'll be ready to leave."

"Are you still at the church?"

"Yes. Dominic said not to leave until Julio picks up Ernesto. He said he doesn't want me exposed unless it's absolutely necessary. But

I don't know why. Deporting me does nothing. We're going back to Mexico anyway."

"No. He's right. They might pick you up just to question you about me. They might charge you with something just to draw me in. I don't know. It's all far fetched, but we can't take any chances. We can't make a mistake. We're too close to the end of this for something to go wrong."

He thought for a moment. "The only thing you have to do tomorrow is go to the bank and withdraw our money."

"Why don't we just wire it to my family's bank in Mexico?"

"We can't," Carlos said, shaking his head as if she were in the room with him. "The government monitors large money transfers to try to get drug dealers. And don't take it in cash. Do you still have the three thousand I left with you?"

"Most of it."

"Good. Take that with you and get a cashiers check for the rest, and we'll mail it to your family by UPS. And there's something else. In the bottom dresser drawer is a safe deposit key. That's where I kept the money from the phony papers I sold. Didn't want you to know about it because . . . well, you understand. There's another five thousand. Get another cashiers check at a different bank for that and mail it, too."

"Okay. As soon as I finish at the bank, we'll be on our way. Erika won't be coming. She wants to stay in America."

"That's probably a good choice. She'll live better here. She's made good friends, so she won't be alone."

"We should make it to Kingman by five o'clock or so tomorrow. I can't wait to see you."

"I know. I know. Did you talk to your parents?"

"Yes. They're going to find us a place to stay until we decide where we'll live. But what then?"

Carlos squeezed his forehead. "I'm not sure. Maybe back to the oil fields. Maybe I can work in a hotel. My English is pretty good now. We'll have to see what happens."

"As long as we're all together," she said.

"That's right. And we *will* be," Carlos replied firmly. "When did you last talk to Dominic?"

"Yesterday. He's been very helpful."

"He has his reasons. You didn't mention anything about going back to Mexico, did you?"

"No, not a word. But he said he'd meet us in Kingman in a day or two to help get us settled in."

Carlos grunted. "We should be gone by then." He hesitated for a moment. "Marisol, take the gun. Just in case."

"Oh, Carlos, do I have to do that? I hate that thing. I'm afraid of it."

"We may need it. If Dominic somehow finds out what we're going to do, I don't know how he'll react," he said, knowing full well how Dominic would respond—murderously. "There's no need to be afraid of it. I showed you how to use it and you fired it. You know the sound and the recoil. Be sure the hammer is on an empty chamber in the cylinder, just like I showed you. Then there's no chance of a round going off accidentally."

Chapter Forty-Two

The day after Carlos spoke to Marisol, he glanced out the window and froze when he saw the crimson Escalade pull up to the motel office. Why was he here now? He said he'd show up in a few days. By then, Carlos and his family would be long gone. Was he suspicious? Did he find something out?

He rubbed his temples and stared down at the floor, thinking hard. Should he make a run for it? Not enough time. Pretend he wasn't here? No. His pickup was just outside his room. Dominic would recognize it.

The phone startled him.

"There's a Dominic Juarez here to see you. Do you know him?"

"Yes," Carlos said. "Yes, send him over."

Carlos breathed in deeply, deeply enough for his lungs to ache. *Try to look normal. Try to look happy to see him.*

Minutes later, the Escalade pulled in front of his room and Dominic got out. Carlos's mouth went dry as he opened the door and greeted him with a wide grin.

"How are you?" Dominic asked.

"I'm fine. And thank you," Carlos said. "Thank you for all your help."

It was a sincere remark. Even though he knew Dominic had ulterior motives, he was still appreciative for what he'd done for his family.

"It was nothing, *amigo*," Carlos replied. "I take care of my people."

Carlos motioned to the table and chairs near the window. "Come in. Have a seat. How are things going?"

"We'll have a place for you soon. The counterfeit documents are being corrected. They should hold up in California, but surely here in Arizona. As soon as you're settled, I'll have you selling them again."

"Good," Carlos said, hoping nothing in his demeanor would give away his plans.

"Feeling better?" Dominic asked. "The worst is behind you, and before you know it you'll be in the money again."

Carlos forced a smile. "Yes, I feel better. And I'll be even better when my family gets here," he said, and thought his voice sounded a little wobbly.

Neither spoke for a few moments, and Carlos sensed that Dominic was apprehensive, mistrustful.

"I talked to my wife yesterday," Carlos said. "They'll be on their way as soon as Ernesto is out of the hospital.

"That's good to hear," Dominic said, studying Carlos's face as if he was peering straight through his eyes and into his brain.

Sweat dotted Carlos's forehead. "I'm looking forward to getting back to work. I'm tired of being on the run. I want to keep myself occupied, and I need the money."

"Something wrong?" Dominic asked. "You seem nervous."

Carlos smiled and shook his head as nonchalantly as he could. "No, it's nothing. I guess I'm just relieved. Happy all this trouble is over and that my life will go back to normal."

"You sure that's it?"

"Sure. What else could it be? Maybe I'm still nervous about the whole thing. Can't get it all out of my mind. I've been like that since I got picked up. Can't completely get rid of it. I still worry something might go wrong."

"Don't concern yourself. You're free and clear now. Enjoy your time with your family."

"Sounds good."

Dominic got up. "Well, I've got things to do. I'll get back to you in day or so."

When Dominic drove away, Carlos walked into the bathroom and rinsed his face with cold water. He lay on the bed with his arm across his forehead. Was he being paranoid? Had he been able to hide his fear? Was Dominic really suspicious?

He paced with his hands on his hips. He couldn't give Dominic time to find out what he was up to. As soon as Marisol and Julio arrived with the kids they'd leave and make their run for the border.

Carlos packed his belongings, then sat on the curb outside his room, checking his wristwatch every few minutes. Almost five o'clock. They should be here soon.

Again, he jumped when his cell phone rang.

"We're going to be late," Marisol said.

"What happened?" Carlos asked anxiously.

"Car trouble. Fan belt snapped. We're in the repair shop now. In Essex, about eighty miles away. They said it wouldn't take long to fix, but Julio's car is old, and they have to order the belt. It could take an hour or two before it's delivered."

"Jesus *dulce*. Sweet Jesus," Carlos said, rubbing the back of his neck. One or two hours? One or two minutes would have been too long. "Okay. Nothing we can do about it. We'll have to deal with it. No choice."

"I know, Carlos. But I can't stand this any more. I want to be with you. I *need* to be with you."

Carlos's eyes teared. But he had to be strong for her. He couldn't show his fear. "You will be. Don't worry. Just a few hours more and we'll be together. You've been brave through all this. Don't lose your courage now."

She was silent, and Carlos could almost see the tears rolling down her cheeks. "I won't," she said. "I promise."

"Good. That's my Marisol. Call me when you're on your way."

Carlos sat on the bed holding his drooping head in his hands, paralyzed by disappointment. Then he got up. He had to do something.

Had to move, go someplace. He stepped outside and began walking, not knowing where, but just walking and waiting for her to call.

He ended up in a bar, ordered a Dos Equis, and lit a cigarillo. More waiting. Endless, endless waiting. He looked again at his watch. Only forty minutes had passed since Marisol called. Forty incessant, tormenting minutes. How many more? When would they get here? When would they begin the journey back to Mexico and away from this nightmare?

She called just after he returned to the motel. They were on the road and would be there in an hour and a half. Once more, his gaze went to his watch. Six-thirty. They should be here by eight—unless something else goes wrong.

Chapter Forty-Three

Carlos stood outside in the dark watching cars pass on the highway next to the motel. He glanced once more at his watch. Ten minutes to 8:00. They should be here soon. He tried to stifle his angst, to find some iota of patience. But he trembled in anticipation, longing to see his wife and children.

A car slowed. Then, the beams of its headlights swept along the walls of the motel as it pulled into the parking lot. He squinted.

It was them.

The car barely stopped when the passenger door flew open and Marisol rushed to him.

They embraced and kissed. Then, Marisol stood back and stared at him, her face streaked with tears. "Oh, at last," she said and embraced him again. "Oh, Carlos, I love you, and it was terrible without you. I missed you so much, I didn't think I could live."

"I know," he said, squeezing her tightly. "This will never happen again. Never." He looked over her shoulder and saw his children approaching as Julio stood near the car holding the baby. Carlos squatted as the children neared, then hugged and kissed each one.

"Are you okay, Papa?" Jorge asked. "Are you going away again?"

"No, no. I'm not going away. Not ever again. I'll be with you all the time now."

The children's broad smiles radiated love and warmth and happiness. He looked at Ernesto. "And how are you? You had your mother and me worried to death."

"I'm okay, Papa. It wasn't that bad. And I'm doing real good now."

They walked to Julio. Marisol took the baby. Carlos lifted the blanket from the baby's head and smiled as he looked at his daughter. He kissed her lightly on the forehead and pulled the blanket down again. Then, he turned to Julio and threw his arms around him.

"How are you, my friend, my dear good friend?"

"I'm well. I'm fine. And I can't tell you how good it is to see you."

"And good to see you, too," Carlos said and stepped back. "Julio, I am so sorry I couldn't be with you in your sorrow to share your pain."

Julio sighed. "I know, my friend. I understand. I know you felt the hurt as I did, and I know that you would have been with me if you could have. These are terrible times."

Carlos grabbed Julio's upper arms and squeezed them. "But that's over now, Julio. Now, we'll be okay. But we have to move fast."

Carlos told them to follow him as he went to his room for his suitcase.

"You all use the bathroom and rinse your faces. Be quick. We've got to leave in a few minutes."

"Why such a hurry?" Marisol asked.

Carlos gripped his suitcase and took her and Julio outside and explained. Minutes later, the children came out.

"All ready to go," Ernesto said.

Carlos smiled. But only momentarily—only until he saw the Escalade and another car pull into the parking lot and five men get out and walk toward him. With the light of the motel sign and the highway's street lamps behind them, they were vague, almost ghost-like silhouettes.

"Marisol," Carlos said, "get in the car with the kids. Get in the driver's seat and be prepared to go the second I say so. Fast."

"What's happen—"

"Get in the car! Now! Quickly!"

Carlos turned to face the approaching men.

"How are you, Carlos?" Dominic asked in an almost friendly tone. "It must be good to see your family again."

"It is." Carlos was getting to be an expert at faking calmness. "Very good," he said, and from the corner of his eye, saw Julio move next to him.

Dominic came within four feet of Carlos and stopped. Carlos knew he wouldn't come closer. But the men he'd brought with him were nearing and surrounding him and Julio.

"And where would you all be going?" Dominic asked. "Taking in the night air?"

"No. We're going to have dinner."

"At this time of night? It's after eight."

"They had a long drive. The kids are hungry."

Dominic's face was menacing. His eyes narrowed and his smile exuded evil as he pointed at Carlos' suitcase. "Do you always take your luggage with you when you go out to eat?"

"No, that's just—"

"Don't lie to me!" Dominic shouted. "You're running out on me, aren't you, you son-of-a-bitch. I sensed it this morning. Good act, but it didn't fool me. So, I had my boys stake this place out. I figured you were up to something like this. After all I did for you. You owe me! And you'll pay, you ungrateful bastard."

This was it.

And Carlos knew it immediately, knew it when the cars pulled into the parking lot.

He had to be fast.

Dominick most likely expected it. But he still didn't see it coming. Carlos was a blur, stepping forward and catching Dominic hard on the chin, collapsing him like a marionette whose strings were suddenly severed.

"Go, Marisol! Go!" Carlos shouted as the other men ran toward him.

Julio tackled one of them. Marisol started the car.

Carlos knew Dominic was out cold, at least for the moment. As the other men neared him, he kicked one in the kneecap, making him stumble forward into Carlos's solid left hook, felling him instantly.

But then came the shattering blow to Carlos's right cheek, ripping open a gash, sending him reeling back and almost into unconsciousness.

That wasn't a fist.

That wasn't flesh and bone.

Brass knuckles.

He stumbled back into Julio's car. But it shouldn't be here. Marisol should have driven away by now. He wanted to shout at her to go, but the brass knuckles dug into his ribs and doubled him over huffing out a huge breath of air. Again, the brass knuckles, this time on the back of his neck.

Dizziness. Weakness.

Sparkling, rotating silver dots.

Then, his face on the pavement.

He saw Julio on top of the man he'd tackled, punching wildly at his face, until another of Dominic's men grabbed him around the neck from the rear and threw him to the ground.

Carlos tried pushing himself to his hands and knees. A kick to his rib cage. He fell down flat. A shoe burrowed into his side, then to the top of his head, slamming it hard against the pavement.

Carlos groaned, but with his last bit of strength, his last bit of consciousness, he reached behind his assailant's leg and pulled hard.

No good.

Another kick. And then he felt himself being rolled onto his back, gazing up at two monstrous, blurry shapes. Carlos put his arms over his head as the bottom of a shoe appeared above his face.

Dominic stepped forward. "Stop!" he shouted. "Stop! Or you'll kill him. And I want to do that." He rubbed his chin. "Still got that powerhouse right, eh, Carlos? Well, it won't do you any good tonight. Stand him up."

As he was lifted, Carlos saw Julio lying face down on the ground, unconscious.

"Nobody does this to me!" Dominic said. "Nobody!"

Groggy, his head hanging to one side and doubled over from the pain in his ribs, Carlos struggled to stay on his feet. If not for the men holding him under his armpits, he would have toppled.

Breathing heavily, and the world around him spinning, Carlos managed to speak. "At least leave my wife and children alone. Please.

That's all I ask. They can't hurt you. You know they can't call the police." His head dropped to his chest. "They're going to Mexico for good. You'll never see them again."

Dominic's lips spread into that thin, sinister smile as he reached into his jacket pocket and withdrew a Glock nine millimeter. "You'll be dead before you know what I decide to do with them," he said as he pulled back the gun's slide, springing a round into the chamber.

Dominic raised the weapon. Carlos shut his eyes tightly.

The shot echoed thunderously in the night.

Carlos stiffened. His ears buzzed. Stunned, he opened his eyes as Dominic stumbled back a step and dropped heavily to the ground.

"Get out of here!" Marisol shouted. "Take your boss and get out of here! Get out or I'll kill you all!" she screamed and walked from behind Julio's car, brandishing the snub-nose revolver like Maria in the last scene of *West Side Story*.

The men rushed to Dominic, picked him up, and dragged him to the Escalade. Off balance and weak, Carlos maintained an unsteady stance, head hung and bent over, his arms clutching his ribs. Marisol put her arm around him and helped him to the side of the car, where he slumped and sat on the ground.

"The kids," he said. "Are the kids okay?"

Marisol squatted next to him. "They're fine. I had them lay down in the back seat. I'll check on them now," she said, then opened the back door of the car. Carlos heard them talking softly, then asked, "Julio. How is Julio?"

"I think I'm all right," Julio said as he staggered toward Carlos, leaning on the car's hood. Squeezing his teeth tightly shut, he slowly sat next to Carlos. "Are you okay?"

Carlos nodded. "I should be. Need to get my breath back. There are ribs broken, have to be to cause this much pain. And my face. That, too."

"Jorge, come with me," Marisol said and rushed into the motel room. Moments later, Jorge ran to the ice machine with a plastic bucket. Marisol hurried out with water-soaked towels and delicately cleaned the gaping gash on Carlos's cheek and told him to press it hard against the wound. Then, she cleaned Julio's face, also cut and bleeding, though not nearly as badly as Carlos's. Jorge arrived, and

Marisol put ice into two clean towels and had Carlos and Julio press them against their facial wounds.

Carlos took Marisol's arm. "We've got to leave. Now! Immediately! The police will be here soon. Someone must have heard all the noise, the gunshot."

Marisol's mouth opened. "We can't, Carlos. We can't leave. You're hurt too badly. You've got to see a doctor, go to a hospital."

Carlos shook his head. "No. We've got to leave. I can live with this until we get to Mexico. I'll see a doctor there. We can stop at another motel thirty or forty miles from here. I can lie down and rest, and you can go to a drugstore and get some disinfectant and bandages and whatever else you need to patch me up." He turned to Julio. "Can you make it?"

"Yes. And Marisol, Carlos is right. We've got to get out of here."

"All right. All right. Can you drive, Julio?"

Julio nodded. Scowling, he pulled himself to his feet. "I'll take the kids. You drive Carlos in the pickup. I'll lead. You stay close behind."

"Okay," she said and went to the back seat to soothe the children. "Everything will be all right now."

"What about Papa?" Christian asked, fear molding his face.

"He'll be fine," she said and hugged him. "It's okay, now. Don't worry. We'll be safe. We'll take Papa to a nice place and help him get better. Then we'll go to Mexico."

She helped Carlos into the pickup, holding him by his arms as he groaned and struggled into the passenger seat. As she got into the pickup and started the engine, Carlos took her hand. "You . . . you should have gone when I told you," he said, gasping for breath between the words.

She looked at him. "I couldn't, Carlos. I just couldn't. After I started the car, I froze, just froze. I was petrified. I couldn't even scream." She looked down for a moment, then back at Carlos. "Then, something happened. I don't know what. But all of a sudden, I felt blood rushing through me and my heart pounding through my whole body. I heard what he said about killing you and me and the kids, and before I knew it, my hand was in my purse and wrapped around the gun. I barely remember shooting him."

Carlos nodded heavily. "All right," he said, his teeth clenched. He leaned over and kissed her on the cheek. "I was angry at first. Wanted you out of here. But if you'd gone I'd be on the ground dead or bleeding to death right now. You saved my life."

Just before driving away, Marisol slapped her forehead. "I know what to do. I'll call Dr. Menendez. Maybe he'll come to help. He always liked you and me, and he loved the kids. He delivered Alexis. I'm sure he'll do something for us."

"Good idea," Carlos said, then smiled and nudged her lightly. "You're a pretty good lady to have around in a tight spot."

She kissed him and ran her fingers through his hair. "I love you," she said and followed Julio as he drove away.

Carlos's gaze rarely drifted from the rearview mirror, waiting fearfully for the whirling red lights and whooping sirens. An hour later, they were at another motel, taking one room for Marisol and Carlos and another for Julio and the children, because Marisol didn't want them to see their father so horribly beaten.

She called Dr. Menendez, and when she hung up told Carlos the doctor couldn't come because it was too far and would take too long, and he had a full load of patient appointments the next day. But he knew a doctor near them and would have him come by tomorrow. "He told me what to get at the drugstore and how to treat you and Julio."

When she left, Carlos lay quietly in bed pressing the ice-filled towel against his wound with a terrifying thought resonating through his brain—*what if they come after us?*

Chapter Forty-Four

Mike's palms were clammy. Perspiration saturated his forehead. His heart pounded. His fear was greater than any he'd ever felt in his life. Not even under fire in Vietnam was he so consumed by fear. It was visceral, and he felt it in every cell of his body.

They'd wanted to give him a sedative, but he refused. Time to man up, to find his courage and face this straight on. Now, he questioned that decision—but wouldn't back away from it.

Morning sunshine flooded the room, and the sky was clear. Ordinarily, that would lighten his mood. But now, all he felt was dread—deep, uncontrollable dread. Would he ever again be able to enjoy another sunny morning? Another blue sky?

Josephine put her hand on his as they waited for nurses and orderlies to take Mike to the operating room. It was three days since he'd been shot and today a team of neuro-surgeons would examine Mike to see what, if anything, could be done to end the paralysis.

"Well," Mike said, "this is it, Jo. Here's where we find out if you've got an invalid on your hands."

"You'll never be an invalid to me. Don't talk that way."

"We've got to face reality. I'll probably be in a wheelchair the rest of my life."

"I'll push you wherever you want to go."

"I think I'll get one of the motorized ones and juice up the engine. Then, I can chase you all over the house."

Josephine grinned. "You would, too. Dirty old man."

"Why change now?"

"Always with the jokes."

"The humor helps."

Mike pulled her down to him. "We'll be fine. I promise. It could be worse. At least I can still put my arms around you." He sighed. "Other people have gotten past things like this. It'll be hard at first, but I'll adapt and you will, too."

She smiled and kissed him. "I know."

"Any word on Manny?"

"He's still unconscious and in critical condition. I think I'll stop by to visit with Arianna in intensive care while you're in the operating room. It'll keep me occupied."

"Good idea. Are the girls coming?"

"Should be here any minute."

His daughters arrived just as the orderlies came for Mike. They hugged and kissed him, and he marveled now at how much they meant to him. They wore happy faces but he knew they must be terrified.

They walked beside him as he was wheeled away, Josephine holding his hand. He kept his face expressionless, hiding his concern. But as they approached the operating room, his fear subsided, and he felt a strange serenity. Had the emotional overload shut down his feelings? Raw bravery? No. Not that either. Then it came to him. He'd finally accepted his fate, whatever it would be. And now, a stoic courage lifted his spirits. In a few hours he'd know his destiny. And, at this point, he was glad for that—regardless of the result.

He squeezed Josephine's hand. "You know, babe, I'm feeling a lot better all of a sudden. I almost feel calm. Whatever happens, happens.

I've got you and the girls, and we have good friends and family. We'll still live a good, happy life."

They stopped. Josephine and his daughters kissed him. As he was pushed in, he glanced over his shoulder. The girls waved, and Josephine threw him a kiss.

Chapter Forty-Five

Carlos healed quickly after the doctor treated him. Three days later, he felt well enough to travel. But he was concerned about carrying all the cash they had—about $5,000, so the day before they left, he got a cashier's check for $3,000, which he mailed to Marisol's family. He pocketed $200 and put $1,800 in an envelope and stuffed it in his shave kit.

They left early the next morning. Cradling the baby, Marisol rode in the pickup with Carlos. The boys were with Julio. They stopped for the night, just past Phoenix, and the following day arrived at the border in Nogales by early afternoon. Carlos remembered that it wasn't far from here that he entered America eleven years ago.

"Finally," he said to Marisol. "Finally, we're finished with the nightmare."

Julio was just in front of them as they crawled in a long line of cars and crossed the border. Then, Carlos's short sense of relief became apprehension when he saw Mexican border guards stopping cars to check identification. One of the guards, wearing a Stetson and mirrored sunglasses, approached.

"Something wrong, officer?" Carlos asked.

"Identification," the guard said.

"Is there a problem? Some kind of spot check?"

The guard held out his hand. "Identification."

Carlos pulled his wallet from his back pocket. He withdrew his driver's license and handed it to the guard, who glanced at it and handed it back. "You'll have to go through customs. Pull into a parking space over there," he said, pointing to the white stucco customs house.

"What's going on?" Carlos asked.

"Just go into the customs house. Take your baggage with you. Show your identification to the guard inside the entrance, and he'll take over from there."

Carlos nodded and pulled away. As he parked, Marisol turned to Carlos. "Why us?"

He shook his head. "I don't know. They didn't have Julio pull over," he said, nodding toward Julio's car parked on the side of the road about a hundred yards ahead. "Maybe they just do random searches. There's no reason for them to single us out."

"I hope so."

They got out of the pickup, and Carlos unstrapped and grabbed their two suitcases from the truckbed, then walked inside with Marisol. He showed his driver's license to the guard, who looked at him with narrowed eyes, then stepped back, placing his hand on his holstered revolver. He called over another guard as he looked out the window. "Which vehicle is yours?" he asked Carlos.

"The black pickup truck."

"Search that pickup," the first guard told the other, pointing at Carlos's vehicle. He looked at Carlos. "Follow me."

He led them past two lines of people waiting to have their baggage inspected and walked to a door in the rear of the building. The guard opened it and led them down a dank, narrow corridor to a small office.

"Wait here," the guard said and entered the office, shutting the door behind him.

They were silent as they waited, then Marisol grabbed Carlos's hand. "I thought we were out of trouble."

"I know," Carlos said. "I thought so, too." He pulled Marisol close. "Listen, we've made it this far. We'll be okay. Just don't panic. Maybe—"

The guard came out. "Go inside," he said, holding the door open to a small room with light coming from a smudged window and a florescent ceiling fixture. Two dented file cabinets were against one wall, and a man at the cluttered metal desk sat staring at a computer screen to his left.

He gestured to two chairs in front of his desk. "Have a seat," he said without looking at them. All they could see was the back of his balding head.

They sat, and a minute later the man took off his glasses and turned to them, the jowls of his blubbery face sagging and his fat belly flopping over the top of his trousers. Heavy eyebrows covered his drooping eyes. "How old is the baby?" he asked Marisol.

"Ten months."

"My last grandson is eleven months. He drives my daughter crazy. Cries all the time."

"No," Marisol said, still rocking the baby, "she's very seldom a problem."

"My name is Lucio Cruz," the man said. "I'm supervisor of this facility."

"*Tanto gusto*," Carlos said.

"*Egualmente*," Cruz replied. "Well, Mr. Castellano, do you know why you've been brought to me?"

Carlos shook his head. "No. No, I really don't. We've done nothing wrong."

Cruz leaned back. "Really. Nothing wrong?"

"That's right. Nothing."

Cruz drummed his fingers. Then, he bent forward across his desk. "Lying gets you nowhere, Mr. Castellano."

"I'm not lying. We haven't done anything wrong."

Cruz nodded. "We'll see. Put your bags on the desk and open them."

Carlos put Marisol's suitcase on the desk and opened it. Cruz rummaged through the contents, then closed it and pushed it to Carlos. "The other one," Cruz said.

Carlos complied. Cruz searched through the bag, pulled out the shaving kit, and opened it. He took out the cash-filled envelope and lifted the flap, then fingered the hundred-dollar bills with a knowing smile. "Well, well. What a surprise." He tossed the envelope to Carlos. "How much is there?"

"Eighteen hundred. We're taking it to our families. Is there something wrong with that?"

Cruz didn't reply. He looked at Marisol. "Your handbag."

Marisol froze. She just looked at Cruz, eyes wide and unblinking. Carlos took her purse, remembering that the gun was in it, and handed it to Cruz.

Cruz moved some items around and then pulled out the revolver. "And this? What's this for?"

"Mexico is a dangerous place these days. We're driving all the way to Mexico City. Who knows what could happen?"

"Unfortunately, you're right about that. But—"

Carlos wanted to remain calm, but Cruz's condescending attitude grated him. "Why were we brought here?" he said sharply. "Why us? Yes, there's the money and the gun, but I've explained all that. Why are you harassing us?"

"Because, Mr. Castellano," Cruz said loudly. "Because our embassy got a tip saying you would be crossing the border and that there was a warrant for your arrest in Arizona. A warrant for the attempted murder of a Dominic Juarez four days ago. The tipster said you'd have this gun and probably a large stash of money. That's why you were brought to me, Mr. Castellano. And I'd watch my tone of voice if I were you."

Marisol began crying, then stopped and wiped away her tears. Her face went taut, and her jaws flexed. "That was me. I shot him. He was about to kill my husband. And maybe me and my children. So, yes, I shot him. You'd have done the same. Anyone would. It was self-defense!"

Cruz's mouth opened, surprised by Marisol's defiance.

"Perhaps. But you are fugitives in America. I could have you arrested and extradited back there."

"I'm sure you can," Marisol shot back. "And you'd do it without the slightest concern about—"

Carlos grabbed Marisol's arm. "That's enough. Stay quiet now."

Marisol's head whipped around to face him. She started to speak, but Carlos said, "Marisol, stay quiet. Please. This is making things worse."

Marisol again began to speak, but the baby started crying. Marisol held her tightly and began rocking and her speaking softly into her ear.

Carlos turned to Cruz. "You said you *could* arrest us and have us extradited. You didn't say you *would*. Does that mean you might not?"

Cruz leaned back in the chair and folded his hands over his belly. "Perhaps. It depends. I have many responsibilities. And I believe your wife. It probably was self-defense. You don't appear to be criminals."

"What responsibilities?" Carlos asked and now knew what was happening.

"I mentioned one grandchild," Cruz said. "I have four. And one of my children still lives with me. How many children do you have?"

"The baby here is the fourth."

"Then you know how difficult it can be making ends meet. This is a good job, but it's still difficult feeding and clothing so many people."

"I understand. We were lucky enough to earn well in America, and my job will be waiting for me when I return. Is there some way I could help you?"

"That's possible. All my grandchildren need new clothes. Anything you can contribute would be appreciated."

"Would a hundred American dollars help?"

Cruz tilted his head. "We've been having inflation problems here in Mexico. I don't think that would go too far. And you have eighteen hundred dollars in that envelope. I'd say half of that would convince me to let you go."

Carlos tensed with anger. The greedy son-of-a-bitch. He'd risked his life for this money, and now this fat, greasy piece of horse shit wanted $900 of it. But he restrained himself. "Half? Half and you release us, no questions asked."

"That's correct."

Carlos peeled off nine hundred-dollar bills and handed them to Cruz. "Excellent," Cruz said and handed Carlos the gun. "Now, you may leave. Have a pleasant trip."

Chapter Forty-Six

Mike opened his eyes, disoriented. He shifted them from side to side, then fixed on Josephine and his three daughters surrounding his bed. Josephine's lips were tightly pursed. She leaned and kissed him on the forehead. "How are you?"

"I feel okay. Just a little groggy. How did . . ."

Josephine wrapped her arms around him and pressed her cheek against his. He felt a tear fall and instantly knew. He closed his eyes and rolled his head away, then turned back and reached out with both hands to his wife and daughters. They grasped them.

"Dad, it's—" Becky started to say.

But Mike shook his head. "Don't say anything just yet, okay, sweetheart. Let's just . . . let's just be quiet for a few seconds."

He swallowed hard, his Adam's apple popping up and down, then stared at the ceiling. He wanted to try to move his legs, but didn't. He was afraid. Afraid he wouldn't be able to. Afraid he'd spend his life in a wheelchair. He breathed deeply and looked at Josephine. "Well, I guess things didn't go well in the operating room."

She squeezed his hand. "No. Not as well as we wanted. But Mike, it's not as bad as it could have been."

His eyes widened. "What? Did you—"

"It's a partial paralysis. Your left leg will be normal after physical therapy. But your right leg. . . ." Her voice broke. "Your right leg . . . they couldn't repair . . ." She looked away.

Becky stepped forward. "They couldn't repair all the nerves properly, Dad. Your right leg is partially paralyzed. There was nothing more they could do."

Mike exhaled deeply and looked at Josephine. "So, do we get the wheelchair new or used?"

She kissed his hand. "There won't be a wheelchair, Mike. Your right leg will have some feeling and some strength. The doctor said you'll be able to get by with a cane."

His feelings were jumbled. His right leg was gone, pretty much useless. But his other leg would recover, and he wouldn't be wheelchair bound.

"Well," Mike said, "I guess that's not too bad. I mean, one good leg is better than none. I can live with that. I can adapt to that. Hell, in a way, you could say I kind of dodged a bullet."

Patti moved toward him. "Bad choice of words, Dad."

They laughed, and Mike pulled Patti close to him. "I love you."

She bowed her head. "I love you, too, Dad. More than ever. I was so stupid. Can you ever forgive me?"

He leaned over and kissed her. "I already have."

She embraced him, and the others did the same.

"When is Marco coming in?"

"Day after tomorrow. He's got some loose ends to tie up."

"I'm looking forward to meeting him."

"And he can't wait to meet you."

Mike smiled. "Okay," he said. "Let's pull ourselves together. This is a bump in the road. That's all. I've been healthy and fit all my life. Now, one leg is paralyzed. What the hell. All my other equipment still works and—" A shiver went through him. "That's true, isn't it, Jo? I mean everything else—"

Josephine beamed. "Yes, Mike. Everything else is fine. You don't have to worry about it."

Mike's head dropped, and he expelled a huge sigh of relief. "Wow! For a moment there I was afraid . . . well, you know."

They laughed, and Mike said, "Now, I *do* feel pretty good."

"Me, too," Josephine said.

"Can you dance using a cane?" he asked.

"I don't know," Josephine said. "But if it's possible, you'll find a way. Oh. By the way, the president called, and I told him about your condition. He was sad, Mike, very sad. He said he'll get back to you later."

"That's fine. I'll cheer him up."

Orderlies wheeled Mike back into his hospital room. Beams of sunlight streaked into the room, and the sky was crystal blue. Mike inhaled deeply. "Maybe I *will* still be able to enjoy a beautiful day after all."

"What?" Josephine asked.

Mike smiled. "Nothing, babe. Nothing at all."

Mike went home a week later. Some feeling returned to his right leg, and he was walking well with the cane. A physical therapist came every morning, and a nurse was assigned to visit him twice daily. He considered that excessive, but went along with it at the urging of his wife and daughters. He stayed in touch with his office and became impatient to return to work. Some things he could take care of at home, but he wanted to be back at his desk in the middle of the action.

Shortly after returning home, capitol security informed him that the two gunmen were definitely high-ranking members of the *Reconquista* movement with long arrest records. Murder warrants had been issued for them almost three years ago. They were two of the most extreme members of the organization and had talked openly about assassinating the governor after the immigration bill passed but weren't taken seriously. When Mike defied the Supreme Court ruling, however, and when one of their members was killed at an immigrant rally, they decided to make good on what, up until then, seemed an idle threat.

They must have thought they might get away with the assassination, Mike was told, because two other members of the group were waiting in a getaway car. Both were arrested as accomplices. Meanwhile, local and state police were investigating other *Reconquistas*, hoping to find any with outstanding warrants and to unearth any other plots. Law enforcement in other states had been alerted and was conducting similar crackdowns.

How the guns got past security was still a mystery, but it was assumed that someone with a security clearance smuggled them in. That investigation was ongoing and everyone with a clearance would be questioned.

Mike's chief concern, however, was Mendoza. He called the hospital and Arianna daily. Finally, the good news came. Mendoza had regained consciousness and was off the critical list. He was still in intensive care but his condition had stabilized and the doctors believed he'd most likely pull through.

When Mike heard Mendoza was in a regular hospital room two days later, he called him immediately. "How you holding up, Manny?"

"Pretty well, all things considered. But this delays my getting to Diaz. I was looking forward to that."

"Me, too. But for now just concentrate on getting back on your feet."

"Doctor said I'm doing well. How about you? Arianna told me about your leg. I'm sorry, Mike. Really sorry."

"It's all right, Manny. I'm okay. I'm adjusting. I'm using that cane like a pro now."

"Glad to hear it. They say I should be out of here in four or five days."

"That's great. We'll keep your seat open."

But even the welcome news about Mendoza came with a moral dilemma. At dinner that night, Mike told Josephine, "Normally, Manny would be looking at eight to ten years. But with his record and with him helping the investigation, I think they'll go easy on him. At least that's what the AG told me. I hope so. That would save me a lot of soul searching."

"Are you thinking what I think you're thinking?"

Mike nodded, and for at least the twentieth time considered pardoning his friend if he got a stiff sentence. "Jo, it's a real problem.

You know how I feel about Manny. We're tight. But how can I pardon him and not the others? I just can't do that.

"It's a tough call. But look at how many low lifes have been pardoned, those scum bags that Clinton let loose. Mark Rich. The FALN people. So, why shouldn't Manny get a break? Ah," Mike grunted and waved his hand. "I'm going back and forth with this."

Josephine touched Mike's arm. "Have you thought that Manny wouldn't want you to pardon him?"

Mike scratched his forehead. "That's a good point. You're probably right. He wouldn't. Damn! I wish John was here. He'd put it into perspective."

"It's a conscience call, Mike. You've got to feel comfortable with yourself."

"It's simply not the right thing to do," Mike said. "He broke the law. If he's convicted . . . I hate to say this, but if he's convicted, he's got to pay a price. You know that. I can't bend the rules for him."

Chapter Forty-Seven

Two seemingly endless weeks went by before Mike returned to work. Walking with his cane through the corridors to his office, he was greeted by applause and cheers. He stopped to chat, shake hands, and get hugs, thanking people along the way. Entering his office, he looked around and sucked in the surroundings. It was good to be back.

He spent the morning getting updates from his aides, attorney general, legal counsel, and department heads. Cost-cutting measures were progressing, the immigration law was proving highly successful, and six sanctuary mayors had agreed to Mike's compromise.

As Mike dove back into his duties, Senator Stern glanced up at her outer office as Josephine strolled in unannounced, wearing a dark blue pants suit, her long black hair in a pony tail swaying from side to side. She approached the senator's secretary, and moments later Stern's intercom buzzed.

"Governor DiGrasso's wife is here," her secretary said. "She wants to meet with you. Says it won't take much time."

A long silence. Then, "Send her in."

Stern knew what was happening and braced herself. There was no delicate way to handle this. She'd been had. DiGrasso had come clean with his wife, and Stern's leverage was gone. She sighed. She had this coming and just wanted to get it over with. She went to the door presenting a warm smile.

She gestured to her desk. "Please come in, Mrs. DiGrasso." They'd met several times at social functions, and Stern had been congenial but never engaged in lengthy conversations. Josephine took a seat in front of Stern's desk. Stern sat across from her, putting her hands on the desk and interlocking her fingers. "Well," she said, "what can I do for you?"

Josephine stared at Stern for a few seconds before saying, "Does the name Karina Sanchez mean anything to you?"

Stern remembered asking Mike that question when she tried to blackmail him over the affair. She looked down to her desk, then up at Josephine. "I thought that's why you came. And I'm not surprised that the governor told you. All I can say is that politics can sometimes be . . ." she hesitated, "let's say, unpleasant."

Josephine sneered. "Unpleasant? Is that what you call threatening a person's marriage? Unpleasant?" She leaned forward, eyes narrowed. Stern saw Josephine's fury, almost felt the hard stare, like lasers striking her retinas. "I'd say it's more like swimming in pond scum. I've heard about people as vicious as you, but never had the . . . let's say, unpleasant, experience of meeting one."

"Mrs. DiGrasso, I know how you must feel—"

"No, you don't. Someone like you couldn't possibly imagine how I feel. You belong in a sewer with the rest of the vermin. How the hell can you live with yourself? What in your life made you capable of doing something like that?"

"Mrs. DiGrasso, it's not necessary to resort to insults and name calling. I'm not proud of what I did. I just—"

"But you did it anyway. Over one stinking piece of legislation. Just to have your way. To satisfy . . . what would you call it, a pet peeve?"

Stern flushed. Her voice rose. "It's far more than that. If your husband gets away with this—"

"I *know* about all that," Josephine snapped. "Did it ever occur to you that *you* might be wrong? That you threatened my husband and jeopardized my marriage because *you* misjudged, *you* made a mistake."

"And your husband? What if he's wrong?"

Josephine shoved her finger at Stern. "He wouldn't have blackmailed you! He wouldn't have destroyed a marriage. He couldn't come close to being that kind of person. But you are. I won't forget this, and neither will Mike. Fasten your seat belt, lady, you're in for a rough ride."

"I don't respond well to threats."

"That wasn't a threat! That was a promise! Mike and I have settled this. I know that affair was a fluke. It meant nothing to him. We love each other, and our marriage is intact. So, your game didn't play out well there."

Josephine stood. Stern pushed away from her desk, not knowing what Josephine would do.

"And," Josephine said, "just in case you're thinking of splashing this in the newspapers, think again. It won't harm Mike's standing one bit. People don't care much about a sixteen-year-old sexual indiscretion. Besides, we're in a post Bill Clinton age. In fact, if you let the newspapers in on this, the only thing that'll happen is that it'll reveal you for what you are—a spiteful, venomous, vindictive bitch who'll do anything to get her way."

She didn't wait for an answer, just turned and walked out.

Stern's breathing was heavy after Josephine left. But she knew Josephine was right. Exposing the governor's affair wouldn't help get the new immigration bill. She put her elbows on the desk and massaged her temples. Forget it. It's insignificant. Her fight was with the governor, not his wife. And she was still confident she'd win, even though the blackmail threat had been neutralized.

Chapter Forty-Eight

Mike heard it on the news as he ate breakfast in his office, and the only surprise for him was that it took so long for the Supreme Court to act. Perhaps it had held off until he recovered from his wounds. The court's spokesman looked and sounded solemn as he announced that all nine justices agreed the governor of California would be cited for contempt of court.

"What else?" Mike said aloud. A bum leg, restraining order, possible impeachment, contempt of court. He'd seen it all coming but still felt the weight of it on his shoulders.

Mendoza called. "You're really catching it from all angles."

Mike smiled. "Sure am. I'm beginning to feel like a one-legged man in an ass-kicking contest."

"A very apt analogy."

Mike laughed. "Yeah, pardon the pun. I didn't think of that. How are you doing? Must be good getting back to work."

"Sure is. How you holding up with everything that's happening?"

"I'm fine, Manny. Don't worry about me. This was bound to happen."

"How do you think the president will react? I don't think you're going to arrest yourself, so he's the only one who can enforce the contempt citation."

"I don't know, Manny. That's his call."

"Anyway," Mendoza said, "I've done some checking around, and there are definitely rumors of impeachment. Some of our guys are wavering with this thing. If Stern can flip a lot of our folks, she might pull it off."

"Even if they do impeach, the Senate has to vote me out of office, and I don't think that'll happen, do you?"

"No, but I can't be sure. Still, even if the Senate doesn't vote you out, the impeachment is a terrible blemish on your career and reputation."

"*C'est la vie,*" Mike said. "That's life. I'll deal with it. Maybe I'll get a sympathy vote."

"Could be. You never know. Okay, Mike. I'll keep you up to date."

Mike was barely off the phone with Mendoza when the president called. "How are you, Mike?"

"I'm doing fine, Mr. President."

"Glad to hear it. I'm here with your two state senators. We've been talking and think that now that you're up and about, we should meet."

"Whenever and wherever you like."

"Let's make it Camp David. Day after tomorrow. That'll give us both time to clear up immediate business and reschedule appointments. My chopper will pick you up at the airport."

Chapter Forty-Nine

Mike did paperwork during most of the flight to Camp David, looking through legislative and budget proposals, highlighting some sections and making notations in the margins. Outside, the sky was a clear powder blue, and the large white cumulous clouds beneath extended as far as he could see.

After a late lunch, Mike had a glass of wine, then reclined his seat. He dozed off for forty-five minutes and awoke shortly before his plane landed at Reagan National Airport at 4:30 p.m., eastern time. It taxied to another secure area where *Marine One*, the presidential helicopter, was waiting. One of the pilots took his bag and walked with Mike to the chopper. Mike felt the cold immediately and zipped up his wool-lined black leather jacket.

Half an hour later, the helicopter touched down at Camp David. A limousine waited at the edge of the heliport, and a young navy ensign got out and approached, his breath forming vapor clouds, and took Mike's bag. Ballard had brought him to Camp David twice before, so Mike knew that it was staffed by navy personnel, and that troops from the marine barracks in Washington, D.C. provided security.

"The president sends his greetings, sir," the sailor said, then loaded Mike's bag into the limo and drove him to his cabin, stopping only at the guard post in front of the access road.

Mike remembered the other visits he'd made here and the quiet ambience and beauty of the surroundings. But those were vacations, pleasure visits with nothing for all of them to do but enjoy. Tomorrow was another matter. He hoped he'd do well, not overact or underact.

The thick growth of stately trees along the road was covered with snow, but Mike recalled Camp David in autumn, when the large variety of trees made the rocky terrain an artist's palette of colors. Night hadn't yet fallen, and Mike caught a glimpse of a mountaintop just as the sun disappeared behind it, spreading a crimson incandescence over the landscape.

At the cabin, the ensign took Mike's bag and walked him to the door, the snow squeaking and crunching under their feet.

"The meeting will be at nine tomorrow morning, sir," the ensign said. "Can I get you anything? Something to eat, maybe?"

Mike said no and dismissed him. He stepped into a spacious living room with a kitchenette to his right. The refrigerator was well stocked, and a few bottles of wine and brandy were in a cabinet above the sink. He unpacked in the bedroom, then poured a glass of wine, put on his coat and sat on the porch bench to take in the fresh, chilly night air.

Only branches creaking as they bent in the wind broke the evening's silence. He stared at the night sky. Peeking through the leafless trees, a bright gold crescent moon glowed in a dark sky filled with sparkling stars, diamonds on a dark velvet backdrop.

The peaceful atmosphere led his thoughts once more to the enormity of what he was doing. He again questioned himself. How could he be so sure what he was doing was right? What if he and the others were wrong and the consequences were dire? When did he acquire such moral certitude? He'd been plagued by all this from the very start. But who wouldn't have doubts? Lincoln certainly must have questioned the loss of so many lives to preserve the Union. The Founders, too, probably had doubts about their rebellion.

Ah! Forget the second guessing, he thought. Do what you think is right and accept the consequences.

He swirled the last of his wine in the glass and drank it. Standing, he took one last deep breath of the crisp clean air and went inside.

Breakfast came to his cabin at 7:30 the next morning and at ten minutes to nine, another ensign arrived and took him to the president's lodge. It was a cold morning but bright sunlight glittered on the snow. As they approached the lodge, Mike noted how well its stone and hardwood construction blended with the rustic surroundings. Nearby, a flagstone terrace and picnic area enhanced the setting.

Entering the foyer of the lodge, the ensign took Mike's jacket and led him to a spacious combined living and dining room, where a huge stone fireplace in the center of the wall on his right dominated the surroundings, its crackling fire radiating heat and flickering light. A gleaming chandelier hung in the center of the room, just above the long wooden conference table where the president sat with three others.

Ballard stood and walked to his friend. "Good to see you, Mike," he said, holding out his hand. "How are you? You look great and you handle that cane like it was part of your body."

Mike took Ballard's hand. "Yeah. It's almost like I don't know I'm using it. It's become practically natural."

"Come and join us," Ballard said, putting his hand on Mike's back as he walked him slowly to the table. Both of California's U.S. senators, Mary Blanchard and Steve Murray, were at the table with Karl Rostoff. They stood and greeted Mike. Everyone wore casual clothes—jeans and flannel woodsman shirts—except for Mike, who wore blue slacks and a gray button-down shirt.

Coffee pitchers and mugs were in the center of the table with water pitchers and glasses on each side. "Coffee, Mike?"

"No thanks. I've had my caffeine fix for the day."

Ballard sat near the middle of the table, with the fireplace to his back and signaled Mike to sit at his left as the others took their seats across from them.

"Once again," Ballard said, "my deepest condolences on John Stone. I know you two were very close."

"Thank you. He was a good man."

"I know," Ballard said. "I only met him once. At your inauguration. But he was immediately likeable. And very knowledgeable. It must be a very painful loss."

"Very," Mike said. "But I'm adjusting. It gets a little easier every day."

"That's good," Ballard said. "And how about the speaker, Mendoza?"

"He's doing well and he's back on the job. But he's still got to face corruption charges."

"I heard. I'm sorry. I know he's a friend of yours, too."

"Thank you, Mr. President. I appreciate that."

Ballard put his hands flat on the table. "All right, let's get on with the business at hand. We all know why we're here."

He turned to Mike. "And before we start, Mike, let me say that you have no enemies in this room. You know I agree with the point you're trying to make. But what you're doing is pushing the issue too far too fast. We think we can deal with it in a way that doesn't cause a national commotion and where we won't be butting heads."

Nice touch, Marty, Mike thought. *Make it seem like you're trying to soothe me before opening fire.*

"That's right, Mike," Blanchard said. Mike thought she looked like Nicole Kidman—slender with light red hair, blue eyes, and thin nose and lips. "I agree with you one-hundred percent about the courts. But if you continue with what you're doing, there's going to be chaos."

"I'm with Mary," Steve Murray said. A former professional linebacker, he was six-foot-three and heavyset. "This is an issue that needs to be settled, should have been settled years ago. But what you're doing is going to shake up the system."

"Maybe it needs a little shaking," Mike said. "This judicial activism has to stop. Federalism is being scrapped. Checks and balances are being ignored. Maybe a shakeup is all that'll work. The country's strong. We'll make it through this and most likely be better off for it."

Hmm. That sounded kind of stiff. I practiced these remarks for hours. Maybe I overdid it. Just relax. Let it come out naturally.

"And maybe not," Ballard said, dropping his left arm over the back of his chair and turning to Mike. "If we can avoid this, we've got to do it."

"Well, you know, Mr. President," Mike replied, spreading his hands, "I'm not crazy about doing this. But something needs to be done. If you folks can pull a rabbit out of a hat, believe me, I'll be happy as anyone."

He almost smiled. *That's better. Keep it up.*

Rostoff said, "We've been looking at options. One is passing legislation to restrict the court from ruling on certain cases."

Mike shook his head. "You can't be sure you'll get the legislation passed. You've got thin majorities in both Houses. And there are plenty of politicians who like what the judges are doing. The woman who's fighting me hardest back home is thrilled by an activist judiciary."

"There are quite a few people in the Senate who are with you on this," said Blanchard. "Even some of the opposition is leaning in our direction. Nothing official, just cloakroom talk. But I think there's a good chance some of them will be on our side."

Ballard leaned toward Mike and put his hand on the back of the governor's chair. "I'll do everything I can to get that legislation through. I carry weight on the hill. A lot of those people owe me big time, and I can put the pressure on when I have to."

"All right," Mike said, his eyes scanning them, "suppose you pass the legislation. What if the court declares it unconstitutional? Then you're in the same bind I am."

Evading Mike's remark, Rostoff said, "Another option is legislation that gives congress a two-thirds majority veto on certain court decisions. That might be doable."

"Same fleas, different dog," Mike said. "You can't guarantee it'll pass and it could be ruled unconstitutional. Face it, the only way to do that would be with a constitutional amendment. That would take years, and the amendment might not be ratified." *Wow. Not bad. Where'd I come up with that dog and fleas thing?*

The discussion continued for an hour and an half with Mike parrying every argument. The president looked frustrated. Crossing his legs toward Mike, he looked directly into his eyes.

"Mike, this isn't going to be easy for you. You've already got a problem in your own state, a revolt from what I hear. Looks like that new immigration bill is going to pass, mainly because of defections from your side. That should tell you something. Maybe you need to reconsider."

"I can deal with that. I expected it, and I can handle the flack. What's the worst that can happen?"

"Huh! I don't even want to think about that," Ballard said. "Listen, Mike, you're the last person I want to lock horns with. You're a bull when you think you're right. It's one of your best traits, and one of your worst. If you believe in something, it's damn the torpedoes, full speed ahead. It's not something I want. We've been friends a long time. But if you don't change your mind on this, I'll be forced to take action. And I have many means at my disposal, many options."

Damn, Marty. You missed your calling. Should have been an actor. Had the president rehearsed any of this?

"I know that. I'm prepared for the consequences. But most of the people in my state support this. And from what I've read, so do most Americans. I don't want a confrontation either. But, with all due respect, I'm just not backing off of this."

The president leaned back in his chair and looked at the others. "Well, we've hit a log jam. We're getting nowhere. Let's take a break before lunch, then come back and try to hammer something out after we eat."

"Excuse me, Mr. President," Mike said. "I'll stick around if you like, but we've been at this since nine o'clock and, no insult intended," he said, looking at the others, "I haven't heard anything to sway me. Everything we've discussed I've already considered. I don't see the point of going on with this. I'd like to head back home."

Ballard shrugged. "Well, I'm not going to tie you to a chair. If you want to leave, that's okay, but I hope you change your mind, because I don't see how this can work out well for you. I'll give it more thought, lots of it. But I can't imagine a satisfactory conclusion unless you make some concessions."

"I wish I could," Mike said. "I really wish I could."

Ballard held out his hand. "Well, at least keep an open mind as the situation develops."

Mike shook the president's hand. "I will."

"All right. Go pack. I'll have an ensign pick you up in half an hour."

Blanchard and Murray stood and shook hands with Mike. "Thanks for your time," Mike said. "Sorry we couldn't work something out."

Chapter Fifty

Mike followed events apprehensively as the press and Ballard's opposition party fumed over the president's prolonged inaction on the California controversy. Public criticism was intense. Protesters marched outside the White House, and Mike guessed that legislators, even in Ballard's own party, were deluged by phone calls, e-mails, and tweets from constituents demanding Ballard do something.

But Mike knew there was another body of citizens who weren't in the least put off by what he was doing. In fact, some conservatives praised Mike. On TV, radio, and in newspaper editorials, they said it was about time someone stood up against "judicial tyranny," and they pressed home the argument that federal courts were exercising power not given by the Constitution.

Ballard's press secretary had told reporters only that the president was considering the issue but delayed his meeting with DiGrasso until the governor fully recovered from his wounds. But now that the president had personally spoken with him, he'd make his decision.

Finally, three days after meeting Mike at Camp David, Ballard called a press conference. Mike watched it in his office. Sipping coffee, he bent forward, anxious to see how Ballard would handle the discussion. Nearly seventy reporters filled the White House press room, representing media from around the world. The confrontation in California was international news.

Everyone stood as Ballard stepped to the podium with the presidential seal emblazoned on its front. After greeting the president, the reporters sat, and Ballard opened with a brief statement.

"As you probably expected, I'm here to address developments in California. In fact, for weeks that's been a key priority for my advisors and me. Needless to say, there were some very heated discussions. I listened to everyone with an open mind, but at some point a decision had to be made. And I've made it. I'll give you a short rundown of our discussions and open the floor for questions."

Mike could feel the tension in the room as Ballard lowered his head and paused for a moment, as if collecting his thoughts. He wrapped his fingers around the edges of the podium and looked up.

"This was a drastic, disturbing action that Governor DiGrasso took," Ballard said. "Very serious. But there was no easy way out of this, no exactly correct solution. If I didn't take action, the repercussions could be serious, perhaps eroding the credibility of the Supreme Court and the position of the judiciary in our government. I heard this over and over again. It's a good, solid, logical position. The central question then became what I could do to enforce the court order. That became my focus."

Again, Ballard hesitated. He pursed his lips and glanced upward for a second before continuing. Mike thought Ballard's face looked as if he were considering another course of action. The only sounds were cameras clicking, a few chairs squeaking, and an occasional cough.

"I finally came to the conclusion that every suggestion regarding federal action was unworkable and excessive. And, to put it briefly, I intend to do nothing to enforce the court's order. I'll take your questions now."

Dead silence—as if the reporters weren't sure they'd heard Ballard correctly. Then, they began whispering to each other, shaking their heads, scribbling in notebooks. No doubt some had expected a less-than-forceful move to get Mike to comply with the court's ruling, even if just a gesture, a show of disapproval. But it was unlikely that anyone anticipated the president would take no action at all.

Tradition is to give the *Associated Press* correspondent the first question, so the other reporters waited as Ballard pointed to her. She was an experienced reporter, but even she seemed flustered by the president's decision, lowering her notebook to her side and appearing to ad lib her question.

"Mr. President, what were some of the actions you and your advisors considered?"

"Well, of course, federalizing the California National Guard to enforce the court's ruling came up. I gave that some serious thought. But I concluded that it was too dramatic and had too many unexpected pitfalls."

"What pitfalls?"

"What would the National Guard do? Picture this. Soldiers pushing their way into the California Capitol Building and taking out the governor in handcuffs. What if he resisted arrest? Would they throw him on the ground? Would they put his hands on the wall and spread his legs? It's something I was not prepared to see all over the news."

The *AP* reporter began to speak, but Ballard continued. "In fact, let's take that scenario further. Suppose members of his legislature who agreed with him tried to block the troops. Or, what if citizens lined up around the Capitol Building to stand in the way of the soldiers? What if the police wouldn't cooperate? What a spectacle that would be. Would you want me to declare war on California?"

Mike leaned back and smiled. "Nicely done, Marty."

The reporter asked, "Anything else?"

"Of course we talked about withdrawing considerable federal funds from California. That had a lot of support. But I was more persuaded by those who said that it might not work and could hurt innocent people who depend on that money. It made no sense to me, and would perhaps even be unconscionable, to subject California's residents to unnecessary hardship just to twist the governor's arm. And I can tell you from personal experience, Governor DiGrasso is not someone who responds well to arm twisting. My feeling is that it would only have reinforced his resolve."

Ballard pointed to the ABC reporter in the first row of seats. "Perhaps, Mr. President, if Californians experienced some of those hardships, their attitude toward the governor might change. The whole political atmosphere might shift and force him to make concessions."

Ballard smiled. "Have you checked the polls coming out of California lately? All of them show solid support for the governor. And that's true nationally as well. Governor DiGrasso's actions have gotten the people thinking about whether the federal courts have the right to make certain rulings. Besides that, this illegal immigration problem has been festering for decades, and now it's come to a head. The people wanted something done, and Governor DiGrasso did it. I don't believe most people in this country would endorse cutting federal funds to his state."

Mike raised the volume slightly. He got up and filled his coffee cup, then returned to his desk and sat as Ballard called on a *Fox News* reporter. Mike knew that Ballard liked going through the national TV stations first. They often had the most penetrating questions, and he wanted to get them out of the way.

The correspondent was tall and thick set with a receding hairline. "Mr. President, what other actions were considered, and why did you decide against them?"

"Some of my advisors suggested that we again meet personally with Governor DiGrasso. But we'd already done that at Camp David. It wasn't just me. It was Chief of Staff Rostoff and both of California's senators. We were as persuasive as we could possibly be. We offered alternatives. We tried the carrot and the stick. The governor countered every argument we made. I'm certain that another meeting would not have changed his mind. We used all the verbal ammunition we had, but he dug his heels in and just wouldn't budge. He can be a bulldog."

"Huh," Mike grunted. "I guess that was supposed to be a compliment."

Ballard pointed to the CBS correspondent, a comely blonde and former Miss New York. Her hair fell to just below her shoulders, and her dark-blue dress accentuated her hourglass figure. "You and Governor DiGrasso have been friends for many years. Did that in any way influence your decision?"

Ballard stared silently at her. Then, he said, "You know, I was sure someone would ask a question like that. And to tell you the truth,

I'm a little offended by it. The answer is no. Absolutely not. Yes, I've known Governor DiGrasso for more than thirty years, and I regard him highly and consider him a friend. But the idea that I would let my personal relationship interfere with my judgment regarding the country's system of jurisprudence is simply ridiculous and, frankly, a little out of line."

Clearly caught off guard, the reporter's mouth opened and she moved backward a half step. But she recovered quickly. "I didn't mean to insult you, sir. But it's a question that needed to be asked. I apologize if it offended you. But I think there are many people who are wondering about that."

"Apology accepted," Ballard said. "And I suppose I owe you one as well for snapping at you like that."

The room went as quiet as an empty church.

"Cat got your tongues?" Ballard joked, and a *New York Times* reporter took the challenge. "Do you think it's proper, that it's good for the country, to have a Supreme Court decision be ignored by a state's chief executive? This is almost unprecedented. Aren't you concerned about the groundwork it sets and how it will affect our judicial system?"

A smile creased Ballard's lips. "I'm glad you said *almost* unprecedented. You apparently know your history. This isn't the first time a court ruling has been defied. And what was the result? Nothing. The whole system didn't come crashing down. And it won't now either."

He began to call another reporter, but hesitated and went on. "Maybe I shouldn't say this, but I will. You could make a strong case that Governor DiGrasso is right to ignore the court. I'm not going to go over his philosophy and reasoning. He's done a very good job of articulating that himself. All of you know my position. I've said it time and again. I think federal courts are meddling in affairs where they have no constitutional authority. I just regret very much that it's brought us to this point."

The Washington correspondent from the *Los Angeles Times* asked the next question. "You may agree with the governor's philosophy, but are you condoning what he's doing?"

"This is not a matter of condoning his actions or whether what he's doing is right," Ballard replied, "legally or ethically. He's done it. I had to deal with that reality and decide what measures could be applied to it. And there were none that struck me as even remotely appropriate, much less good for the country. I wish this had played out differently. But it didn't and the situation is what it is."

Ballard looked at a gaggle of foreign correspondents in the middle of the room and saw a reporter with a BBC logo on his blazer and pointed to him.

"Are you concerned how this will be perceived overseas, sir?" the reporter asked in a crisp, well-articulated English accent.

"Well, of course, I'm concerned about their reactions, especially our British friends, who are always watching developments in the colonies."

He waited until the laughter died. "We consider how other countries view us. But this is a purely domestic issue and in no way affects our foreign friends. I'm doing what I think is best, and they're free to form their own opinions about it."

Ballard moved a step back from the podium and held a hand up, signaling the reporters to hold their questions. "Let's look at this objectively. Ask yourself if this situation is as terrible as it's being made out to be. What are the deadly consequences? Frankly, I don't see them. The foundations of our government aren't crumbling. Trembling a bit maybe, but far from crumbling.

"Next to most other nations, America is still young, still having some growing pains, still evolving. I don't take what's happened lightly. But I don't consider it a national crisis. In fact, I honestly think that an occasional domestic flare-up like this may be for the best. Helps us fine tune the way our government operates. That's not a bad thing. Jefferson once said that a little revolution now and then might be good for the country. Maybe that's what this is. A sort of little revolution that could do us more good than harm."

The room was momentarily quiet except for some whispers and shuffling of papers. Ballard took advantage of the lull.

"I think that's the best way to look at this," he concluded. "And, on that at least somewhat optimistic note, I'll close this conference. Ladies and gentlemen, thank you for being here."

Mike clicked off the TV and exhaled deeply. "Done," he said out loud. "Once and for all, done."

He waited an hour before calling the president. The first operator connected him with another, who connected him to the president's secretary.

"I'll buzz him," she said, and moments later told Mike that the president would call him back on the secure line. Shortly, Mike's phone rang.

"Congratulations," Mike said. "You handled that conference beautifully."

"Thanks, Mike. Your praise is always welcome."

"You made a good case for not intervening. I think we're going to change a lot of minds."

"Yeah, I believe we will. But I'm going to be taking some heavy flack for a while. And that's all right. Whatever happens is worth the price. This needed to be done. I'll tell you one thing, Mike. I'm glad we're at the finish line. I've had second thoughts about the whole thing ever since we decided to do it."

"You, too, Marty? It's been in the back of my mind the whole time. I was thinking about it again just the other night at Camp David. This is enormous, historic."

"Yeah, it's a political earthquake. But it's best for the country in the long run."

"I think so, too," Mike said. "I know the Founders would agree."

Ballard laughed. "Maybe we should consider this 'The Founders' plot.'"

Mike smiled. "I think they'd like that."

Epilogue

Initially, it seemed Ballard had put one out of the park. But the preponderance of reporting and commentary in the days after the news conference was generally negative, even vitriolic. As the attacks became more vociferous and the spin doctors plied their trade, public opinion gradually shifted, not greatly, but enough to encourage the president's opposition party to speak out more harshly than it had. The senate minority leader said Ballard had "weaseled out of a serious crisis rather than grapple with it."

Two days after the president's news conference, House and Senate opposition leaders held their own. They clearly smelled blood. From the start, the conference was a scorching assault on the president. His decision "was an act of weakness." He'd "proven himself unable to deal with a serious blow to the judiciary."

The House minority leader even reopened the question of Ballard's friendship with Mike. "I don't care if it irritates President Ballard or not. I'm not some cutesy reporter. And I say that his friendship with the California governor strongly influenced his decision, whether he admits it or not." Moreover, she hinted at impeachment hearings and a thorough investigation of how the president reached his decision.

The president fired back that the opposition was playing politics and had offered no solutions. "If they had an answer to the problem, they should have put it on the table," he told reporters. "This is partisan nonsense and serves no useful purpose. It's no more than a distraction, sleight of hand, and it's time to put it behind us and get back to doing the people's business."

Meanwhile, the issue was at the center of countless editorials, TV commentaries, and radio talk shows. The battle of the pundits and the war of words in the Beltway went on for weeks.

But it all came to nothing. Six months later, Ballard's favorability rating had fallen, but if he could run again, he'd most likely win. In California, Mike's poll numbers were high.

The public debate focused attention on judicial review, and as the people learned more, attitudes shifted. National polls showed that most Americans—although disturbed by defying federal courts—agreed that these courts had accumulated too much power. The controversy gradually subsided, and the separation of government powers once again assumed the balance that the Founders intended.

Elizabeth Stern didn't get her new immigration bill. And her attempt at impeachment withered on the vine. It was a serious loss of face that greatly diminished her standing and influence. She wasn't rendered politically impotent, but she didn't carry the weight she once did. Moreover, she'd expended much of her political capital by calling in favors and making promises, and she'd persuaded others to do the same, weakening them also. She could still wheel and deal and twist some arms, but no longer had the aura of a fearsome legislative figure.

The California immigration law proved highly successful. Increasing numbers of illegal aliens were rounded up and deported. Many left the state, and the previous flood of illegals was now a trickle. And all the sanctuary city mayors eventually agreed to Mike's compromise.

Other states, under pressure from the federal government because of their immigration laws, breathed a sigh of relief. At the same time, the governor of Colorado ignored a federal court ruling that a state law which required the names and faces of child molesters be posted on the state's website was unconstitutional.

Patti and Marco were married three months after they returned, and a year later Mike was a grandfather. Mendoza was convicted on corruption charges. The judge, however, considered his help with the investigation, his record in law enforcement and politics, as well as his character witnesses, and cut his sentence to six months in prison and two years of community service.

Carlos, his family, and Julio made it safely to Mexico City, where they lived better than most people there. Even after bribing corrupt Mexican officials, they still had enough of the money they'd saved in America to buy a building with four apartments, two of which they rented out. They formed a subcontracting company providing drywall and plastering services. Two years later, Julio remarried. Marisol had a fifth child.